A native Northwesterner with the
Stefanie Sloane credits her parents' ⟨...⟩
not to mention their decision to live i⟨...⟩
– for her love of books. A childhood spent lost in the pages
of countless novels led Stefanie to college where she majored
in English. No one was more surprised than Stefanie when
she actually put her degree to use and landed a job in
Amazon.com's Books editorial department. She spent over
five years reading for a living before retiring to concentrate on
her own stories. Stefanie currently resides with her family
in Seattle. You can find out more about Stefanie and her
books at www.stefaniesloane.com and www.facebook.com/
stefaniesloane, or by following her on Twitter @stefaniesloane.

Praise for Stefanie Sloane and her intoxicating novels:

'Smart, sensuous, and sparkling with wit' Julia Quinn

'Sloane cements her reputation with a powerfully emotional,
sexually charged story that will keep you up all night'
Romantic Times

'Stefanie Sloane writes utterly delectable and seductive
Regency romance!' Teresa Medeiros

'Captivating . . . With her fresh, original voice, Stefanie Sloane
will charm her way into readers' hearts' Susan Wiggs, *New
York Times* bestselling author

'Fabulous . . . everything readers of Regency romance crave'
Amanda Quick, *New York Times* bestselling author

'Perfect blend of tender romance and heart stopping
adventure!' *Fresh Fiction*

By Stefanie Sloane

Regency Rogue Series
The Devil In Disguise
The Angel In My Arms
The Sinner Who Seduced Me
The Saint Who Stole My Heart
The Scoundrel Takes A Bride
The Wicked Widow Meets Her Match

One Perfect Christmas (e-novella)

STEFANIE SLOANE

The Sinner Who Seduced Me

headline
ETERNAL

Published by arrangement with Ballantine Books,
an imprint of The Random House Publishing Group,
a division of Random House LLC.

First published in paperback in Great Britain in 2015
by HEADLINE ETERNAL
An imprint of HEADLINE PUBLISHING GROUP

1

Cataloguing in Publication Data is available from the British Library

ISBN 978 1 4722 2847 5

Offset in Sabon by Avon DataSet Ltd, Bidford-on-Avon, Warwickshire

Printed and bound by CPI Group (UK) Ltd, Croydon, CR0 4YY

HEADLINE PUBLISHING GROUP
An Hachette UK Company
338 Euston Road
London NW1 3BH

www.headlineeternal.com
www.headline.co.uk
www.hachette.co.uk

For Randall.
No flowery words or clever turns of phrase.
Just know that you own my heart
and you always will.

1

Late Summer 1811
PARIS, FRANCE

"Crimson?" the male voice drawled in disbelief. *"Vraiment?"*

Lady Clarissa Collins steadied her hand as she brushed the bright hue onto the canvas. She stepped back and narrowed her violet eyes critically over the voluptuous female model draped across the blue damask divan. The elegant sofa was placed several yards away from her easel and angled toward the outer studio wall. The late morning sun poured through the windows that made up the southern wall of the space, bathing the nearly naked woman in warm golden light.

Clarissa considered the canvas once again and used the tip of her little finger to barely smudge the fresh paint before nodding with satisfied decisiveness. "Now, Bernard, observe. Would you like to ask me again?"

Bernard St. Michelle, preeminent portrait painter of Paris and indeed all of Europe, frowned, lowered his thick black eyebrows into a forbidding vee, and turned toward the model. "You may go."

The woman lazily reached for her dressing gown and rose, nodding to both before disappearing down the hall.

Bernard meticulously unrolled a white linen sleeve down one lean forearm and then the other. "Clarissa, how long have I been a painter?" he asked, his Gallic accent more pronounced.

Clarissa dipped her brush into a jug of turpentine and vigorously swished the bristles back and forth. She knew the answer to Bernard's question, of course. In fact, she knew the entire conversation that was about to take place, since they'd had it too many times to count.

"Longer than I," she answered, tapping the brush hard against the earthenware pitcher before dunking it a second time, resuming the swishing motions with more force.

Bernard adjusted his cuffs just so. "And while you were learning to dance and capture the attention of unsuspecting young men in London, what was I doing?"

Clarissa pulled the brush from the jar and rubbed the bristles with a paint-stained rag. Her grip was too tight, the pressure too fierce, and the slim wooden brush handle broke in two. "Destroying your tools?" she ventured, tossing the snapped end of the brush handle to the floor.

Bernard sighed deeply, ignoring the broken wood as he walked to where Clarissa stood. "I was working in London too, cherie, honing my craft during the Peace of Amiens. Even when the war broke out, I painted night and day—"

"Until returning to Paris—in the hull of a blockade runner, no less," Clarissa interrupted. "I know, Bernard. And I will remember if I live to be two hundred and two."

"Then you know that when I question your work, you must listen? I believe that I've earned such respect. Don't you?"

He was right, of course. Since returning to Paris, Bernard's popularity with the ton had grown, his limited availability making him only more desirable. Sheer genius combined with the adoration of the elite was difficult to deny.

Clarissa eyed the other brushes in the pitcher, the urge to break wood calling to her like a siren. "But I was right, Bernard. The touch of crimson to define the subject's lip line is exactly what was needed."

"That is hardly the point, my dear—and you know it." Bernard pushed the table with the pitcher of brushes and the clutter of stained rags, paints, and palette knives beyond Clarissa's reach. "How can you expect to grow as an artist if you do not allow the world—and others with more experience—to inform your work?"

His midnight black hair had escaped its queue and feathered about his temples like so many brushstrokes, piled one atop another.

No matter how hard she tried, Clarissa could never stay angry at Bernard—especially when he was right. And since the day she'd met him, he'd been right about everything, unlike the long list of French painting masters who, despite her talent, had refused to take her as an apprentice because she was female.

Five years earlier, when their world in England had come crashing down, Clarissa had agreed to flee with her mother to Paris. The prospect of studying with François Gérard or Jacques-Louis David had held all her hope for the future. When both artists scoffed at her request simply because she was a woman, Clarissa dismissed them as the idiots they clearly were and moved on, working her way down a list of suitable teachers in Paris.

Despite her impressive portfolio of work, everyone she approached refused, until she was left with one: Bernard St. Michelle, the highly respected and, arguably, most talented painter on the European continent. She'd not placed St. Michelle higher on her list, having overheard that even male artists of her caliber could not secure a position with him.

But when she'd found herself with nothing to lose, she'd had her finest painting delivered to him—signed "C. Collins"—and St. Michelle had granted her a personal interview. Clarissa had procured suitable men's clothing and made her way to his studio, intent on letting her art speak for itself rather than her sex doing all the talking.

He'd agreed to take her on and, with a handshake, the deal was sealed. Clarissa had taken particular pleasure in ripping the beaver hat from her head and revealing her topknot of glossy black curls.

Bernard had only sighed deeply and instructed her to arrive by eight in the morning—no earlier, no later—then told her to go.

Though he was her senior by only a handful of years, Bernard had become a mentor and friend, father and confidant. As trustworthy as he was endlessly talented. And he'd taught her more about her art and her life in the last five years than she'd learned in the previous nineteen.

The memory of just how much she owed this man had Clarissa sighing, her annoyance evaporating. She placed the flat of her palms on Bernard's cheeks, cupping his face, and gently squeezed. "At least I did not throw the brush this time, *oui?*"

He raised a thick black eyebrow in agreement. "Nor did you shout. Improvement, indeed, my dear. The fire in your heart is beginning to meld with the sense in your head. One day you will be the finest portrait painter the world has ever seen. Such self-possession will be of great value when working with the aristocracy."

"That, and my beaver hat," Clarissa replied teasingly, playfully pinching Bernard's face before turning to attend to the remaining brushes.

The sound of the front door slamming below followed by the heavy tread of feet on the stairs caught Clarissa's attention.

"Jean-Marc?" she asked, referring to Bernard's paramour.

"No." Bernard shook his head, waving her toward the dressing screen in the corner. "He attends to his mama today," he whispered. "Go."

Clarissa complied, leaving the brushes to the turpentine and tiptoeing quickly toward the colorful screen. She'd made use of the hiding place many times before when delivery boys or Bernard's friends had dropped in unexpectedly. A strategically placed peephole located in the upper corner of a painted butterfly's wing allowed her to see all that was happening without revealing her presence.

She'd barely whisked out of sight when three men entered the spacious studio.

"*Bonjour, messieurs,*" Bernard greeted them in his native French.

"Bernard St. Michelle?" the tallest of the three men asked. He was perhaps Bernard's age, with small, glistening, black eyes and a balding head.

Bernard nodded. "Yes. And who might you be?"

The ratlike man stepped closer to view Clarissa's canvas, eyeing the painting with a lascivious gleam before turning back to Bernard. "I'm a man with a business proposition that I feel certain you will not refuse."

"If you're in need of my services, I'm afraid you will leave here disappointed. I am committed to the Comte de Claudel until next year," Bernard replied, his tone remaining even.

The Rat licked his thin lips. "Are you certain?" he inquired, gripping the carved silver top of his walking cane. With a quick twist, he pulled out a slim épée, the lethal fencing sword sliding silently from its hiding place. "Because, as I mentioned before, I'm quite certain you'll find this proposal impossible to refuse." He raised the blade and brought it down with force on the canvas. The painting ripped in two, a jagged cut appearing down the center of the model's reclining body. "And I am never wrong," he said, the words remarkable for their total lack of emotion.

Clarissa bit her hand to stifle the scream building in her throat. The men were more than common street ruffians and she was sensible enough, even when outraged by the wanton destruction of her canvas, to know when to keep quiet.

Bernard regarded the painting with quiet concern. "You have my attention, monsieur."

The two men positioned behind the Rat smirked in unison, their broad heads nodding with approval.

"You'll leave in three days' time for London to paint a portrait for a wealthy Canadian. There will be compensation, of course, as would be expected. And lodging . . ." the ratlike man paused and flicked a disdainful gaze about the cluttered studio, ". . . that will suit your needs."

Bernard folded his arms across his chest. "And the comte?"

With a swift, smooth flick of his wrist, the man slashed the blade at Bernard and a thin line of blood appeared on his face. "Tell the comte what you will. It makes no difference to me."

"And if I do not?"

"If you do not?" the Rat parroted disbelievingly. Without warning, he lunged at the dressing screen, the blade slashing the painted silk covering until all that stood was the wooden frame. "Then my employer, Durand, will kill the girl—and her mother, for good measure."

An instinctive survival response had sent Clarissa

stepping back and away from the deadly tip of the weapon. Now she was exposed by the shredded silk screen and she lunged at the swordsman, raking her nails against his cheek. "Not if I kill you first," she spat out.

The Rat stood motionless, seemingly suspended by his utter surprise at Clarissa's attack. The neckless pair stared at the unexpected sight of the slender woman in blue dimity attacking their superior.

Of the four men, Bernard recovered first, grabbing Clarissa and shoving her protectively behind him. "Three days, gentlemen. I trust you'll stand by your word?"

The Rat touched his face, dabbing at the blood left by Clarissa's nails before licking the red stain clean from his fingertip. "Three days. No more, no less," he confirmed, his cold, menacing smile directed at Clarissa before he turned toward the hallway. The muscular pair of henchmen followed behind, their heavy footfalls growing more muted, until the outer door to the street below slammed and they were gone.

Bernard turned, his face set in stark lines.

"Do you remember what I said regarding the fire in your heart and the sense in your head?" he asked, clutching Clarissa's arms so tightly the skin beneath his hands turned white.

"Yes," she answered, wincing at the pressure of his fingers, a thousand unanswered questions threatening to spill from her lips.

"I was wrong."

Clarissa eased from beneath his hands and lifted the hem of her smock, pressing it firmly against the line of blood welling on Bernard's cheek. "Who were those men?" she asked, unable to control the tremble in her voice.

"Your guess is as good as mine," Bernard said grimly,

his dark gaze meeting Clarissa's wide eyes. "But I may know someone who can tell us more."

James Marlowe detested salt water. Swimming was all well and good, but taking in repeated mouthfuls of the briny liquid was, in a word, hell. He dug his heels into the wet sand and looked out over the black water of the English Channel. A full moon rode high in the night sky, illuminating the crest and curl of the rolling waves.

He'd known from the beginning that penetrating Napoleon's darkest of organizations, Les Moines—The Monks—would be difficult. But when Henry Prescott, Viscount Carmichael, asked, one hardly thought in terms of ease.

He spat once, then twice, grimacing when the salty taste failed to disappear. James was an agent within the Young Corinthians, an elite British government spy organization that operated outside the bounds of normal channels.

Carmichael was the liaison between the spies and those in control of the British government at the highest level—and those at the top were anxious to be rid of Bonaparte. When intelligence reports revealed Les Moines's troublesome strides toward securing Napoleon's dreams of adding Russia and Britain to his continental empire, Carmichael was tasked with putting an end to their efforts—once and for all—by fair means or foul.

James untucked his sodden linen shirt, pulling it free of his waistband, and rolled his aching shoulders. Carmichael had made it clear that no one but himself would know the true nature of James's assignment. He'd have very little in the way of resources other than his skill and wits. James was well aware that eventually all within the Young Corinthians would assume he had betrayed his compatriots and become a traitor to Crown and Country. It was not a role he relished, but he'd rather take it on himself than have Carmichael hand it off to one of his fellow Corinthians. Compared to others, he had little to lose—and no one to care if he died while carrying out his assignment.

And so he'd agreed. It had taken over a year to secure his footing within the organization, and six months more to prove his dedication to the cause, establishing a place in the despicable group.

Which had landed him squarely on the beach of St. Aldhelm's Isle, where he'd done battle with his fellow Corinthians mere hours before. His most recent undertaking for Les Moines had had him hunting for emeralds in the wilds of Dorset. He'd managed to ensure that the jewels would not fall into Napoleon's hands, but not without incident. The time had come to reveal himself as a traitor to his fellow Corinthian agents, and thus he'd been shot at by a baronet's daughter while trying to board a boat. Acting on instinct, he'd sunk below the waves and swum until his lungs nearly burst. When he'd surfaced, the Corinthians were gone, leaving the world to mourn the loss of James Marlowe, traitor.

He doubted anyone would spend more than a passing moment regretting his "death."

Out on the dark water, a light flickered, rising and falling on the swell of the waves.

He shoved himself up from the wet sand, standing as the light drew brighter with the approach of a boat that was scheduled to retrieve both James and the jewels.

There would be hell to pay for the loss of the emeralds, he thought, and his apparent untimely demise would be a nuisance. But James was well versed in the art of improvising.

"*Un beau soir pour aller nager, oui?*" one of the men called out, the other crewmen responding to his sally with hearty laughter as they shipped their oars.

A lovely evening for a swim, James silently repeated the man's words in English, grinding his teeth with the effort it took to keep from snarling a reply. He walked to the water's edge and stepped in, the wet sand sucking at his boots as he waded through the surf to the waiting boat.

"Merriment not from you, Marlowe?" the man asked in broken English as he offered James his hand.

James hauled himself up into the small skiff, the boat rocking as he took a seat near the bow. "The emeralds are gone," he growled in French, hardly having the patience for Morel's butchering of his mother tongue.

"Oh," Morel replied matter-of-factly in his sailors' patois. "They'll likely kill you, then. It was a pleasure knowing you."

A second rousing chorus of laughter broke out as the men lowered their oars and began to row. Morel pounded James on the back with a beefy hand. "I am joking, of course. Dixon and his men will see to the emeralds."

James knew Morel was wrong. There was no way the traitorous Mr. Dixon could retrieve the emeralds—now that they were in the possession of the Corinthians. Still, James saw no benefit in answering the man either way, so he simply nodded and looked out toward the waiting ship that would take him to France.

"Still, if I were you," Morel suggested, "I would give some thought to explaining yourself. Your aristocratic English face will only get you so far."

As if on cue, Morel's motley gang erupted in rough laughter once again.

"How long is the crossing to France?" James asked, ignoring Morel's comment.

"Twelve hours. Anxious to be rid of your country?"

James deducted twelve hours from the coming months it would take to bring down Les Moines. The sale of the emeralds had been intended to fund Napoleon's fight. With the jewels now in safe hands, James was that much closer to slapping the hell out of the organization.

"Something like that."

"Clarissa, do sit down." Isabelle Collins, daughter of the Comte de Tulaine, the estranged wife of Robert Collins, the Marquess of Westbridge, and Clarissa's beloved mother patted the space next to her on the gold settee.

"Mother, please," Clarissa groaned. She pressed her forehead to the cool glass panes of the window. Below, Parisian society strolled past 123 rue de la Fontaine, blissfully unaware of the tempest of emotion within Clarissa and Isabelle's home. "How you can sit still is beyond me."

"I am hungry and thirsty. Now, do come and sit, *chérie*."

Clarissa lifted her head and turned, taking in her mother's somber face. "We are in danger—Bernard is in danger," she began, sitting down and taking the offered cup of tea. "I've been to the studio, his home. He is nowhere to be found."

"Not even at the tavern?" Isabelle asked in a whisper.

Clarissa reached for a fourth sugar cube and pitched it into the cup. "No," she replied grimly, "not even the tavern."

"I feel sure Monsieur St. Michelle would not want to involve you further." Isabelle patted Clarissa's arm reassuringly, though her darkened eyes betrayed her concern.

Clarissa returned her cup to the silver tray with a snap, the sweetened brew sloshing over the sides and onto the plate of biscuits. "But I *am* involved—*we* are involved, Mother. Those horrible men threatened both of us. I've no idea how, but they knew I was there, as if they'd been watching Bernard's studio."

Isabelle traced the rim of her delicate cup with the tip of her forefinger, frowning in thought. "*Chérie*, could they not have heard your footsteps?"

"Even so, how did they know of you?" Clarissa countered.

"What young woman does not possess a mother?"

Unable to sit still, Clarissa rose from the settee and began to pace the plush carpet. Her muslin skirts swirled about her ankles, echoing her agitation. "Mother, this is all too coincidental. I cannot believe their knowledge can be explained so easily."

Isabelle gently set her cup and saucer on the tray, then cleared her throat. "Clarissa, *chérie*, there is no need to be so dramatic."

"On the contrary—this is hardly my emotions at play," Clarissa countered, clasping her hands behind her back as she stalked the length of the room and back.

She was afraid. Deep within her bones, she was terrified, and for good reason. Her mother's response, however, was hardly surprising. Before they had left London to live in France, Isabelle could not have been a more doting mother, loving wife, and caring friend. Her beauty and charm were matched only by the love she lavished on all those fortunate enough to be in her life.

And then her husband's flagrant affair came to light. The other woman was never identified, nor would Clarissa's father deny or confirm, but the damage was done all the same. Isabelle shut tight her heart and escaped into herself, choosing existence over emotion, the safety of distance over the danger of involvement.

Her father's betrayal had destroyed Clarissa as well, though her response could not have been more different from her mother's. She was enraged. She was embittered. She craved revenge.

For Clarissa, the betrayal was twofold, with the most important men in her life disappointing her in the worst way. For just as her father had set light to the happiness and security of her well-fashioned world, James had seen fit to burn it to the ground. James Marlowe, youngest son of the Baron of Richmond, the love of Clarissa's life, had destroyed her world as surely as her father had set fire to Isabelle's.

"My dear," Isabelle said in a controlled tone, interrupting Clarissa's thoughts. "Let us not quarrel yet again on this point."

Clarissa stopped pacing and moved quickly to her mother, dropping to her knees. "*Maman,* we are different, you and I—this you know all too well. You find weakness in love. I find my strength. I love Bernard, for he's been both mentor and dear friend to me here in Paris. I owe him far more than I can ever repay. Therefore I must ensure his safety. I simply could not do anything else. Can you understand?"

Isabelle took Clarissa's hand and kissed it, holding it to her cheek as though it were the greatest of treasures. "I do, *chérie,* I do. But what is to be done? It seems that St. Michelle does not want your help. And do not forget: You are one woman against three ruffians. Hardly enviable odds."

"True enough," Clarissa agreed, "though perhaps not insurmountable."

2

If there was one thing James had learned from his previous trips to Paris it was this: Expect the unexpected. Tout et Plus was just that. A brothel located in the heart of Montmarte, the establishment went far beyond any house of ill repute within the confines of London—or all of England, James would have ventured to guess.

Beautiful women, in a dazzling variety of luscious shapes, coloring, and sizes, strolled about the main dining area while even more danced upon the stage near the front, their varying degrees of undress the perfect accompaniment to their provocative show. Low candlelight and miles of sapphire velvet draped across every available surface made one feel as if in a heated dream, while the slow, rhythmic music from the group of musicians near the dancers put one's mind in the mood for activities best undertaken behind closed doors.

A petite woman with long, chestnut curls, carrying a shepherd's crook, stepped into James's line of vision. She wore a white bonnet festooned with satin pansies, silk stockings, garters, and nothing else. Her backside was so round and firm, James could have bit into it right then and there. He scrubbed his hand over his chin and looked at the Les Moines agent sitting next to him. "This is a test, is it not?"

The man, who'd only given his last name of "Durand" when asked, continued to stare at the stage, emitting a low growl in response.

"I'll take that as a yes," James muttered, tossing back his brandy in one swallow. He'd assumed the lost emeralds would cost him some ground within Les Moines, and they had. But even worse, he'd yet to meet anyone beyond Durand's ranking, which, as best James could tell, fell somewhere within the middle of the hierarchy. Being assigned such operatives meant he was further along than the likes of Morel, but still nowhere near trusted enough to meet face-to-face with the ringleader.

Over the last two days he'd been ordered to appear at a series of bars, parks, and now Tout et Plus. Each time, a different operative had interrogated him regarding the loss of the emeralds—to catch him in a lie, no doubt. It was hardly an issue for James, lying was as natural to him as breathing at this point in his career, but it was supremely frustrating. The emeralds had been nonnegotiable, that he knew, but Les Moines were proving to be even more suspicious and prepared than the Corinthians had originally thought.

James suspected that a grand gesture was in order. He simply wasn't sure what would be grand enough in the eyes of Les Moines.

"And the last emerald?" Durand asked, his dull gaze never leaving the stage.

James looked at the man's extraordinarily ordinary face once again. "To the best of my knowledge the Corinthians are in possession of it—unless Dixon was successful on your behalf?"

Durand reached for an ornate snuffbox on the table, opened it, and raised a pinch to his hooked nose. "That is of no consequence to you."

The shepherdess began to sway back and forth to the music, arching her back ever so slightly as she did so.

"All right, Durand. Let us get to the point. What must I do to make up for the loss of the emeralds?"

"Finally, a pertinent question," Durand replied, toss-ing the snuffbox onto the table.

James was known for many things. Patience was not one of them. He'd never cared for verbal sparring, and the past hour spent in Durand's company had not in-duced him to change his mind. Still, he bided his time and busied himself with thoughts of the shepherdess as he waited for the man to continue.

"There is a rich Canadian with dreams of rising in the ranks of the British aristocracy," Durand began, his eyes settling once again on the dancing girls. "He wishes to have his daughter's portrait painted by a particular Parisian artist—apparently this is a mark of some im-portance, yes?"

James had never made it his business to study the whims of London society, but he'd spent enough time with the ton to know that the right assets could greatly enhance one's social position, and thus a daughter's de-sirability on the marriage mart.

"Yes," he said noncommittally, gesturing for Durand to continue.

"This Canadian, he has more money than sense. If we secure the services of the artist, he will pay all that we need—and more."

James focused his gaze on the dancers and waited, not wanting to appear overly eager. "And where do I fit in all of this?"

"The Canadian is too busy with his work to travel fur-ther. He insists that the artist come to him in London."

James looked at Durand once again. "Why?" he asked.

"His daughter is readying for her presentation before the English court," Durand answered with a sneer of disapproval. "And with the money in his possession, we cannot force the issue."

"So the artist must go to the Canadian," James said simply.

Durand waved away an offer of more drink from a buxom woman wearing fairy wings. "That is where you fit in."

"Convincing the artist to sail for London? Really, Durand, is that all?" James was sure there had to be something more to the assignment.

"You cannot possibly be as stupid as you look." Durand replied, growling as the fairy attempted to fill his glass a second time. "You will accompany the artist to London and make sure that he completes the portrait and the Canadian pays what he has promised. And if you do not," Durand turned and looked directly at James, "you will die."

"Fair enough," James replied honestly. After all, he and Durand were more alike than not. Both operated in a world where life and death were merely currency to be traded. Though James had no idea how he might manage to steal the money before it fell into Les Moines's hands and escape with his head intact, he wouldn't let that detail keep him awake at night.

"Now," Durand said, standing abruptly, "you will find the shepherdess upstairs. Third door on the right. This building was once a monastery; ironic, no?"

The fairy appeared again, but this time Durand allowed her to approach. He kissed her outstretched hand then slung her over his shoulder and slapped her bare bum. "Do not keep her waiting or she'll use the crook," he warned before disappearing down a long corridor.

Death was, without a doubt, not worth losing sleep over, James reflected. As a younger man, he'd thought differently; the love of one woman and her happiness had been more important to him than anything else could ever be. But she'd cast him out, claiming he knew little of true love. And in time, he'd come to agree.

No, death was hardly worth lost sleep. But a shepherdess? Well, that was an entirely different matter. And James intended to show her how very little like a monk he really was.

Clarissa looked to the heavens and offered up a small prayer of thanks for her mother's predictability. It was Wednesday, which meant that Isabelle was at the Musée Napoleon with her childhood friend Madeline Moreau. The two women would stroll through the Greek antiquities before proceeding to the sculptures, where they would linger for a time before making their way to a café for refreshments.

Isabelle had penned a note to Madeline, telling her she could not come, but Clarissa had convinced her to recant and keep to their regular Wednesday schedule.

She had given the performance of a lifetime, Clarissa thought, as she hurried toward Bernard's studio, her petite maid, Sophia, struggling to keep up. She'd promised her mother she would not set foot outside their home the entire day. Isabelle was firmly convinced that Bernard's trouble was better handled by the artist himself. She had kissed Clarissa on first one cheek, then the other, and commended her for making such a sound choice.

Of course, the moment her mother had left for the museum, Clarissa had called for Sophia. Within the hour, she was dressed in a pale violet walking gown, her hair upswept in a sensible yet fetching style, and a parasol with a particularly sharp point was in her gloved hands.

She nervously twirled the parasol now. Her mother had been right when she'd suggested that Clarissa's emotions played a large part in her daughter's life. As far as she was concerned, this was hardly a fact to deny, though it did have a habit of landing her in interesting situations.

"Interesting?" Clarissa said out loud. No, not interesting, she reflected. Perhaps "challenging" was a more appropriate description. Be that as it may, she thought with conviction, she was not about to close herself off from involvement or attachment with other people as her mother had done. She'd feel the weight of the world, even if it meant that in the end it would crush her.

She turned onto rue Marcadet and at last could see the street entrance of the slim row house where Bernard's atelier was located. One of the neckless twin bodyguards stood outside the door, his vacant gaze fastened somewhere beyond Clarissa's shoulder. A cold tendril of fear wrapped itself about her spine.

She stopped abruptly and turned to face Sophia. "Here," she began earnestly, reaching into her reticule and retrieving a handful of coins. "Wait for me at the café."

Sophia nodded obediently and took the proffered coins, hurrying across the street and into the small shop.

Clarissa lifted the hem of her skirt and ran, coming to a skidding halt in front of one twin. His bulk blocked the door, preventing her entry.

She pointed her parasol at the giant's chest. "Move," she demanded, her voice brisk and commanding.

The bulky twin easily twisted the makeshift weapon from Clarissa's hold, and with a quick snap broke it in two.

"Impressive. You're capable of breaking a parasol. Congratulations." Undaunted by the show of strength, Clarissa fixed him with an intimidating, icy stare. "Let me pass. Now."

He only smiled, then stepped aside to let her by. "It is your funeral, mademoiselle."

Clarissa bit the inside of her cheek and brushed past him, turning the familiar heavy door handle with one hand and pushing with the other. She paused for a moment at the foot of the stairs. She was committed to her course now. Even if she wanted to change her mind—which she didn't—she could hardly turn back. The giant's cold smile implied that he looked forward with anticipation to her confronting whatever was waiting for her upstairs. And just as likely, he would enjoy the prospect of crushing her in much the same way he'd destroyed the parasol. She assumed the other henchman waited upstairs with the man she'd attacked three days before.

And there was Bernard.

Clarissa tucked a few stray hairs into place, licked her lips, and squared her shoulders before ascending the stairs as though she were attending the ball of the season. There was no question that she would be defeated. But she would not, under any circumstances, be outclassed.

"Is he dead?" James asked, eyeing the painter collapsed in the corner. Upon meeting the indelicate twins, he'd insisted that he visit the artist alone. Durand had refused and that had been that.

There was some satisfaction in being right, he thought to himself as the twin rolled the man over with his foot. But not at the moment.

"He's breathing, but his arm doesn't look right."

James crossed the room and looked down at St. Michelle. "You broke it, you imbecile."

The twin cocked his head to the side and looked again. "At least he's not dead," he offered, starting at the sound of someone on the stairs.

"Oh, lovely, your brother. Perhaps he can break the other arm for us, then?" James said angrily, kicking at an upended table and splintering one of its slim legs.

He stalked to the windows and surveyed the district below. The situation had quickly gone from bad to worse. When James arrived at the artist's studio, St. Michelle, drunk as James had ever seen a man, had flatly refused to take the job in London. James countered, St. Michelle balked. James threatened, St. Michelle spewed nonsense concerning his rights as an artist.

And then the twin had lost his temper and thrown the man across the room.

"Oh, my God, Bernard!"

James spun around at the sound of a woman's voice.

It couldn't possibly be.

He caught a flash of pale skin, raven-black hair, and violet fabric as she rushed toward St. Michelle, dropping to her knees and bending low over the fallen man.

"What have you done?" the woman demanded, twisting to look over her shoulder at the men. Her appalled gaze reached James and she froze, eyes widening with shock.

But it was.

Those violet eyes, which he'd thought never to see again, narrowed in anger and outrage as her gaze swept swiftly over him before returning to meet his.

"You!" Clarissa's voice was choked with emotion.

"No, mademoiselle, not I. Him," James replied lightly, pointing to the twin. "He is responsible for this—well, that's not entirely true. But the broken arm was certainly all his doing."

Every inch of his body wanted to react to the sight of her. Rumors had raced through London when she and her mother had fled to Paris five years before, but James had never entertained the possibility of seeing her again.

"How can you—"

"Allow such a thing to happen?" James interrupted, silencing her, at least for the moment. "It's simple, really.

St. Michelle had a choice to make. Clearly, he made the wrong one."

He could not let his feelings get in the way. Revealing the fact that he and Clarissa knew each other would pique even the twin's limited interest.

St. Michelle groaned in pain and clutched Clarissa's arm. She quickly pulled off her pelisse, bundled it into a makeshift pillow, and carefully tucked it under the artist's head. "Do not move," she ordered, then stood. "He has a broken arm. How do you miscreants propose he paint your portrait now?"

"At least he's not dead," the twin offered a second time.

Clarissa moved about the room at an efficient clip, gathering a basin of water, lavender soap, and clean cloth rags. She was familiar with the space, even proprietary. "He might as well be dead," she hissed. "Without the use of his right arm, he cannot paint. And if he cannot paint, what good is he to you?"

Understanding finally dawned on the giant's face. He rubbed his bald head in consternation before shoving his hands into his pockets. "What do we do now?"

"Yes, what *do* we do now?" Clarissa repeated as she knotted two of the rags into a sling.

St. Michelle groaned again.

"Give me a moment to think," James growled. He'd not spent a year and a half of his life on this assignment only to be bested by a brainless giant.

"This portrait, who commissioned it?" Clarissa asked as she wiped smears of blood from St. Michelle's bruised and cut face.

James scrubbed one hand over his forehead. "A Canadian, newly arrived in England," he said wearily.

"I can assume, then, that this Canadian has never met Monsieur St. Michelle before?"

St. Michelle's good hand grasped Clarissa's. "No, do not even think of such a thing."

"It would be easy enough, my friend," Clarissa said gently but firmly, prying his fingers free so she could continue her ministrations to his battered face. "I fooled you once, so why not the Canadian? Besides, my talent is up for the task, would you not agree?"

The giant frowned. "What are you two going on about?"

James's jaw clenched. She couldn't possibly be proposing that she . . . No. It could not be, though her presence here in St. Michelle's studio made much more sense now. She'd spoken often of her desire to study with a great artist—and lamented that being female would make success difficult, if not impossible. Clarissa's talent had been enormous, astonishing, five years ago. James could only assume that her artistic skills had grown under the tutelage of St. Michelle.

But not enough to risk her further involvement with Les Moines, he thought grimly.

"I will go in his place," Clarissa stated firmly, rising to her feet to face the men.

The twin wrinkled his bulbous nose. "But you're a woman."

Clarissa's mouth compressed into a thin, straight line. "Yes, a woman, with enough talent to pass for St. Michelle. And," she paused, planting a hand firmly on each hip, "your only hope. I've masqueraded as a man successfully before. Let's see if I can manage it again, shall we?"

"No," James and St. Michelle roared in unison.

The twin held up one beefy hand. "Wait a minute." He took Clarissa's upper arm and dragged her to a window close to where the artist lay. "Look there, out the window," he commanded.

Clarissa complied, tilting her head and peering upward to let the sunlight fully reveal her face.

The giant looked from Clarissa to St. Michelle and back again, his feeble brain comparing the two. "I think it might work. She's close enough to the same height, her voice is husky, her coloring is similar, and her breasts are flatter than my grandmother's crêpes," he stated, pointing toward her bosom beneath the high-necked violet gown. "With a morning coat and cravat—well, yes, it just might work."

"Not a chance in hell," James bit out. "I will not leave this to a woman."

Clarissa batted the twin's hovering hand away from her bosom as if it were no more than an annoying gnat and turned toward James. "You've no choice. If this Canadian has his heart set on a St. Michelle portrait, no other artist will be acceptable—and you well know it."

"She's right," the twin said.

James wanted to hit the bastard. "Durand will never agree."

"Not that I would presume to know this Durand nor his affinity for common sense, but perhaps speaking with him would be prudent?" Clarissa said stiffly, directing her question to the henchman. "But first, a doctor is needed. Please, on your way to inform your superior, summon Monsieur Leveque and bid him come at once."

She turned her back on the men to kneel once more at St. Michelle's side and reassure him that all would be well.

Not bloody likely, James thought, though he kept the conviction to himself.

Clarissa waited until she heard the door slam shut below before peering out the small studio window that looked out on the building's front steps. She bit the inside of her cheek as she watched James confer with the ruffians and then stride off down the avenue, one giant keeping pace beside him while the other remained to stand guard at the entrance.

Not until James disappeared did she press the torn rags clutched in her hands to her face, giving way to the storm of tears that had been building since she entered the studio.

"You are weeping?" Bernard asked, groaning from the effort.

Clarissa was unable to respond. Sobs shook her shoulders, easing the overwhelming tension of the last moments and the effort needed to hold them in. At last, she patted her face dry and took three deep breaths.

"I *was* weeping, and now," she replied, turning to face Bernard, "I am not." She resolutely walked to him and bent over, catching his shoulders in a gentle but determined grip. "To the divan with you."

Bernard awkwardly sat up, then used his one good arm to scrabble and push himself to his feet. "You cannot do this, Clarissa. You've no idea who those men are."

"Then tell me," she said simply.

They reached the divan and Clarissa helped lower Bernard as gently as she could, propping his legs up on an old wooden bench before settling in on the floor next to him.

"The 'Durand' that the man mentioned," Bernard began, protectively holding his injured arm close to his chest, "is well known to all within the Parisian underworld. He dabbles in legitimate businesses, but his real interest lies in somewhat darker undertakings—thievery, kidnapping. Even murder. Antoine said Durand is rumored to have ties to Napoleon."

"And you trust the word of your barkeep?" Clarissa asked skeptically.

"Implicitly."

Clarissa sensed she was painfully close to crying again. How could James have gotten himself involved with such men? She hated him for what he'd done to her—in some ways she hated him even more now than when it had happened—but to think that he was capable of treason.

"Why did you not run when Antoine told you this?" she demanded, swiping at an errant tear dampening her cheek.

Bernard closed his eyes tightly. "I did. I made it as far as Orly before this sent me back." He clumsily reached into his coat pocket and pulled out a scrap of paper.

Clarissa sighed at the sight of it. Some months back, after Bernard was discovered sleeping in the kitchens of a tavern in Rouen, she'd insisted that he record his name and address on the scrap and carry it with him at all times. Apparently he'd been drunk in Orly and someone had found the slip of paper and sent him home.

"I would have protested my return if I'd been able," Bernard assured her. "As for you, I suppose it was too much to hope that you'd stay out of all this."

It was not the first time Bernard had attempted to fix a problem with copious amounts of drink, but Clarissa saw little point in bringing that up now. "Yes, my friend, it was."

"In that case, you must run," he said in all seriousness, as though it were a simple matter.

Clarissa eyed him wearily. "I'll do no such thing."

Bernard crumpled the note in his fist. "Be sensible, do not let your pride get in the way of your safety. You are afraid—as well you should be. Escape before it is too late." He tossed the scrap and Clarissa watched it land on the paint-stained floor near the broken table.

Fear was just one of many emotions Clarissa had encountered since waking this morning—all of them were unwelcome. "You're right. I am terrified. But one man guards the door below and the other two will return soon enough. It is too late for escape. Our fate is in my hands."

Durand stared at the neckless twin, his displeasure evident. "You broke the man's arm?"

Neckless moved restlessly in his seat. "How could I have known he would land on his arm?"

"And you brought Marlowe here, without consulting me?" Durand pressed, his hands gripping the mahogany desk that occupied most of the northern wall of his office.

"Time was of the essence," Neckless answered anxiously, nudging James with his elbow. "Tell him."

It hadn't been at all difficult to convince the twin that a meeting with Durand could not wait. James had seen fit to work the man into a lather over the injured artist, advising the lackwit that Durand would be livid over such a mistake. The twin had hastily agreed and called for a carriage at once.

They'd ended up not far from Tout et Plus in the 3rd arrondissement, where the questionable intersected with the respectable.

James looked at the twin from the corner of his eye, nearly feeling sorry for the man. Durand would have his head for the day's work. Such was the nature of the game they played.

"As I see it," James answered, distancing himself from the twin's efforts, "we've very little choice in the matter. Either the girl masquerades as St. Michelle or we call off the deal altogether. There's no time to find another artist—nor, dare I say, would we find one competent enough to undertake the portrait. The girl is our only hope."

Durand cursed and slammed his fist against the desk.

"And if I agree? What assurance do I have that this bitch will cooperate?"

"Threaten to kill St. Michelle?" Neckless offered enthusiastically.

Durand looked at James. "Will this be enough?"

"From what I witnessed, there is true affection between the two. Perhaps taking the man into our custody would convince the girl—"

"Or the mother," Neckless interrupted, rubbing his hands together. "Yes, the mother. I've been watching their house long enough to know that the two are very close. Take the mother and the girl will do anything you ask."

James resisted the urge to clout the twin across the face, and instead watched Durand take in the information with disturbing interest. James knew damned well that the twin was correct. Clarissa's mother was all that she had left in the world. As such, he could not let this happen.

"The mother, you say?" Durand asked, drumming his fingers on the desk.

"Come now, the last thing we need is a weeping mama on our hands. St. Michelle will do nicely—and all that he'll require is an unlimited supply of wine. The mother would prove exhausting, I assure you."

James knew that he needed to tread lightly. One false move, one slim indication that he valued the needs of Clarissa and her mother over those of Les Moines, and Durand would pounce with pantherlike swiftness, putting an end to James and all that he'd worked for.

Durand ceased drumming and looked straight at James. "We've dealt with such women before."

"And the girl? If it is true that her mother and she are indeed as close as we believe, what if the pressure is too much and she's unable to go through with the plan?"

James held tight to his restraint as he teetered on the

precipice. He was doing everything in his power to keep Clarissa and her mother safe, but he was afraid it wasn't nearly enough.

"It is your job to ensure that she does," Durand replied dryly, then stood from his chair and walked around the desk. "Go," he told James. "I've unfinished business with this one."

Every inch of James's body tensed with the desire to argue, but he fought against it and stood, nodding to Durand. Neckless caught his eye with a pleading look, but James only turned toward the door and left. He couldn't do anything for the man now without compromising his own position. There was no point in offering hope when there was none to be had.

3

The carriage rolled to a slow stop behind another carriage waiting just outside 123 rue de la Fontaine, Clarissa's home. The door suddenly opened and one of the overgrown brothers appeared first, followed by Lady Westbridge and a second man, whose arm was wound tightly about the woman's waist. She was pale though composed, a glacial calm in her eyes as she looked quickly up and down the street.

She'd hardly aged in the five years since James had seen her on that fateful night he'd been refused entry to Westbridge House but had forced his way in, making it only as far as the entryway before four footmen wrestled him to the floor.

Lady Isabelle had appeared at the top of the stairs and called his name before descending. She'd gripped the banister for dear life as though she barely had the strength to walk. After insisting that the men release James, she'd offered him her hand. He'd held fast to her slim, soft fingers, hardly able to believe that it had all come to this point.

Some months before, when James had been recruited into the Young Corinthians, Robert Collins, the Marquess of Westbridge, had taken him under his wing. James had been grateful for the man's help with his first official case as a Corinthian and eager to learn all that he could. He'd looked forward to dinner with the marquess and his family, for James's gratitude had grown into true admiration and affection for Westbridge.

He couldn't have known that he'd meet the love of his life that evening. Lady Clarissa walked into the drawing room and straight into his heart. James had never pondered love before. As the second son of a baron he allowed himself to harbor hopes for a wife with money but never one he would love.

But Clarissa bowled him over with her beauty and independent nature. She was an emotional creature, something many men would tire of easily. But James admired her for it, her honesty rather refreshing.

She'd loved him unabashedly, giving of herself and her time as if James was the most important person in the world to her.

And then the rumors had begun. Whispers of an affair between Clarissa's father and a well-known courtesan were far too delicious for the ton to ignore, and naturally, the talk had made its way to Isabelle's ears.

The woman had been devastated and Clarissa right along with her. "Theirs had been a love match," she'd sobbed when she told James the news. She'd looked to him for support and assurance that he would never do such a thing to her.

The problem was that James suspected the rumors were false. The marquess had been on assignment, the courtesan a Young Corinthian informant. But he could hardly admit as much to Clarissa. So he'd assured her that, no, he would never even entertain the thought of betraying her trust.

He'd held her close and calmed her. Then suggested that perhaps the rumors were just that—unsubstantiated and quite possibly false. James could not stomach the idea that all of society, most especially Westbridge's own family, thought the marquess capable of such betrayal. He felt it his duty to in some small way defend the man.

Clarissa had flown into a rage, claiming that James's support for the man who had broken her mother's heart and so dreadfully disappointed his daughter showed how little he knew of the true nature of love.

James had erupted as well, declaring Clarissa's inability to trust him revealed she was not the woman he'd believed her to be.

She'd told him to leave and never return.

He'd assured her he would do just as she asked.

And yet he'd found himself on her doorstep, holding Lady Isabelle's hand and searching for the words that would put everything back in order.

No words had come.

Lady Isabelle's eyes had filled with tears when she told him to leave her daughter's life forever.

"Sir?"

The voice pulled James from the painful memory and he turned to look at the man sitting next to him.

"Yes, Dupont," he answered the tailor, watching as the marchioness was forced into the carriage. The twin climbed in after her while the other man slammed the door shut and yelled for the coachman to drive on.

James turned when Dupont pulled an ornate gold pocket watch from his waistcoat pocket and consulted the time. "I have an appointment in an hour."

"Of course," James concurred, turning to the carriage door and opening it. He stepped from the coach and waited as Dupont alighted, a serviceable satchel in hand. They started up the steps, nodding at the man who stood guard outside the front door.

"Dupont," the burly man said by way of hello.

"Simon," the tailor answered simply, gesturing for the man to open the door.

He complied, pushing the red lacquered door wide enough for the two to step inside.

A young maid met them in the foyer, her body shaking as she dipped a polite curtsy.

"Upstairs, I presume?" James asked, moving toward the stairs.

The maid threw herself bodily in his path. "I'll ask my lady to come down. You will wait here."

James nodded and watched the girl practically fly to the upper floor, disappearing down an east-facing hall.

Dupont checked his pocket watch a second time.

Clarissa's irate voice echoed from above. "Am I to understand that he requires my presence below? You may tell the man I'd rather ride a horse—"

The tirade was cut short by the sound of a door slamming shut. The maid appeared shortly after, descending the stairs at a markedly slower pace. "I'm afraid Lady Clarissa is indisposed at the moment."

James looked at Dupont. "Shall we?"

"We shall," the tiny tailor confirmed, hefting his satchel in one hand and awaiting James's sign.

The maid reached the bottom of the stairs and readied to curtsy again, obviously hopeful that the men would take their leave.

"Now," James said to Dupont.

The tailor ran toward the stairs just as James reached for the maid and held her still.

"Do not follow," he warned the maid, releasing her. "Or I'll have reason to be angry."

The girl blanched at the thought and scurried toward the back of the house.

James took the stairs two at a time, discovering Dupont waiting for him just in front of the only closed door.

"Coward," James taunted.

"Smart," the man countered, stepping aside so that James might enter first.

James raised his hand to knock, then thought better of it. The element of surprise would prove beneficial in this situation—or at the very least, would hopefully ensure fewer injuries for himself and Dupont.

He noiselessly turned the polished brass handle, pushed the door open, and stepped in, allowing Dupont to slip in behind him before slamming it shut.

"How dare you!" Clarissa sat bolt upright in the middle of her bed, a multitude of embellished pillows in shades of blue surrounding her. She wore only a thin white night shift, and her hair was undone, cascading all around her shoulders and falling in a spill of glossy raven black silk reaching below where the coverlet met her waist.

She threw a pillow at James's head. He caught it neatly before it hit him square in the face. "How could you let them take her?" She'd been crying, he could tell. Her violet eyes were reddened, her lids swollen.

"They'll not harm her, I promise," James answered, needing to calm her. *It would be so easy,* he thought to himself, the desire to hold and comfort her surging free and surfacing from where he'd buried it five years ago. Two steps, three at the most, and he would be at her side.

"Your promises mean nothing to me," she said, fixing him with a cold glare. "You know that."

"It's all that I can offer you—and it's all that you'll get from the men I work for. Please, Clarissa, you've no other choice." James fingered the brocade fabric of the pillow, wanting to tear it in two. "Your mother will be taken to the country and treated with the utmost respect, I assure you. It's in the organization's best interest too."

"Of course," she replied, her voice devoid of emotion. "I'd forgotten that you've everything to gain from keeping me happy—at least for now." She paused and wiped the tears from her cheeks. "Clearly, the money this Canadian is willing to pay for the portrait is of great importance to you. If you wish to receive the payment, you'll provide proof of my mother's continuing safety. If not, I'll make sure that not a penny of the portrait fee returns to Paris. Do you understand?"

James tossed the pillow back, the small, rectangular frippery landing at the end of the bed. "Of course." He knew Clarissa like the back of his hand. If she said that she would make the money disappear, she would. And probably destroy the painting as well.

"Letters. I'll require letters from my mother. Written in her own hand," Clarissa added, drumming her fingers against the coverlet.

James wanted to hoot with delight over the woman's clever scheme, but knew he could not. "I'll ask Durand—"

"No," she interrupted, staring him straight in the eye. "You'll tell your superior that this is required—or I'll not move from this chamber. Do we understand each other?"

Dupont cleared his throat. "I've a little under an hour." He bent to open his satchel. "I suggest we begin."

James returned Clarissa's fierce stare with one of his own before nodding at the tailor.

"What is going on?" Clarissa asked incredulously, pulling the coverlet higher to drape around her shoulders.

"I'll warn you, I've little experience with gowns." Dupont continued, efficiently producing a measuring tape, scissors, a length of chalk, and a small metal box of pins from his kit. "And with our time nearly gone. Well, I'll do what can be done, but I'm hardly a miracle worker."

"What. Is. Going. On?" Clarissa ground out for the second time.

James addressed Dupont first. "She'll require five suits, complete with shirts, vests, breeches—everything."

The man nodded, his experience in working with Les Moines clear from his lack of surprise. "Very well. Please, come and stand here," he directed Clarissa, pointing to where a woven rose twined intricately with an ivy pattern just at the corner of the carpet.

"Clarissa, we must be sure your appearance as St. Michelle is believable. You cannot travel to England without the proper attire," James explained. "Do as Dupont has asked—and do it quickly. The cobbler will be here any minute."

"Laurent?" Dupont inquired. "You do not want to keep that man waiting. Come, mademoiselle, there is no time to lose."

Clarissa tossed her hair back over her right shoulder and rose from the bed, coming to stand in exactly the spot that Dupont had indicated.

"Thank you." James leaned against the oak door and folded his arms over his chest. His casual pose was deceptive. His muscles were strung tight as he fought to control the urge to carry Clarissa out of the house to safety.

Clearly unaware of the conflict of emotions that tore at James, Clarissa's stormy violet eyes shot daggers at him. She held out her arms and allowed Dupont to begin. "Do not thank me. This is not for you—not now, not ever."

After a day fraught with worry, Clarissa climbed the stairs and sought her mother's room. She pulled a brush through her long hair and stared into the triple dressing-table mirror in her mother's chamber. The maid had turned down the bed out of habit, then hastily attempted to remake it, until Clarissa assured her she needn't.

There was something comforting about the turned-down bed. As if at any moment her mother would walk through the chamber door and wonder at Clarissa's presence in her room. Clarissa pulled the brush through her thick fall of hair again and waited, but her mother did not appear.

She'd not even told Isabelle of seeing James again, Clarissa thought. By the time she arrived home from caring for Bernard, it was far too late to discuss such matters. And Clarissa hadn't really had the time to properly consider James. The danger of the situation had kept her mind spinning with concern. The sight of him in Bernard's studio flashed in her mind. There was a hint of the young man she'd known, his deep brown hair and umber eyes the same. But he'd grown into a more commanding male, his cheekbones and nose more chiseled, his physique honed to muscled perfection.

"James," Clarissa said his name out loud, then dragged the brush so hard through her hair that her scalp tingled. He'd broken her heart when he'd sided with her father five years before. He'd even gone so far as to question the quality of her love—as if her refusal to believe her father's innocence meant she'd somehow failed James.

She set the brush down on the mahogany table. James had convinced Clarissa of his love. Shown her with his embraces and told her time and again. She'd believed him, because she wanted to, and also needed to. Other men had paid her pretty compliments and pretended to find her emotional nature charming. But she'd always seen through their flattery, no matter how much they tried to convince her otherwise.

James had recognized Clarissa's nature for what it was—an essential part of her, no more changeable than her arms or legs. He'd understood the value in her temperament, come to appreciate her rich emotional exuberance. And when he'd left, claiming her heart had gotten the better of her head, she was inconsolable.

She pulled her long, thick hair over her shoulder and began to plait it. The last five years in Paris under Bernard's tutelage had done wonders to restore Clarissa. He'd made her see that a balance between the two was ideal—a blending of mind and emotion allowed her to discover the truth in her subject while remaining objective enough to be authentic in her work.

She'd worked hard to forget all that James had wrought. Yet here he was in her life again.

Clarissa finished with the braid and stood, walking to her mother's bed. She'd thought to speak with her mother that very morning about him, after she'd had the opportunity to think on things. But she'd overslept, dreams of the Rat and the neckless twins plaguing her the entire night.

She lifted the skirt of her pale blue muslin night rail and climbed into her mother's bed, slipping under the coverlet with one of the pillows tucked into her arms. The linens smelled of her mother, the delicate hint of rose both comforting and distressing to Clarissa.

She cried herself to sleep, fearing for the morning but knowing full well that dawn would come.

"Do you require assistance?"

James stood outside Clarissa's door, with Dupont by his side.

"No!" Clarissa ground out, and silence fell over the house once again.

He'd been required to recount through the door his hasty conversation with Durand regarding the marchioness's safety. The man had acquiesced to Clarissa's demand that her mother be allowed to write to her, though James felt they could not spare a moment lest the Frenchman's word suddenly became worthless.

Clarissa had accepted the newly tailored garments then promptly slammed the door in his face. And that, by James's estimation, had been nearly twenty minutes before.

The tailor began to pace. "I wasn't sure how to accommodate her . . ." he trailed off. "There's a length of linen," he continued, his short legs covering the hall with surprising speed. "She'll need to wrap it thusly." He stopped in front of James and began to demonstrate on his own stout torso.

Behind them, the door opened and she stood in the threshold.

The two men turned in unison and looked at her.

"A fine job, if I do say so myself," Dupont exclaimed with delight, pulling Clarissa forward and gesturing for her to turn slowly. "The binding looks to have worked well," he said distractedly, eyeing her breasts critically. "And the breeches! Well, if I didn't know better, I would assume those to be the legs of a gentleman. Mind you, your build made the task far easier than if you possessed a more feminine form . . ."

James ignored Dupont's observations and simply watched Clarissa revolve. He had to agree with Dupont—the binding worked, as did the breeches. If he were to encounter her on the street, James would not look twice. Even her hair, tucked up beneath a hat, was passable, though they would have to cut it off before reaching England. But he *knew* her—remembered every intimate detail of her body, which made the moment that much more bizarre.

"If you two are done, I'll need some assistance with the boots." Clarissa turned on her stockinged heels and returned to her room. "Dupont," she called after the tailor.

"The remainder of the clothing is downstairs. Please make sure that it is carefully packed," the tailor requested of James, then joined Clarissa, closing the door behind him.

4

"Are you comfortable?"

Clarissa swept the dark, dank ship's cabin with a critical eye, then looked at James. "Not in the least. Did you specifically request the most inhospitable of ships or was it merely my luck?"

James took one step toward the scarred lattice-backed chair where Clarissa sat, the planked floor creaking ominously under his boots. Then he stopped, uttered some sort of oath, and turned abruptly toward the captain's bed situated along the wall of the low-ceilinged cabin.

This would be the first significant amount of time they would spend in each other's company since their unexpected reunion. Clarissa had insisted James accompany her on horseback rather than ride in the carriage. And then she'd shut herself up in her room for the entirety of their stop last night. Clarissa couldn't help but miss the distance that had so conveniently separated them until now.

"There is a blockade in effect, Clarissa. Besides, it is important that we not be seen. Our presence will draw less attention in a ship of this nature rather than a more 'hospitable' vessel," he said tightly.

"By nature, I assume you refer to the fact that it is piloted by common criminals?"

Clarissa sat straighter in order to gain some relief

from the tightly wound fabric about her chest. Unwanted emotion churned in her stomach. Anger? Fear? Certainly, though there was something else. Something she didn't want to consider too closely.

"Are you well?" James asked, leaning against the opposite wall and folding his arms across his chest.

Clarissa breathed as deeply as she could, the binding fabric chafing against her skin as she did so. "Why would you ask such a question? No, of course I'm not well. You've placed my mother in danger, forced me into service, and torn me from my home." She rose from the chair and leaned her head against the wall, the wood rough beneath her forehead as she attempted to draw another, deeper breath. "Really, James, you've grown lack-witted in our time apart," she added caustically, her head beginning to spin.

Dimly, she heard the sound of footsteps, then his hands were upon her, ripping the linen shirt from her waistband, before slipping them beneath the soft fabric.

"What do you think you're doing?" she demanded, batting at his hands as she tried to escape his hold.

He spun her around and yanked the bindings loose, quickly unraveling her with deft skill. "When I asked if you were well, I was referring to your physical state. This," he paused, holding a fistful of the bindings at her eye level before tossing the length of fabric on the floor, "was slowly suffocating you."

Clarissa stared at the length of soft white fabric on the floor, drawing in welcome draughts of briny sea air while she caught her breath. "I'm sorry," she said simply, unable to look at him.

"For what, Clarissa?" he asked, gently catching her chin and turning her face up to his.

His touch was just as she remembered. Firm, yet gentle. "It's been so long, and yet I've fallen into our old pattern."

He cupped her cheek in his hand, his eyes searching hers. "Of quarreling? Yes, it has been quite some time, but I remember that part clearly."

Clarissa shrank back, pressing against the rough wall behind her. James's nearness suddenly threatened to overwhelm her senses. "It takes two to quarrel—"

"Clarissa," he interrupted, laying one finger against her lips. "Please, I've no desire to fight with you. What's in the past is just that—in the past." He removed his finger and stepped back, gesturing for Clarissa to take the chair while he lay down on the bed.

She instantly missed the feel of his skin on hers—and hated herself for it. She knew he was right. There was no point in wasting time when her mother was in danger. And James was, in all likelihood, her only hope of assuring her mother's safety. Durand and the rest of his gang were hardly the sort to inspire confidence in their promise to leave Isabelle unharmed if Clarissa completed her assignment.

And to succeed, she needed James's help.

Still, his transformation troubled Clarissa; his ability to remain calm and rational in her presence confused her. Or was it her response to him that frayed her nerves? She watched as he effortlessly folded his arms and cradled his skull in his intertwined fingers.

"And the present?" she queried, suddenly needing to think upon anything else but their shared past.

He appeared to be rocking slowly back and forth, the movement of the waves below providing an easy rhythm. "Once we arrive in Dover, we'll travel by coach to Bennett's London home—no more than a two-day ride. You'll begin the painting no later than—"

"You misunderstand me," Clarissa interrupted, tucking the tails of the linen shirt into her snug breeches. "What I meant was, how did you find yourself here, in the employ of such men?"

James dropped one booted foot to the floor. "Why do you want to know?" he asked, shifting to look at her.

"Why?" Clarissa parroted in disbelief. "Although you broke my heart, you were, at one time, an honorable man, James." She struggled to remain calm. "I suppose I'm curious, that's all. Why would the son of a British peer cast his lot with such a crew?"

James turned his head and stared once again at the low ceiling above him. "I broke your heart? Is that how you remember it?" he asked, his voice a low murmur.

"How else should I remember it? My father ripped apart the fabric of his marriage by taking a mistress and exposing my mother to the worst sort of pain imaginable. And you refused to lend your support to me—and my mother—at what was arguably the most difficult time in our lives—"

"You would not listen to reason," he interrupted, his tone bitterly savage.

Clarissa gasped and clapped a hand across her mouth.

"And I've no doubt you'll not listen to reason now," James added, abruptly swinging his legs over the side of the bed and rising. "I've already told you, I've no desire to quarrel with you. How I came to work for Les Moines is of no consequence to you. Complete the painting so that you may return to Paris and your mother. That is all you need think on."

He snatched the single lantern that lit the cabin and stalked toward the door.

"Where are you going—and why must you take the only light?" Clarissa asked, her throat thick with emotion.

James turned, fixing her with a stony gaze. "To fetch a pair of scissors, and I assumed you'd rather not alert the blockade ships to our presence with the light."

"Wait, why would you need a pair of scissors?"

"For your hair." He closed the lantern's shutters then

stepped over the threshold, slamming the door behind him.

Clarissa picked up the rickety chair and threw it against the door, finding satisfaction in the sound of the ancient wood splintering as it broke apart.

James took the narrow steps to the top deck two at a time, welcoming the briny air that hit him full in the face once he reached the top. The cabin below had been filled with Clarissa's delicate flowery scent. Even now, it teased his nostrils and stroked his senses into painful awareness.

The ship's captain was on the bridge. Not wanting to converse, James turned in the opposite direction, successfully skirting a handful of sailors as he made his way to the stern. Looking out over the darkening sky and the sea below, James grimly acknowledged that dealing with Clarissa was going to be far more difficult than he'd first estimated. Even after all the time that had passed since they'd parted, she could still cut him to the quick like no other. The fire in her eyes and hurt in her voice made him ache just as before. His first instinct was to react with passion and heat—no thought for the consequences, no ability to see beyond the moment.

A steady rain had begun, but James didn't seek shelter, remaining at the rail. The moisture slowly seeped its way through his clothing, and yet he stayed. He hoped the damp would wash away the essence of her. He flexed his fingers, the smooth satin of her silky skin remaining on the tips. He'd prepared himself for her dramatic response to—well, in all honesty, everything involving her. But the smell of her? The feel of her? Her soft body under his hands as he'd pulled the shirt from her waistband and unwound the bindings from her breasts? It was too soon for such contact, clearly.

The rain began to beat at him in earnest and the wind joined in, whipping about James in an ominous fashion. He'd forgotten what it was like with Clarissa. Once, she'd consumed his every thought and he, hers, until they'd not known where one began and the other ended. And then she'd taken it all from him.

He gripped the railing as the ship began to pitch, widening his stance to keep his balance on the rolling deck. There was no point in revisiting the past, he thought grimly. He'd done so countless times after Clarissa had departed London for the Continent, and in the years that followed. It always ended the same way: James heartbroken, with nothing left but his work with the Young Corinthians. She'd turned her back on him once, refusing to listen. God willing, she would not fail him this time. He only hoped her love for her mother meant more to Clarissa than the love she'd once professed for him.

"You broke my heart," he muttered. Clarissa's words were as unbelievable to him now as they had been when she'd first uttered them five years before in her mother's parlor.

If he'd been able to tell her the truth back then, perhaps she might have continued to trust him. A wave splashed over the railing, further soaking James, but he hardly noticed. She should have trusted him, he thought bitterly. With or without an explanation, Clarissa should have believed him when he'd assured her he loved her. And she hadn't.

A deckhand rushed up to James, pointing just beyond his shoulder. "A nasty one's coming in. Best get belowdecks, sir."

James turned to see a growing thicket of black clouds rolling on the horizon, the storm's ferocity threatening as it ate up the sky.

"Get me a pair of scissors. I'll wait here," James instructed the deckhand with authority. "Now," he snapped, causing the man to jump and run toward the bridge.

Clarissa was a vain woman—something she had always readily admitted. James had secretly found this charming, though he'd teased her relentlessly for the weakness. Above all else, she'd valued her hair. Long, silken, and so black the thick mane had a bluish sheen, Clarissa's hair was beautiful.

James looked out at the choppy waters. He'd known she would have to cut it if they were to have any hope of substituting her for St. Michelle.

But he'd been cruel to announce it in such a dismissive way. He'd done it on purpose. Her insinuation that he was now a dishonorable man had cut deep—far more than it should have considering the company he was keeping.

The deckhand slid to a stop at James's side and handed the scissors over. "Blimey," he proclaimed, looking out at the storm nipping at their heels. "It's going to be a nasty one," he said.

"You've no idea," James replied before turning for the stairs.

Clarissa had found great satisfaction in throwing the chair. For a moment. Then she'd quickly regretted its demise, since the less James realized his ability to vex her, the better. And he'd surely know she'd vented her temper by breaking the chair. She'd sighed, gathered up the broken bits, and dropped them into an empty chest at the foot of the built-in bed.

And then she'd cried. She tried to stave it off, afraid that James would return and find her sniveling in the corner. Of course the man would realize he still held the ability to irritate, but did she really need to shed tears over the fact? Nevertheless, her emotions had gotten the best of her—again—and she'd climbed into the hard bed, pulled the coarse bed linens up about her head, and sobbed.

James wasn't the man she remembered. Clarissa supposed that was to be expected, at least to a certain extent. She'd been changed forever by their involvement, and logically, it made sense that he had been, too. But it was more than that. When he'd placed his hand on her chin and looked into her eyes, she thought she'd seen a flash of the man she'd known and loved. But the moment had passed too quickly for her to be sure she'd seen something substantive.

The ship pitched forward, sending Clarissa sliding toward the end of the bed. Before she could right herself, the ship pitched back and she tumbled to her original position, tangled in the bed linens.

The cabin door was wrenched open. James appeared, holding the doorjamb to steady himself as the ship wallowed, then threatened to rock forward again. "Clarissa," he called, his gaze quickly searching the small room until he located her in the bed.

Clarissa attempted to rise from her inelegant position, only to be catapulted to the end of the bed yet again by the rocking ship. "What is going on? Does this have something to do with the blockade?" she demanded.

He stepped into the room and slammed the door shut behind him, throwing the lock. Just as he turned toward Clarissa, the heavy storage chest slid across the floor and smashed into the opposite wall, narrowly missing him. "No, we made it past the ships. We're in the midst of a storm."

Clarissa planted her hands firmly on the mattress on either side of her hips and struggled to push herself upright.

"Stay where you are," James commanded, steadying himself against the wall before staggering across the rolling floor to reach the chest. He grabbed a handle and pulled, dragging the heavy box across the floor and wedging it into the corner at the end of the bed. "This is the safest place for us until the storm passes," he added, climbing in next to her.

Waves crashed into the ship, lifting the vessel and sending the floor pitching at an angle again. Clarissa rolled into James and screamed.

"Clarissa, listen to me." James wrapped his arms around her and dragged her against his chest. "I won't let anything happen to you. Do you believe me?"

Clarissa tried to pull back, but his iron hold on her didn't lessen. The ship's timbers groaned as the waves hammered against the sides. Terrified, she buried her face against his linen shirt, comforted by the warm, hard wall of his chest and the solid, reassuring beat of his heart. "Why should I?" she ground out, squeezing her eyes shut.

"Clarissa, look at me!"

The sharp command was colored with a faint hint of desperation. Compelled, Clarissa opened her eyes and tipped her face up to his. There was a glimmer of the man she'd once known there, deep within his umber eyes. She felt sure this time. Not that it would change their shared past, but it was something.

"I do. I do believe you," she whispered, uncertain whether he heard her over the wind howling just beyond the ship's walls. Had she uttered the truth? She couldn't know . . . not yet. But she needed to believe in something—in someone—right now more than anything.

He tightened his grip, giving her a small smile as he nodded. "It's about bloody time."

Cries from above rang out just as a loud, cracking noise reverberated throughout the cabin. Clarissa screamed again. James lowered his cheek to rest against the crown of her head.

"Perhaps I should see if I can be of any use above-deck," he said, shifting as though to leave her.

Clarissa held tightly to his arm as the ship shifted and swayed. "You're needed here," she said resolutely.

James looked at the door. "Clarissa, I've some sailing experience. This may be the best way to keep you safe—"

"Do not make me regret the words I spoke mere moments ago, James."

He settled back against the wall, taking her with him, tucked securely within the circle of his arms.

His embrace was unexpectedly comforting. Though the ship threatened to break apart at any moment, held safe in James's arms Clarissa felt as though everything would, somehow, be all right. He was, for better or for worse, she acknowledged, her only ally.

"A truce, then?" Clarissa offered, settling more fully against him.

"Truce," James agreed, bracing against the bed's wooden frame as yet another wave slammed against the ship.

"Must we?" Clarissa sat on the trunk, her back to James.

The ship had bobbed in the roiling sea for hours, the storm finally settling near dawn. James had held Clarissa the entire time, inquiring after her painting, which he knew from past experience would distract her. She'd fallen asleep at some point, and yet he'd held tight, telling himself it was for her safety.

The slower speed of the ship and the sounds coming from the top deck told him they were nearing the port of Dover. James had it on good authority that the captain had an understanding with several of the customs officials, which would make their putting into port much simpler than their taking leave of Calais had been.

"We must." With scissors in one hand, he gathered Clarissa's hair into the other. The thick, black strands nearly slipped free as he paused, scissors poised and ready. "May I?" he asked, though the question was only a formality.

Clarissa nodded without speaking, and with genuine regret James made the first cut, the length of long silken hair falling to the floor.

She gasped, but to her credit remained still.

"It will grow back," James reassured her as he gathered another fistful and cut. He made quick work of the chore, wanting the moment to be over—for both of them.

When he stepped in front of her to reach the silky bangs that fell in an ebony fan over her forehead, he nearly faltered at the stark lack of emotion in Clarissa's eyes. Then he steeled himself and resolutely wielded the scissors before stepping back to assess her close-cropped hair.

"Well?" Clarissa asked somberly as she stared at his boots.

"You look . . . you look beautiful," James answered, disbelief in his voice. He hadn't thought it possible for Clarissa to look any lovelier. But the short hair emphasized her distinctive features and drew the eye to her long, bare neck in a most disruptive manner.

Clarissa lifted trembling fingers, running them through the shorn locks. "Impossible," she muttered, tears welling and threatening to spill down her cheeks. "Well, there's no going back now."

"There never was," James confirmed, his mouth a grim line.

Clarissa's steady gaze was bleak as it met his. She looked away, rising from the chest to brush the clinging bits of ebony silk hair from her shoulders. "No, I suppose there was not."

5

"Well, it is—"

"Pretentious. Excessive. Ridiculous?" James suggested with sarcasm as he and Clarissa took in Kenwood House from the coach window. The treacherous Channel crossing followed by the two days drive from Dover had hardly put him in a good mood. Still, the home was perhaps the single largest estate he'd ever laid eyes on.

Clarissa brushed off his mood with a feminine huff. "I'll admit it is somewhat overgrown. But if it's money you're after, it appears you've come to the right place."

James couldn't argue with Clarissa's logic. From the little he knew of Canadian financier Joshua Bennett, the house was only the beginning. A fortune made in banking and trade guaranteed Bennett had enough money to do as he pleased—which, apparently, included living on the largest estate in the whole of England.

He should be thankful for the man's well-lined pockets. But something within him made James critical of such ostentation.

"I do hope I have my own wing," Clarissa added sarcastically.

James chuckled. "Making fun of me now?"

"Perhaps," Clarissa replied, straightening her cravat.

The carriage slowed, rolling to a full stop on the gravel drive, just in front of a monstrous portico supported by Grecian columns. No less than six liveried servants stood at attention, waiting for the two to alight.

"James," Clarissa murmured as she patted self-consciously at her hair. "What if . . ." She paused, then folded her hands in her lap. She was shaking. Slightly, but still, her nerves were jangled.

James took his hat from the seat beside him and donned it, allowing Clarissa a moment to recover. "You'll finish the painting. I've never known you to fail."

"Hmm?" she replied, turning to look at him. "Oh, no. I'm not concerned in the slightest over my work." Her hand shifted to touch her short locks again and she looped sections of the black silk about her finger. "No. I'm worried about my role. Do you think I'll pass for a man?"

James had pondered this very question for most of the carriage ride. Clarissa had quizzed him relentlessly concerning his sex. Everything, from breeches to women had been thoroughly discussed. And while Clarissa was an eager and intelligent student, James couldn't quite see her as a man.

Still, if bravado was worth anything, Clarissa had a fighting chance. Or so he desperately hoped.

"Well, first things first. Stop fussing about with your hair in that manner," he instructed.

She pulled her hand back as if she'd been burned. "Is that better?"

James cast a critical eye over her countenance, then smiled. "Much improved. Now, repeat after me: 'Bloody son of a pockmarked whore.' "

"Come now, is it really necessary to use such vulgarity—"

"Say it," James commanded.

"Son of a bloody pockmarked whore," Clarissa spat out convincingly.

James thumped her between the shoulder blades,

nearly knocking her off the carriage seat. "Close enough. I do believe we just may pull this off."

She righted herself, frowning fiercely and clearly about to give him a tongue-lashing for the attack on her back. Then understanding dawned and she smiled. "Oh, yes, of course. That's how you congratulate one another. With physical injury."

James chuckled low in his throat. "Precisely. Now, are you ready for your debut, St. Michelle?"

"I've never been more ready in my life," she said resolutely, looking out at the servants who stood at attention, ready to receive them.

James followed her gaze. "Truly?"

"Not in the slightest. But there's hardly any point in telling you I'm terrified. Come, our audience awaits." She reached for the carriage latch and shoved the door wide.

"Monsieur St. Michelle, welcome to Kenwood House. I am Robert." The butler swept a low bow, the powder from his wig puffing, drifting, and filling the air where his head had been only a moment before.

Clarissa nodded in approval. *"Merci,"* she replied in a perfect Parisian accent, then looked about, critically assessing the property. *"Oui,* this will do nicely. Now," she added, gesturing toward James, "my assistant, Lucien Rougier, and I would like to be taken to our rooms. It has been a trying journey for us, you understand."

James remained stoic though his hands itched to swat Clarissa's backside. "Lucien"? Really, they'd never once discussed an alias for him. And if they had, he sure as hell would not have chosen "Lucien."

"Of course." Robert snapped his fingers and two of the waiting footmen hurried to assist the carriage driver, who was wrestling with the baggage. "If you will come with me?" he added, gesturing for them to follow.

Clarissa took the lead, clearly pleased to be in charge of James. "Lucien, I'll require a cold compress and a light repast," she announced commandingly.

"I'll see that both are delivered to your chambers immediately," the servant replied dutifully, nodding in command at the footmen manning the massive main doors. The two leapt into action, opening the panels wide. The butler stepped aside and allowed Clarissa and James to enter, then followed.

"*Non.* I prefer Lucien to oversee my needs for the duration of our stay," Clarissa answered in a bored, matter-of-fact tone as she looked up at the mural on the entryway ceiling. "Cherubs," she commented with a marked lack of expression. "Interesting choice."

The entryway looked large enough to house the inhabitants of most of the northern end of London. The Grecian influence begun on the outside of the house continued here—finely formed fluted columns, cornices, and archways occupying nearly everywhere that Clarissa looked.

The three mounted the grand staircase, James's gaze following the seductive sight of Clarissa's backside swishing in a decidedly feminine sway with each step. He made a mental note to speak with her about this then turned his attention to the butler, who'd come to a stop just past the top of the stairs.

"The family is in residence in the east wing," Robert began, waiting for James and Clarissa to join him. "You will have the west wing to yourselves. We've taken the liberty of preparing a studio for you, Monsieur St. Michelle, though if you find you'd prefer to work elsewhere in the house, please do not hesitate to say so."

"Well," Clarissa began, admiring the artwork as they continued down the hall, "it's impossible for me to say, having not seen the space yet." She turned, arching an eyebrow at James, her eyes amused. "I do enjoy having an entire wing at my disposal, though. *Merci.*"

They walked for what felt like ages to James, through rooms whose purpose he couldn't discern, until they reached yet another hall, with six doors, three on each side.

Robert ceremoniously opened the third door on the right with a flourish, revealing a beautiful suite done entirely in shades of blue. "Monsieur St. Michelle, these are yours. I'll have your trunks sent up straightaway. Mr. Bennett looks forward to meeting you at dinner this evening."

"Thank you, Robert," Clarissa replied, stepping into the room and closing the door behind her.

The butler bowed low and did not rise until he heard the oaken panel thud gently to meet the frame, the latch closing with an audible click. He eyed James with an alert look of understanding. "Follow me," he instructed, a cockney accent seeping through to color his voice. "Don't want to keep St. Michelle waiting. I'll show you where the kitchens are."

James stared for a moment at the door next to Clarissa's. He assumed that across the threshold lay his suite, though at this rate he would not be surprised if his "quarters" were slightly beneath the eaves. "*Oui,*" he answered, already considering just how many vulgarities to use when he spoke with Clarissa regarding the turn of events.

Clarissa stood at the tall windows of her suite, looking out over Kenwood Park and beyond, to where the thick green acres of Hampstead Heath stretched as far as the eye could see. It felt strange to have returned to her home country, especially under such circumstances. She'd never thought to see the isle again, especially without her mother.

She tugged, loosening and then untying the neatly knotted cravat at her neck, unwinding the long length of white linen. Five years ago, she'd found it nearly impossible to leave behind her life in London. But with time she'd come to terms with Paris—who she was and what her life would be. And now here she was, returned from the Continent but unable to tell anyone. Alone, save for James.

Clarissa dropped the length of linen to the floor and turned, moving toward the canopied bed. She would not regret the decision she'd made to trust him, at least with her safety. He may have broken her heart and somehow involved himself with Les Moines, but she could not do without his help.

She sat on the edge of the bed and pulled at one of her boots. Practically speaking, if anything were to happen to Clarissa, James would be in just as much danger as her mother. Which, she supposed, explained why he'd held her the entire stormy night on the ship.

She'd pretended to sleep for the first hour or so in his arms. The warm, muscled wall of his chest had risen and fallen beneath her cheek, his steady deep breaths providing an inordinate amount of comfort. He'd run his fingers through her hair and tested the weight of it, brushing a lock against his face, back and forth, back and forth, finally placing a chaste kiss on her forehead and drawing the covers closer.

Clarissa tugged one last time at the boot then gave up, dropping her foot to the floor and lying back on the silken coverlet. Yes, there was a practical explanation for why James would want her safe. But could the same be said for his actions when he'd thought her asleep?

Or was Clarissa making far more of it than she should? She was too easily ruled by her emotions—there was no point in denying it. And though he'd disappointed her in the worst way, she clearly still held feelings for the man.

"*Lucien?*"

Clarissa sat up so quickly she fell off the edge of the bed and landed on the floor. James stood over her, a tray in his hands. "You surprised me!" she exclaimed, fumbling to stand up.

"I could say the same to you," he replied, setting the tray on the bed before stalking to the windows. "Why on earth did you deviate from my instructions?"

"I suppose I should have anticipated some sort of reaction," Clarissa muttered, eyeing the small cucumber sandwiches before snatching one up and taking a bite. She chewed slowly while James stared at her with an impatient frown. "I was thinking as St. Michelle, is all. 'James' felt rather, oh, I don't know, ordinary for someone with such an artistic temperament. And so Lucien was born. Besides," she paused, taking another bite and chewing before swallowing, "why should I be the only one masquerading behind a persona other than my own?"

"Because that was the bloody plan," he bit out, turning back to glare at the window as though he was readying to punch his fist through the glass.

Silence fell over the room and Clarissa waited. James ran both hands through his hair then folded his arms across his chest, finally turning back toward her. "I apologize for my outburst."

Clarissa swallowed the last bite of sandwich and stared at him, words failing her. Never before had he apologized. At least not so quickly nor without coaxing.

She looked down at her breeches and picked at a piece of lint. "I'm sorry," she whispered. "I did not think before I acted. I should have stayed the course as originally planned," she offered, her gaze returning to rest on him. She mentally chided herself for the instant sense of pleasure she felt at the sight of his eyes softening in response to her words. "Still," she continued, "would you not agree that 'Lucien' is—"

"Clarissa," he said in an exasperated tone.

She could point out that not only had he interrupted her, but his unwillingness to listen to her very sound line of reasoning was, in all honesty, both pigheaded and rude. But if he could keep his temper in check, then so could she. Besides, she was suddenly aware that she was to blame—a revelation that left her quite uncomfortable.

"Yes," she answered hesitantly as she twisted her hands together.

He walked toward her until he stood too close. "Clarissa, I need you to understand—this is not a game."

His scent, a mixture of sandalwood and citrus, teased her senses, the combination stirring memories that made her shiver. She twined her fingers tighter, only faintly aware her knuckles ached from the strain. "Of course I know that, James; how could I not?"

He moved in, his face bent dangerously close to hers. Clarissa feared he might try to kiss her. She feared even more that she wouldn't stop him. But he merely lifted her clasped hands and gently separated her fingers, enclosing them in his warm, hard hands for a brief moment before releasing them.

"Clarissa, the men I work for would think nothing of killing your mother, or St. Michelle, if you should prove incautious and provoke their anger."

She wished his hands were still on hers—then instantly regretted her weakness. "Are you trying to frighten me?" she asked pointedly, taking a second sandwich from the plate and nervously nibbling.

"Yes, that is precisely what I am attempting to do. Please tell me I've been successful."

She nodded, her mouth too full to speak—rather convenient, considering she hardly knew how to respond. Her lungs felt suddenly constricted with too little air and her neck tight, the weight of his words having had the desired effect.

"Good," James said firmly, gently pushing her to a seat on the bed. "Now, we'll need to explain why it will be necessary for me—a mere servant—to occupy the suite adjacent to yours. Thoughts?"

He knelt on one knee and grasped the heel and toe of her polished Hessian, pulling it off with one firm movement.

Clarissa sighed, wiggling her freed toes, and laid back on the bed to hold out her other foot. "Must you reside next door?"

"I've been informed that Les Moines has several men in the house. I'd rather not be separated by stairways should you need me," he replied grimly, tugging the second boot off.

"Oh," Clarissa answered perceptively. "In that case, I'll let it be known that we are lovers."

"Perfect. My name is Lucien and I'm the lover of renowned portrait artist St. Michelle. Why didn't I think of that?"

Clarissa chuckled appreciatively. "All right, then. I will simply throw a French artist's fit if they do not move you at once. Really, James, I had no idea you were quite so provincial."

"And you've lived in Paris far too long, Clarissa," James replied. "You'd best learn how to remove your own boots," he finished, then left without another word.

* * *

Despite himself, James quite liked Joshua Bennett. Their host, currently cutting into a portion of beef with marked enthusiasm, was, well, undeniably likeable. He discussed things one shouldn't, laughed entirely more than was proper, and delighted in his family and life in general.

An altogether awful chap, really, James thought with admiration as he watched Mr. Bennett thump Clarissa on the back for perhaps the thirtieth time that evening.

His wife, Adele, though nowhere near as animated or as boisterous as her husband, was quite charming as well and welcoming in a way that James had never witnessed from any of the ton's grande dames. The Bennetts possessed enough blunt to rival the most significant of English families—enough, they hoped, to secure a titled husband for their daughter Iris.

James lifted his wineglass and, under the pretext of drinking, glanced sideways, down the length of the table to where Iris sat. Her beauty alone would garner interest from this season's bucks, that was simple enough to see. And she'd been tutored to within an inch of her life as well, her impeccable manners and engaging conversation a tribute to her governess's skill.

There was something about the girl, though, that set off alarms for James. A mischievous glint in her eyes, perhaps? He couldn't put his finger on a specific concern, but it was there.

"I am absolutely stuffed, I tell you," Mr. Bennett declared, dropping his knife to clatter upon the nearly empty plate.

Iris delicately cleared her throat, giving her father an admonishing look as she did so. "Mother, let us leave the gentlemen to their cigars," she announced, waiting as a servant quickly approached and held her chair as she rose from the table.

James stood and Mr. Bennett followed, Clarissa only hesitating a moment before she did the same.

Iris and her mother nodded politely before walking arm in arm from the room.

"Well, let's see if we can't find my study, gentlemen," Mr. Bennett said, tossing his serviette carelessly on the table and turning toward the door.

A servant scurried to assist but Bennett waved him off. "If I can track a bear for forty miles and bag him, I can find a study."

The servant bowed dutifully and made way for the man and his companions. James fell into step on Bennett's right while Clarissa lingered, trailing a step or two behind them.

"Bears, monsieur?" James asked, noting Bennett's pleasure at the question. "We understood you to be a banker, *non?*"

Bennett clapped James heartily on the back and laughed. "I like you, Rougier," he said amiably. "Banking is my business, true enough. It's what allowed me all of this," he added, sweeping his hand through the air in reference to Kenwood House. "But hunting is my passion."

They continued through a portrait gallery, where scores of English nobility stared down at them with regal aloofness.

Bennett stopped and looked about, then gestured for James and Clarissa to follow him down a hall that branched off to the right. They continued past five more rooms before Bennett hesitated in front of an oaken door. He pushed it open to reveal a massive mahogany desk flanked by two leather armchairs and a similar one behind.

"Aha!" he cried, stalking across the threshold and walking around the desk to where a table sat, a number of fine decanters and cut crystal glasses waiting.

James settled in one of the armchairs, the buttery-soft leather welcoming his weight. Clarissa took her place in the other chair and carefully crossed her right leg so that her foot rested on her left knee.

"Not that I've experience in the field," James began, watching Bennett pour a generous amount of brandy into three glasses, the amber liquid splashing as he did so, "but handling vast sums of money all day couldn't be that dull."

Bennett handed James and Clarissa their glasses, then took his own in hand, sitting down behind the desk and sighing. "One would think, Rougier, one would think."

He took a long drink and closed his eyes with pleasure as the superior brandy slid down his throat. "And for some it's true—my father, for example. But there's much more than the money. Well, my very presence in England is a perfect example."

"*Pourquoi?*" Clarissa responded, then took a minuscule sip from her glass.

Bennett drained his glass with one more swallow and reached to refill. "Well, I'd much prefer to be at home in Halifax. But, according to Iris, an Englishman is what's needed now. If not for the money, she'd have settled for George Fitzbrooke, as her mother and I had hoped."

Clarissa swallowed, only a slight grimace twisting her lips before she recovered from the unexpected taste of brandy. "I see. Then I've your daughter to thank for my presence."

James detected an accusatory tone in Clarissa's voice, but from the looks of it, Bennett had not.

Their host let out a grunt of displeasure. "Entirely. The girl's had her heart set on the fairy tale for some time—which apparently requires your services. Oh, not that I'm unhappy you're here—quite the contrary, actually. It was a rare piece of luck that I encountered Lord

Mayhue at the Pembrook fete. Everyone had assured me that you were engaged for the entirety of our time here. It was Mayhue who told me otherwise."

James savored the liquor, holding it on his tongue as he contemplated that bit of information. Nothing about Bennett caused James to think the man knew anything of Les Moines, but learning the name of Mayhue was a start—and a good one at that.

"I haven't gone and insulted you, have I?" Bennett asked Clarissa, obviously concerned. "Iris claims I'm the most boorish man to be found in Canada—I'd hoped to avoid such distinction here."

He smiled then, an honest, unaffected beaming friendliness that could not be denied.

Clarissa hesitated and James tensed. They could not afford to offend Bennett so early in the game.

"*Non,* Mr. Bennett, no offense has been taken," Clarissa replied, following up her statement with a hearty drink of her brandy.

"I'm drunk, aren't I?" Clarissa said as James assisted her up the stairs. Her body felt made of lead, each step a Herculean effort.

James tightened his hold about her waist. "Lower your voice, for God's sake. There's no need to shout."

Clarissa hadn't the foggiest idea what the man was talking about. She could barely hear him, let alone her own voice. She was silent, not protesting as he steered her down the hall and into her chamber, where he quickly deposited her in an upholstered chair near the fireplace.

"Wellll," Clarissa demanded, finding it difficult to finish the word.

"Yes," James answered, standing over her with his hands on his hips. "You're drunk."

"In my cups?" Clarissa pressed as she attempted to cross one leg over the other, with little success.

"Yes."

"Foxed?"

James nodded in agreement, then knelt before her and yanked at the knots in her cravat.

"Disguised?" Clarissa asked. "Though I have to admit that I don't understand that one at all. Actually, I don't understand 'foxed' either, but 'disguised' is by far the most mystifying of all."

He ignored her, continuing in silence, undressing her with impersonal precision.

Clarissa found this irritating, for all the wrong reasons. Even in her inebriated state, she realized that what vexed her wasn't the fact that a man was removing her clothing. No, what was truly needling was the fact that he seemed completely unaffected by it.

"I must say," she began, sitting up as he untucked her shirt, "this feels nothing at all like the time you purposely provided me with far too much champagne."

His fingers froze, the top button of her shirt caught halfway through the buttonhole. "You had two glasses, Clarissa, and if I remember correctly, it was you who nicked the champagne from your parents' party."

"Two glasses, is that all?" Clarissa watched as James finished with the buttons and gestured for her to raise her arms. "But isn't that the first time that we made love?"

He pulled one arm free of a sleeve and then the other, tossing the shirt onto the floor. "Clarissa, must we speak of this?" His voice was grim, his tone forbidding.

He set to work on her boots, tugging off first one and then the other, with ease.

"I loved you, you know." Clarissa hadn't meant to say it out loud, but judging from James's abrupt rise to his feet, she'd done just that. "More than anyone before—and anyone since. You needn't have bothered with the champagne that day. I wanted you to—"

James pulled Clarissa upright, standing her on her feet before him, and began to unwind the material about her breasts. "Clarissa, you're drunk. You don't know what you're saying."

She grasped his upper arms to steady herself and looked up into his eyes. "And now here we are, thanks to a spoiled young woman's flights of fancy, thrown together despite everything."

"Clarissa," he pleaded in a low husky tone, finishing with the wrap. He forcefully removed her hands from his arms, his darkened gaze fixed on hers. "There is no point in dredging up the past."

She closed her eyes, swaying with relief at being able to draw deep, unfettered breaths with the wrap removed. James caught her and held her against him, his hands settling at her bare waist. Clarissa set her own hands on his. "I assumed that you wanted all of me too. How could I have been so wrong?"

She opened her eyes and looked at him, catching her breath at the depth of emotion that played over his face. He felt the pain too, deep down in his heart, where she couldn't have known it was hiding.

And then he kissed her hard, his lips bruising hers as he demanded more. His tongue forced her mouth open, plunging with a possessiveness that both terrified and excited Clarissa. He picked her up, the strength of his arms wrapped around her, crushing her bare breasts against his chest. She laced her hands behind his neck as he walked toward the bed, her tongue meeting his with matching ardor.

Then he tossed her in the air and she landed, sprawling on the soft, overstuffed bed.

"Good night, Clarissa," he uttered in a barely measured tone, his breathing labored.

Her head was spinning and she closed her eyes, certain she'd misheard him. But when she looked again, he was gone. She was alone in the beautifully decorated blue room.

6

For Clarissa, sketching was seeing without being seen. Touching the truth of her subject with a few quick strokes of charcoal in those moments of revelation before they retreated and hid their souls away. Beauty, in its truest form, was often stark and sometimes profane in both clarity and cut, from the local fishmonger plying his odorous trade to prostitutes hawking their wares on filthy street corners. Whether the scene was the neighborhood tabby sunning itself in the street or exhausted nannies in the park with their screaming charges—each slice of life revealed itself with flashes of insight to the artist within Clarissa.

She loved the act of creating. But even more, she craved this intimate view of others afforded through her work. Perhaps she yearned for the contact because she herself found it nearly impossible to withhold or conceal herself from others. Her own emotions bubbled up, surfacing with the slightest of provocations. Restraining her natural openness was as foreign to her as living as an elephant in India would be. And so the curiosity, to discover, to understand, deepened her passion and drove her to examine life through her art time and again.

The subject currently under her discerning eye, Mr. Bennett's daughter, Iris, was quite beautiful, that was obvious enough, Clarissa thought. But what would their time together reveal? She took up her charcoal and bent to the work, the precise curve of Iris's cheekbones proving elusive. What lay beneath the exquisite bone structure? Clarissa studied the girl's eyes, a deep blue that held . . . boredom, if Clarissa was correct. And perhaps some impatience, further revealed by the pursing of her heart-shaped mouth. The girl turned at the far-off, muted sound of a dog barking and Clarissa huffed. Iris murmured *"Pardon"* in a more than passable French accent. Yes, Clarissa reflected, Iris was what those in Clarissa's set—when she was part of such a thing— would have called a diamond of the first water.

Clarissa smudged her thumb along the pencil line defining Iris's right cheekbone, the black charcoal stark against pale drawing paper. *"Parfait,"* she declared aloud in a satisfied murmur, tilting her head to admire her sketch. Clarissa herself had been too tall, too flat-chested, and far too unpredictable to have been considered the matrimonial catch of her own London Season. But it had hardly mattered to her. The frothy dresses, delicious shoes, glittering jewels—oh, Clarissa could hardly think on it without crying. It had all been for her. Not to please a man, but to please herself. And it had. She'd never understood those women who'd fought the "restraints" of womanhood. To her way of thinking, anything that accentuated her figure or face only gave people more reason to want to know her. And once they knew her, they couldn't help but appreciate her for everything that she was—unconventional beauty and intelligence.

She looked again at Iris, impressed by the girl's ability to keep her back ramrod straight despite the time that she'd been required to sit and pose. Iris wanted it all— the portrait that would lend her distinction, the husband that would declare her ton-worthy, the distance that England would afford between herself and her Canadian family.

Yes, Iris wanted, perhaps yearned. But Clarissa felt

sure, as she watched the girl's foot tap out a staccato beat on the oaken floor, that Iris hardly knew herself well enough to make such choices. She was young—well trained, but inexperienced. She desired, but she couldn't know why.

Clarissa had not been so very unlike Iris at her age. She'd felt sure of her future simply because there was no reason to question it. She would marry, become a mother, perform the duties required of her station, and so on and so forth. And then she'd met James. He was so wrong for her . . . yet so right. He wasn't bothered by her moodiness—quite the opposite, actually. Their quarrels almost always led to the most meaningful of conversations, and the most passionate of encounters. He encouraged her to challenge him, something no other man had done before, nor since.

Iris had so much still to learn. Clarissa felt sympathetic toward the girl—and angry. If not for Iris and her need to catch an English aristocrat, Clarissa would be safely at home, with her mother by her side. She looked up to examine Iris's brow line and the girl's sharp gaze met hers.

Drat. Clarissa's fingers tightened on the charcoal with a viselike grip and she forced herself to continue. If she was being completely honest, she could not blame Iris, she thought. Nor the girl's parents. After spending time—and drinking the dreadful brandy—the previous evening with James and Mr. Bennett, she had to conclude the Canadian knew nothing of Les Moines's involvement in this scheme. Either that or Mr. Bennett was quite a good actor. Clarissa herself was rather gifted in the dramatic arts and would wager her jar of gold leaf that the man had been telling the truth rather than putting on a performance.

And so that left Les Moines to blame—and by association, James.

"Monsieur St. Michelle," Iris said brightly while keeping her head perfectly still. "Where is Monsieur Rougier? Should he not be assisting you in some way?"

Clarissa rubbed at her jawline in a masculine fashion and wondered for a moment if the girl had the ability to read minds, dismissing the fanciful notion almost at once. "I gave him the afternoon off. There's little the man can do while I'm sketching."

That wasn't entirely true. James had woken Clarissa just before dawn. After forcing her to drink a truly vile concoction that he'd assured her she desperately needed, he'd told her he would be unavailable for most of the day. She'd poked and prodded but he'd refused to cooperate, giving her little information other than that his plans involved other business.

"He seems a rather interesting chap," Iris continued, sighing with relief and slumping for a moment when Clarissa gestured for her to relax.

Iris's purposeful use of the common English term was charming, but Clarissa felt uneasy at her line of questioning. "*Peut-être,*" she answered vaguely, setting the length of charcoal on her drawing table. "Hardly the sort that you hope to attract though, *non?*"

Iris rose from the richly upholstered settee and walked toward Clarissa, her countenance changing as she did so. She squared her shoulders and her chin tilted determinedly. "Monsieur St. Michelle, from what others have told me, you, of all people, would not judge a person for desiring a taste of what the world has to offer."

Ah, Clarissa thought to herself. Even her revealing sketch could not have unearthed this surprising turn. She was torn between admiration for the girl and utter shock. And she couldn't help but be a bit curious about just what tales of the real St. Michelle's escapades had reached England—and whether they were even close to being true. She suspected not. "Really, *mademoiselle,* you cannot believe everything that you hear."

The girl laughed, a hint of wickedness in the sound that confirmed deeper layers yet to be revealed. "I believe your interest in which stories may have been bandied about rather than the state of my virtue proves my point."

"Touché." Clarissa had to give the girl credit; there was more to her than a hopeless romantic in search of her titled prince—though Clarissa could hardly encourage her to set her sights on James. Their time in Hampstead would be difficult enough without such distraction. And that was the truth. In its entirety. Clarissa scrubbed roughly at the charcoal on her fingers with a damp length of linen. *"Je suis désolé.* I cannot allow a dalliance to distract Rougier from his duties."

Iris's brows lowered as she contemplated Clarissa's words, the small vee created by the finely arched eyebrows smoothing away a moment later. "Oh, I see. Well," she paused, looking at the sketch before reaching to gently smudge the edge of one eye with her fingertip. "Sometimes these things cannot be controlled."

She bowed politely and offered Clarissa a bright smile before turning and leaving the studio, silky golden ringlets bobbing gently about her head as she went.

Clarissa took the sketch in hand and promptly tore it in two. "I should have told her James preferred men."

In the kitchen, James lingered at the scarred wooden table where the servants had just finished their midday meal. Though he was full, he reached for a loaf of bread and cut a second piece for himself. He slathered it with butter, drizzling honey over the top before taking a bite.

The last of the maids and footmen scraped their chairs across the stone floor and hurried out of the warm kitchen, save one at the opposite end of the table. The man, nearly as tall as James but rail-thin, eyed the bread. Then he picked up his plate and walked the length of the table to take a seat next to James. He tore a generous portion from the fragrant loaf of bread and spread a thick layer of butter atop it.

"You've got everything you need, then?" the man, introduced as simply Pettibone to James yesterday, mumbled around his first bite, his Adam's apple bobbing as he swallowed.

James suspected there were a number of Les Moines within the household, but this was his first encounter with one. The note left beneath his door last night had been simple and to the point. James would provide progress reports to his contact. The contact, already well entrenched within the household and with a network of men outside, would then pass along the information to Durand in Paris. Conversely, any news deemed necessary for James to receive would be passed through the route in reverse.

James tore off a small bite of crunchy bread crust and chewed slowly. "Yes," he replied, swallowing. "And the mother?"

The clanging of pots at the long trestle tables across the kitchen signaled the beginning of dinner preparations. James knew he had little time before his absence would be noticed by more than just Clarissa.

"Safe—for now. Of course, that could change, depending on how long it takes," the footman answered in flawless English. He dropped his bread onto the pewter plate in front of him. "With the girl in England, there's hardly a need to keep the mother alive for long."

"Durand understands what's at stake if she comes to any harm." James took another bite, not wanting to appear too eager. "And we are speaking of a portrait, after all. It will take some time to complete."

The man frowned slightly and brushed at his coat. "It's not my job to know such things. She's to hurry or there'll be trouble. Tell her." He placed the flat of both palms on the table and stood, shoving the chair back and out of his way. He stopped and pulled what appeared to be a missive from his breast pocket. "From the girl's mother," he offered in explanation, dropping the travel-stained paper on the table then walking from the room.

James retrieved the letter just as a scullery maid approached and set to clearing the table.

From the moment James had recognized Clarissa in St. Michelle's studio, he'd known that timing would be everything. Successfully completing his mission and retrieving the money meant for Les Moines was equally as important as securing the safety of Clarissa and her mother. He felt sure his superior, Carmichael, would agree.

But how could James secure the safety of two women in two different countries at precisely the same time?

The scullery maid very nearly dropped a piece of crockery in his lap, huffing with disgust as she bent awkwardly to avoid him. James took the female servant's silent suggestion that he leave and stood, giving her a friendly smile as he did so. She looked to refuse him the nicety then thought otherwise, her lips curving in a genuine, friendly smile before she turned her back and continued clearing the table.

James strode from the room and turned down the hall toward the servants' stairs, his thoughts once again occupied with Clarissa and the role they played. When he'd first accepted the Corinthian assignment, he'd known it would be challenging. And now? There was no point in telling Clarissa that her mother was in far more serious danger than she'd thought. The weight of such knowledge could only do her work harm—and her heart. The mother/daughter bond had obviously grown stronger over the last five years.

He mounted the narrow stairs, shaking his head with disbelief. Practically speaking, he knew Clarissa wanted to return to Paris as quickly as she could, but her artistic talent could get in the way of efforts to hurry. He'd never seen her accept anything less than the best from herself; James only hoped her skill was up to the challenge of producing quality under pressure.

And that he would be as well.

Pettibone watched the English bastard stride down the hall toward the stairs. Durand, his father and employer, had assured him when reassigning the job to Marlowe that the turncoat deserved the opportunity to prove himself more than Pettibone did. After all, the lying Englishman had deceived the Corinthians into believing he had perished—there was nowhere for the man to turn. The time was ripe for Marlowe's testing. And so he'd bowed to his father's wishes yet again, though something inside of him had snapped.

Pettibone believed such business should be left to the French, not the English. Had he not perfected his crude English accent? Learned to act the British buffoon until it was second nature—a fact that ate at his heart until he couldn't breathe. He'd done all that his father had asked of him and more. It had galled him to have the man reconfirm how little faith he had in his son's abilities. But the fact that the agent was English? Pettibone tasted the bitterness of the blow yet again as he moved toward the stairs. He'd suffered long enough in meaningless roles such as his current one, relegated to waiting hand and foot, like a common slave, while agents with far less skill undertook the worthwhile assignments.

"You'll not get anywhere at that pace," a cheery voice chided from behind. Pettibone turned to find Daphne,

Miss Bennett's maid, standing behind him, a warm apple turnover in her hand.

He smiled at the woman. Not because he wanted to—God forbid. Much to his chagrin, she'd been pestering him for weeks. She tore a small bite from the pathetic pastry and popped it into her mouth.

"I was waiting for you," he replied charmingly, realizing as he watched the lazy cow chew her cud that she could be of some use.

The woman's eyes brightened and she swallowed quickly, wiping plump sticky fingers across her apron. "Is that so?"

There were a number of Les Moines agents within the walls of Kenwood House, but Pettibone thought Daphne might be exactly what his plan needed.

"It is. Walk with me," he urged, offering her his arm. She looked about for somewhere to set the turnover, settling on her pocket before taking his arm.

Pettibone sighed with disgust at the greasy print she'd already managed to leave on his immaculate sleeve.

It would not be easy nor without trouble, but he'd prove to his father once and for all that he was prepared to take his rightful place within the organization—even if it meant losing Bennett's money.

Clarissa had nearly completed the second sketch when James arrived. He knocked politely on the door just as a personal servant would and waited for her to admit him.

"*Entrez,*" Clarissa said firmly, ignoring James's amused look.

He shut the door securely and walked to her, his gaze turning to the two sketches of Iris. "The first one not quite to your liking?"

She picked up the ripped sheets and balled them in her hands. "Oh, the sketch was perfectly acceptable. It is the model that's the problem."

"Come now," James began, taking the ruined pages from her and setting them on the drawing table. "The girl is just that—a girl. What could she have possibly done to cause you problems?"

Clarissa turned away, stalking to the window before halting abruptly, spinning on her heel to return. Her index finger pointed accusingly, hovering near his chest. "I'll tell you what *that* girl did," she began, poking James for emphasis. "That *girl* is taking this portrait no more seriously than tea with the local vicar. She all but called into question my artistic ability."

"Well, in her defense, the only reason you're here . . . wait, let me correct myself. The only reason St. Michelle is here has everything to do with the transient nature of the ton's likes and dislikes. Society tells her she must be painted by St. Michelle, and so her father secures you, despite the difficulties such a demand presents. The most ridiculous fact in all of this is that the painting will, in all likelihood, secure a more desirable connection. That's hardly her fault."

Clarissa considered his words, knowing he spoke the truth. "That's all well and good," she replied, poking him again in the chest. "But what of my abilities as a painter? One does not secure the services of the most lauded artist of one's time only to question the—"

"Do stop poking me," James requested, closing hard fingers over Clarissa's hand and lowering it to her side. "Just what, precisely, did she say or do to insult you?"

"She altered the sketch!" Clarissa snapped. There. She had him!

James ran both hands through his hair as if readying to pull each strand from his scalp. "And when you say 'altered,' is this something similar to when I suggested that your sketch of the Serpentine might require a bit more perspective?"

Clarissa remembered the incident as if it had happened only yesterday. She'd reacted abominably to James's words that day; her sensitivity when it came to both her work and her burgeoning love for him had combined to create one of her more dramatic outbursts.

She'd always hated to be proven wrong. But even more than that, she'd hated that he saw it before she did. He'd yelled in response, claiming his words were in no way meant to harm. And then he'd tipped her head back and kissed her hard and thoroughly, the embrace leading to making love then and there, in her studio.

Clarissa's nipples tingled at the memory, the damp heat gathering between her legs not as unwelcome as she would have liked.

"Clarissa?" James pressed, stirring her from the hazy memory of passion.

"No!" She folded her arms across her bound chest. "Not in the least. No, she touched the sketch—smeared the charcoal, to be exact."

"Contact, then?" he asked, hardly as shocked as he should be.

Annoyed at his refusal to recognize the level of intrusion, yet beginning to see some humor in the situation. Clarissa poked him in the chest yet again. "Precisely."

He clasped her fingers once again, only this time he pressed them against his coat, trapping them. "I'll ask the girl to behave; will that help?"

She could feel his heartbeat beneath her hand. "You'd do that for me?" she asked, suddenly embarrassed by her demands.

"It's my job," he replied simply, squeezing her hand before releasing her. "Now, is there anything else?"

Clarissa turned back to her table before any hint of disappointment registered on her face. Of course it was his job—she was a means to an end, nothing more. She'd nearly given in to the heat that his closeness had inspired and . . . what? Almost kissed him as she'd wanted to since he'd held her close on the ship? Or should she have told him that the chit's openly declared interest toward him was making her act like a lunatic?

Oh, *that* was the issue at hand. *Oh, Lord.* Clarissa nearly burst into tears at the realization. "Yes, actually: Miss Bennett is intent on seducing you."

James mussed his hair, actually succeeding in pulling a strand or two from his head this time. "She's nothing more than a child. And it's not as if she will seduce me against my will."

"Yes, I suppose so." Clarissa managed a smile, turning her attention back to the sketch.

"Clarissa, about last night," James began, drawing her attention to him. "I hope you understand why I removed your clothing."

In all honesty, Clarissa had wakened with very little memory of the evening before. There were a few spotty images of James's face and the feel of his hands on her as he'd undressed her, but that was all. She stared hard at the sketch and the heated memory of his lips on hers flooded her, but she could not say whether this was indeed a memory or simply a figment of her imagination. "I still had my breeches on this morning, James. Perhaps you're mistaken in what transpired?" she said with a shrug, attempting to keep the tone light.

"It was necessary to remove the bindings, Clarissa. As for the boots, I could hardly let you sleep—"

"James, I was only teasing. I'd already arrived at the very same conclusion, I assure you. I hardly suspected you of anything untoward."

He looked far too relieved as he nodded in understanding, piquing Clarissa's curiosity.

"Though I do wonder," she continued, reaching out to smudge a sharp edge in the sketch, "whether I may have done something—or perhaps said something—that I shouldn't have?"

James folded his arms across his chest and sat on the edge of the table. "Why do you ask?"

"I was upset."

"Were you, now?" James queried, looking out the window at the rolling green acres of Kenwood's park.

"You know very well that I was. Why on earth would I have consumed the brandy otherwise?" Clarissa countered, scratching at the sketch with her fingernail. "I was angry with Mr. Bennett for his foolhardy desire to please his daughter at any cost. And for my mother's imprisonment. And with you for bringing me here—for being involved at all."

"So you remember nothing of last night?" he asked quietly, his gaze taking in the sketch with concern.

"Nothing."

He pushed himself off the table and walked toward the door. "Clarissa, you neither did nor said anything that would change the outcome of our allotted time together. Words spoken under the influence of spirits are nothing more than the meanderings of our overtired minds."

Clarissa sighed with relief, though there was something in his claim that made her uneasy.

"And I believe this will bring you some comfort," he added, turning back toward her as he pulled the letter from his pocket and handed it over.

She instantly recognized her mother's delicate handwriting, the sight of it making her heart soar with relief. "Thank you," she offered, hardly able to contain herself.

James nodded and turned around to go.

"And next time, James," she paused and waited for him to look at her.

He stopped just in front of the door and turned, "Yes?"

"Do relieve me of the breeches. I promise I won't hold it against you."

He said nothing in return, only smiled and opened the door to step into the hall, closing the heavy portal quietly behind him.

7

It was well past midnight. James lay with his arms folded beneath his head and studied the silence that surrounded him.

"Do relieve me of my breeches."

He rolled to his right side and punched the feather pillows, dropping his head upon the cool linen. Those words had plagued him since that afternoon. Clarissa had made the comment in fun, but to James . . . well, it had been much more than that.

He'd taken advantage of her their first night at Kenwood not because he could, but because he'd wanted to. More than he'd wanted anything for some time. If he'd had his way they would be lovers again, not as St. Michelle and Lucien, but as Clarissa and James.

He punched at the pillow again then folded his arms across his bare chest, the feel of the soft, expensive sheets almost oppressive. He shouldn't be surprised that his feelings for Clarissa had reappeared. After all, if she'd only trusted him and what he'd had to say concerning her father's purported infidelities, they would, in all likelihood, be together as husband and wife.

He stared at the candle on the nightstand as the flame flickered, casting shadows on the walls. Carmichael had entrusted him with this assignment because James was free from any entanglements that would present a distraction. His parents were deceased and his older brother was well and married, leaving James to himself.

He threw back the covers and looked at his swelling cock. "Clearly, you're distracted."

The sound of his door opening drew James's gaze to the darkness beyond the candlelight. A dim light from the hall outlined a form as it stood still. Then the person moved into the room, gently shutting the door behind them.

James sat up and tossed the covers over himself, concealing his nakedness from the waist down. "I'll not bother with niceties at such a late hour. Who are you and why are you here?"

The figure slowly came closer, a feminine form becoming apparent. James's pulse quickened at the thought that it might be Clarissa, but as his guest reached the pool of light cast from the candle near his bed, James realized he was mistaken.

"Miss Bennett?" he uttered, disbelief lacing his voice.

The girl arched an eyebrow with practiced ease then sat down next to James. "Yes, though I do wish you'd call me Iris." She caught the end of the cream-colored ribbon tied at her waist, the satin sliding easily as she pulled. "Now, as for the why . . ."

Her dressing gown parted as the bow escaped its knot, revealing the outline of first one of Iris's perfectly shaped breasts, and then the other, barely concealed beneath a gauzy night rail. She placed her hands behind her on the bed and leaned back, the wrapper falling entirely open.

"Mademoiselle—"

"Please, Mr. Rougier," she purred, her tone calling to mind things James would rather not think on.

"Iris," he began, taking a pillow and dropping it between himself and the girl, "you do not want this."

Iris nodded. "Oh, but I do."

"*D'accord*. Then I do not want this," he replied, his patience growing thin. "Your parents have come all the way to England to find you a suitable husband. I'll be damned if I'm going to be the one to ruin your chances."

Iris sat up and reached for the pillow, tossing it over her shoulder, then climbed atop James, her knees astride him.

He lifted her off of him and slid from the bed, falling to one knee before regaining his ground and standing.

"Are you absolutely sure you do not want this?" Iris asked, her eyes focused on his still hard cock.

He grabbed for his dressing gown, which he'd tossed over the back of a heavy leather chair, and hastily threw it on, savagely knotting the tie at his waist before replying. "Leave, *s'il vous plaît*."

James was on precarious footing. A dalliance with Iris could be helpful to his case—or incredibly damaging, depending on a number of factors.

Normally he would have happily obliged such a willing bed partner. But his throbbing cock was right; his feelings for Clarissa could not be denied.

He reached for Iris's dressing gown and roughly closed it, tying the sash in one swift movement then picking her up from the bed and forcefully accompanying her to the door.

"I can make your life rather difficult, Lucien," she warned, her lips pursing into a seductive pout. She skimmed his chest with her hand, pushing back the lapel to encircle his left nipple with her fingers.

"Meaning?" he asked, grasping her wrist and forcing her fingers to stop.

She pressed herself against him and rose on her toes so

they were nearly eye to eye, with nary a breath between them. "Allow me to walk from this room and you'll find out."

The feel of her breasts on his chest, the indentation where her thighs met his, grinding up against him. God, James nearly took her right then and there, just to prove that he could.

But things had changed. All of a sudden it wasn't about what one could do, but what one wanted to do. It wasn't enough—she wasn't enough.

He reached for the door, pulling it open wide enough for her to pass. "Good night, Miss Bennett."

She hesitated, disbelief playing across her face before being swifty replaced by anger. "Good night, Mr. Rougier. Sleep well."

He watched her walk down the hall to make certain she didn't turn back. When she'd reached the stairs and started down them, James ducked inside his room and shut the door, leaning against the thick panels. "Sleep well? I doubt I'll ever sleep well again, at least not in Kenwood House."

"Where is she?" Clarissa yelled, kicking at the gravel as she paced back and forth in front of the bench.

James gave her an admonishing look before checking his pocket watch for perhaps the tenth time.

"I assure you, she is nearly an hour late. No timepiece in the world will tell you a different story."

If not for the absence of Iris, Clarissa could say that this was a spectacular day. She'd woken early after a restful night of sleep. The realization that she did indeed still harbor feelings for James had been liberating, her emotional state never at its best when she denied the truth.

She'd risen with the sun and dressed herself, which she

was immensely proud of. It had taken twice as long as it should have, but she'd done it, leaving twelve creased cravats in her wake.

Clarissa paused to admire her work, noting with displeasure the scuff she'd just made on her otherwise brilliantly shined boots. She wouldn't even be out in the garden, on the gravel path—the very gravel that had marred her boots!—if not for the girl. A servant had delivered a note from the girl just as Clarissa was enjoying her first cup of tea in the breakfast room. Iris had requested they meet in the cutting garden for their morning sketches.

Keeping in mind what James had said concerning Miss Bennett's place in the ever-thickening plot, Clarissa had complied and made her way to the cutting garden at the prescribed time. Only she'd found herself in the rose garden rather than the cutting garden. And then James had arrived and the two of them had hastened to the correct garden, only to find no one there.

And Clarissa's spectacular day had become markedly less spectacular from then on.

"Do send a servant to fetch her, won't you?"

"I've already sent two," he snapped, his gaze focused on the back of the house.

Clarissa looked at James, noting again the dark circles under his eyes, which she'd first noticed as they'd walked. She sat down next to him on the bench now and propped her elbows on her knees, as she'd seen countless men do. "You look awful. Did you not sleep well?"

"I find it rather hard to sleep well while dodging a persistent woman," he replied, closing his eyes and lifting his face to the morning sun.

Clarissa's jaw tensed. "I see. So that is what you call it these days. 'Dodging'?"

"No, you do not understand," he ground out, opening his eyes and turning to look at her. "It was Miss Bennett who arrived in my room—completely uninvited and wholly indecent."

"Well, that's rather . . ." Clarissa wasn't sure how to end her sentence. She was far too relieved to hear the word "uninvited."

"Unexpected," he finished for her, brushing distractedly at his fawn breeches. "I imagine it has something to do with her absence this morning."

"What do you mean?"

James's hands rested on his thighs. "She was rather disappointed with my cool reception and warned me that she could make things difficult."

Clarissa's feelings of relief were rapidly fading. "*She* threatened *you*? Has she no idea with whom she's dealing?"

"She knows exactly who I am—personal assistant to St. Michelle. It's hardly unheard of for people in her position to take advantage of those less fortunate—and not of the same class. She may be Canadian, but she's rich."

"Oh, no, you've misunderstood. I was referring to her treatment of St. Michelle—clearly she does not know that she's dealing with the greatest portrait artist the world has ever known," Clarissa replied earnestly, attempting to make James laugh.

"Clarissa," James began, folding his hands in his lap. "The men I work for are expecting to be paid. Even if everything should go according to plan, there's no guarantee . . ." He cleared his throat and surveyed the neat rows of hydrangeas. "Miss Bennett holds the reins here. Without her, you cannot complete the portrait. And without the portrait there will be no payment. And without the payment I've no hopes of keeping you and your mother safe."

Did he truly care what happened to her or her mother? *Why did you ever agree to work for such men?* Clarissa pleaded with James in her mind, as if knowing the truth of his employ would align the facts into something that made sense. She'd feared the worst upon meeting him again—and who would blame her? Any man willing to enter into an alliance with Les Moines would have to own a soul as pitch-black as the depths of hell from which the members of the organization surely came.

But she found herself praying fervently that James was not that man. He'd broken her heart, but surely he could not have forsaken all the good in himself only to embrace the darkness. And for what? Power? Fortune? Clarissa could not begin to imagine. To her, giving up oneself was akin to death.

She stood and began to pace, crossing James's line of sight as she traversed the width of the rows then turned back, repeating the pattern. "What must we do?"

"Whatever she asks, I'm afraid," James replied, his voice laced with frustration.

"But that would require you to—Good Lord, you cannot be suggesting what I think you are suggesting?"

James unclasped his hands and rose, coming to walk beside Clarissa. "It is not as if I've led the life of a hermit," he said in a low tone.

Clarissa didn't know whether to scream or feel impossibly proud that he'd shared such intimate knowledge with her. "I see."

"Please don't tell me we're back to that point," he replied gruffly. "I simply meant to say that such activities may be undertaken by a man without emotional attachments. There is pleasure to be found despite the circumstances."

Clarissa was feeling far closer to the scream. "And was that true with me?"

"Never," he said at once, "which is exactly my point. Do not equate what I *must* do with that spoiled heiress to what we had. One is an obligation. The other was . . ."

"Love," Clarissa finished for him, her eyes set on the gravel that spread out before her on the path.

"Ah, Monsieur St. Michelle, it looks as though there's news of Miss Bennett," James announced, his tone dutiful.

Clarissa looked beyond the rows of flowers to where the second servant they'd sent after Iris approached, a silver tray in his hands.

"I've a plan," she whispered to James. She pulled her coat cuffs down and placed her hands on the lapels, adopting what she hoped was a masculine stance in readiness to receive the servant.

"Have you listened to nothing I've said?" James demanded through clenched teeth.

"Every word."

"Did you enjoy your morning?"

Iris sat across from James and Clarissa in the rose drawing room, one of several reception rooms in Kenwood House—though surely the only one that exactly matched her flower-patterned frock. She looked well rested. Her hair had been coiffed into ridiculous curls near her ears that so many women seemed fond of and her cheeks looked to have been recently pinched. She was supremely pleased with herself.

As was Clarissa, which James found rather odd. For his part, the day had been nothing short of exhausting. And it looked to not let up anytime soon.

"Mademoiselle Bennett," Clarissa began, accepting the restorative cup of tea that Iris offered her. "Shall we speak frankly?"

"I'd like nothing more," Iris replied, pouring a cup for herself then settling into the upholstered settee.

Clarissa took a sip of the brew and swallowed. "Mademoiselle," she began, crossing her legs with ease. "Am I to understand that you've some interest in my assistant—beyond the artistic?"

James felt damned uncomfortable. Two women, speaking as though he weren't even in the room. But the best thing for him to do was remain silent, and so he gritted his teeth and watched.

"Yes, you're correct. And as you've seen firsthand," Iris replied, reaching for a shortbread biscuit from the gilded tray, "I can be quite persuasive." She bit daintily into the delicacy, turning her gaze to James as she slowly chewed then licked at an errant crumb.

Clarissa sipped slowly, her eyes watching one of Iris's feet crossed over the other just beneath the hem of her dress. It tapped the carpet, though James would not have noticed if it were not for Clarissa.

"*C'est vrai,* though I believe I may have a proposition for you that would be infinitely more interesting."

Iris's foot suddenly stopped tapping. "I'm not sure how that would be possible. You see, I find Monsieur Rougier quite *interesting.*"

"Be that as it may," Clarissa said, returning her empty cup to the tray. "A girl in search of excitement would do best to look outside the walls of her own home, *oui?*"

"Meaning?" Iris asked, her foot beginning to tap again as her interest was piqued.

Unfortunately, James knew exactly how Miss Bennett was feeling. The last time Clarissa had seen fit to act of her own accord, James had taken on a new name. There was no telling what the woman was capable of concocting. James could only hope that his threats regarding Les

Moines would persuade her to remain within the realm of awkward and avoid the dangerous altogether.

Clarissa picked at a bit of lint on her waistcoat before answering. "Tell me, mademoiselle, have you heard of the Cyprians' Ball?"

8

"Daphne told me you didn't say a word."

James looked out over the lake, Hampstead Heath beyond, Kenwood House just behind him. The moment the words had fallen from Clarissa's lips he'd known there would be hell to pay; the fact that Iris's maid was employed by Les Moines—now, that he hadn't known. "And what would you have had me do? I am, you'll remember, only a servant."

"Durand assured me you were the man for the job. I'm beginning to have my doubts." The agent, known only to James as Pettibone, released Miss Bennett's matching spaniels from their leads. The brown and white pair ran off toward the lake, yipping with delight.

James clenched his jaw but remained outwardly calm. It was unthinkable that he would not succeed at bringing down Les Moines. But to leave Clarissa and her mother to these men? The mere thought made his blood boil. "And I still am."

Pettibone picked at a speck of lint on his sleeve and flicked it off. "Then you must get control of the woman," he stated, letting out an incredulous laugh. "She is, you'll remember, 'only a woman.' "

"Don't you think I know that?" James bit out, watching the dogs frolic in the water. That the man had dared to use his own words against him was galling. That he was right made the situation even worse. James pictured himself holding Pettibone facedown in the water while the man's limbs flailed wildly, and his jaw eased a touch.

Pettibone let out a piercing whistle and the two dogs came running, skidding to a stop just in front of the man. "You see, that's how it's done. Not the other way around," Pettibone said sarcastically, growling low at the dogs, then bending down to reattach their leads. Both cowered before him, clearly fearful.

And the man's limbs stilled in James's mind, the last bubbles of breath around his submerged face popping one by one. James looked again at the lake, certain he could wrestle Pettibone to the shore and be done with him in no time.

"Most educational," James muttered, the image of Pettibone's dead body still floating in his mind. "Now, as for the Cyprians' Ball, it's tomorrow evening. We'll be in need of—"

"An invitation," Pettibone interrupted, standing upright and pulling a thick folded piece of note paper from the inner pocket of his coat and handing it to James. "Done. Those are hard to come by, so you might want to hand it over to Lady Clarissa for safekeeping."

James grabbed Pettibone by the neck and squeezed. "Let's get this out of the way now, shall we? I've done my best to be a good sport about this, but I'm afraid my patience has run out. You're as inconsequential as I am to Les Moines—otherwise you wouldn't be here in that ridiculous wig, walking dogs and employing maids to do your dirty work. Only, if I manage to do my part, I'll be rewarded with a higher ranking within the organization. Can you say the same?"

Pettibone stared stonily at James, his face flushing to a reddish-purple hue.

"Good. I see that we understand each other."

James squeezed one last time then released the man and stepped back.

"I'll send the tailor and modiste along this afternoon," Pettibone choked out before he spat on the ground.

"The tailor is not necessary," James replied. The last thing he needed was Clarissa trying to bluff her way through a fitting. "Order dominos for Lady Clarissa and myself and send the modiste directly to Miss Bennett."

Pettibone nodded begrudgingly. "Of course." He took up the leads in one hand and turned toward Kenwood House.

"And the Bennetts? I assume you've fabricated a reasonable explanation for the girl's absence from Kenwood House?" James asked, genuinely curious but glad to have a reason to detain Pettibone further since it obviously bothered the man.

"The filthy Canadians managed to worm their way into the Sutter Ball, which takes place the same evening. They'll be gone all night, most likely," Pettibone replied, not even turning around to address James. "As the girl has not officially taken her place in society, she's not allowed to attend. Is that all?"

James savored his newfound power before answering. "Yes, for now—though I do think it would be best if I returned to the house first."

James passed the man on his right and continued without looking back. He could have sworn he felt Pettibone seething as he did so.

Clarissa gently shut her chamber door behind her and leaned against it. She had managed to avoid being alone with James since she'd made the bargain with Iris. A night of scandalous behavior in exchange for his amorous attentions seemed a sensible enough trade to her, but she feared James would feel otherwise.

She peeled off her coat then set to work on the buttons of her waistcoat. Iris had been exceedingly agreeable that afternoon and Clarissa had made real progress on the sketches for the portrait. She hoped to begin on the painting within the next few days—which, once one added in the average amount of time needed to complete the portrait, meant that she could reasonably expect to be reunited with her mother by October at the lastest.

Clarissa reached the last button and freed it with a quick jerk, then sat on the edge of her bed and bent to grasp her right boot. She knew from the letter that her mother was alive. But was she being treated well? This was not the first time such worry had crossed her mind. James had dismissed her concern with the assurance that the marchioness was safe, though he might as well have added "for now." Clarissa had no faith in the promises of the Rat and his cohorts.

She pulled as hard as she could but the boot would not budge. Her chest tightened and she willed herself not to cry.

But it was of no use. She released the glossy soft leather and sat upright, dropping her face into her hands and letting the tears flow. She cried for her mother. She cried for James, whom she wanted to believe in but had every reason not to. And she cried for herself. This charade was proving to be more than even Clarissa thought herself capable of. She'd abandoned her life in England, built another in Paris, and somehow kept her sanity intact. But this was too much. Far, far too much.

The door opened, demanding Clarissa's attention. She wiped her eyes hastily with the cuffs of her linen shirt and looked up to find James. He shut the door behind him and strode across the room angrily, stopping just in front of her.

"Did I not warn you that we were not playing at a pageant? This," he paused, gesturing wildly at the surrounding room, "is not your stage. Les Moines will kill you and your mother if you do not perform exactly as prescribed. Do I make myself clear?"

Clarissa widened her eyes as far as she could in an attempt to keep from crying. "You needn't tell me such things—"

"Is that so? Then please do explain to me why we've committed to escorting Miss Bennett to the Cyprians' Ball," James interrupted, leaning so that his face was directly in front of hers. "What on earth possessed you to have suggested such a thing?"

"You," she whispered, unable to say anything more.

He grasped her upper arms with his powerful hands and shook her. "You're not making sense, Clarissa," he said savagely, his eyes wild with fury. "Tell me!"

Clarissa couldn't keep the tears at bay any longer. A sob ripped from her throat as she struggled to break free of his hold. "You. You're the reason I suggested the Cyprians' Ball. The idea of you with Iris was more than I could take. After everything that's happened, I still want you. I did it for you."

James instantly let go of her arms and stood upright, backing away until he nearly fell into the fireplace. "Are you telling me the truth?" he asked, his voice suddenly stripped of emotion.

"James, I have tried very hard to ignore my feelings. But it's simply not within my power, I must be honest with myself, and you."

Clarissa knew all that she risked in baring her heart to James. But she could no longer deny what she felt. And if she was to accept the traitorous state of her heart, there seemed no logical reason to keep it from James.

"Goddammit, Clarissa," he spat out, his knuckles whitening as he gripped the mantel as if his very life depended on it. "You cannot do this. Not now. I've just . . ."

The man had broken her heart once, so it would not surprise Clarissa to know that he would do so again. But she had to be true to herself, no matter what the cost. "I understand, James. There's no need to be angry. You do not feel the same and I—" Clarissa stopped abruptly. "James, what is it?"

He'd fallen to his knees and dropped his head in his hands. "Please. Stop."

"I'm only being honest. If we're to get through this at all, I can't go on denying my feelings for you," Clarissa said quietly, though the effort forced the tears forth once more.

James lowered his hands and looked at Clarissa, the emotion in his eyes searing her. He flattened his palms on the Aubusson carpet and levered upright, his head hanging as if he didn't have the strength to lift it.

"James, please. Say something," Clarissa pleaded, unable to bear the silence any longer.

He closed the space between them and came to stand over her. "Do you truly want this?" he asked, reaching for one boot and yanking it off before swiftly removing the other.

Clarissa's heart pounded with anticipation. "Yes," she said breathlessly, "more than anything in the world."

He pulled her to stand. With quick efficiency, he set about ridding her of the fine linen shirt, then untied and began to unwind the strip of cloth that bound her breasts. He turned her in a slow, torturous pirouette, placing soft, wet kisses first on her lips, then the base of her skull, just below her collarbone, her left shoulder, and on and on until the cloth was completely undone— as was Clarissa. She closed her eyes as he reached for the front of her breeches and unbuttoned them, then shoved them down the length of her hips, thighs, and calves until they pooled at her feet.

Clarissa opened her eyes and reached for James, holding tightly to him as she pressed a long, lingering kiss on his lips. She suddenly realized how much she'd missed him—the taste of him, the smell of him. The feel of him.

She tugged at his cravat and ripped open his shirt, pressing closer. The hair on his sculpted chest rubbed the sensitive tips of her breasts.

James pushed her onto the bed and leaned over her, his eyes hot and intent. "You're perfect. Just as I remember," he said quietly. His fingertip traced a line from her throat to her belly, the pad of his thumb exploring the indentation of her navel. His hand stroked lower, until he parted her slick folds. Clarissa shuddered with sensation as heat raced through her veins, stealing her breath. His fingers stretched her as his thumb rubbed torturously, until Clarissa widened her legs and reached for him, scoring his shoulders with her fingernails as she urged him closer.

She'd forgotten what it was to need someone so badly that you would surely die if refused. James looked into her eyes, his own hazy with anticipation. Clarissa licked her finger and ran it around her left nipple, pleased when James reached for the front of his breeches and rubbed hard. She grabbed at the weight of her breast, kneading it as he watched, his excitement only fueling her own.

James suddenly reached for Clarissa and dragged her to the edge of the bed. He dropped to his knees again and his tongue found her now swollen folds. Clarissa recognized the intense sense of urgency. James had brought her to this point many times before. But it all felt new somehow. She clawed at the bedding, taking up fistfuls of sheets as her body rose higher and higher.

All that Clarissa could think of was the powerful sensation building within her being. His tongue strokes quickened and Clarissa's breathing altered, urgent sighs escaping her lips as she held tightly to the linens. Her hips bucked as his tongue dove deeper, reaching to her very core. His hands gripped her thighs and she shattered into a million pieces, the very room disappearing until all Clarissa experienced was absolute pleasure.

She cried out, releasing with the sound of all of the fear and anger, the sense of betrayal and longing she'd kept pent up. "Oh God, James. I've been a fool. I forgive you, James," she said, continuing to pant as she slowly returned to consciousness.

James suddenly loomed over her and set a hand on each side of her head. "For what?"

"Must I say the words? Really, it is I who should ask for your forgiveness. I held on to what you did to me for far too long. I forgive you. It's as simple as that," Clarissa replied softly, then turned to kiss his wrist.

His face transformed as though a chilling north wind had blown through, turning from heat and need to a cold, stone mask. "But you told me that you couldn't lie to yourself anymore, nor to me."

Clarissa stared at James and the scene suddenly came into crystal-clear focus, the pleasure of mere moments before replaced with a growing sense of dread. "That I wanted you, James. I could no longer lie about my desire."

James pushed himself from the bed. "I cannot believe this is happening."

Clarissa propped herself up and self-consciously folded her arms across her breasts. "Nor can I, I assure you."

James fastened the buttons on his shirt and adjusted the cuffs of his coat. A cool remoteness settled over his countenance that chilled Clarissa to the bone. "Do sleep well, Clarissa." His voice was brusque. "We've a busy night of debauchery ahead of us—though, I can now attest to the fact that you're well up to the task."

The words slammed into Clarissa's heart with all the force she felt sure James had intended. She reached for a pillow and threw it at his retreating form.

He opened the door and walked out, not bothering to look back as he slammed it.

Shaken and wounded, Clarissa crawled to the top of the bed, where the rest of the pillows lay. She chose a small, rectangular one with silken tassels, curled herself beneath the soft bedding, and screamed into the pillow until her voice disappeared.

It had taken all of three minutes for James to realize he could not stay in his chamber. Nor was the library acceptable, not even the kitchens, where the tantalizing smells of the day's stewed apples only made his stomach roil.

He'd taken up a lamp pilfered from the servants' hall and bolted from Kenwood House, running through the gardens and across the endless expanse of lawns and wooded areas until he'd reached the lake.

He didn't even bother removing his clothing. Just jumped right in, swimming until he could hardly feel his arms and legs. Sadly, his cock and balls continued to ache, but as James looked up into the starry sky, he knew the situation was his own fault.

He floated faceup, willing his heart to seal back up into the charred bit of flesh and blood he'd managed to salvage after Clarissa had destroyed it the last time.

At last, he turned onto his belly and slowly swam for shore. His feet touched the sandy bottom and he waded the rest of the way, collapsing near where he'd met with Pettibone earlier that day.

Though Pettibone was a snide, corrupt ass, he'd been right. James needed to take control, and fast. If the past hour had proven anything, it was that he was far weaker than he'd ever been before when it came to Clarissa. He'd begun this assignment resolute and focused, but that had faded as he began to remember what it was that made him fall in love with her.

He'd been stupid and careless and now he was paying the price.

A shooting star whizzed through the sky high above. James watched it fly, squeezing his eyes shut and wishing aloud. "Let me remember what it was that drove us apart. Let me remember and never forget."

The feeling in his arms began to return. And so he dove back into the water, intent on swimming until he felt nothing at all.

9

"Really Monsieur Rougier, you are a devil," Iris teased archly, leaning across the space that separated the carriage seats and patting him lightly on the thigh.

Clarissa watched with disgust as James flashed a smile to match the description. Though it was well past midnight and dark within the coach, she turned her head and looked out the carriage window to distract herself from her companions.

They'd left the leafy boundaries of the heath and arrived somewhere in London, that much she could discern. The soft, rutted roads had been replaced by cobblestone. Lamplight provided a dim view of buildings and carriages lined up here and there, but it was far too dark for Clarissa to secure her bearings.

Oddly enough, the feeling was becoming familiar to her. She'd not known what to expect from James after their . . . She hardly even knew how to think on their encounter. What had begun as the sweetest of physical reunions had ended as nothing more than a mistake.

The wheel hit a rut in the road and the carriage pitched slightly, causing Clarissa's leg to press against James's. She slid to the outer wall as if she'd been burned and stole a glimpse at James. He was busily engaged at the present with Iris, colorfully describing for her all that she could expect to see that evening.

The touch had gone unnoticed. At least by James. For

that matter, their night together had produced the same effect. He'd been so tender earlier, so attentive. He'd bared his heart with his touch, his thoughts with few but loving words. However, the moment their misunderstanding had been revealed, he'd shuttered himself from her and become the man she'd met in Paris.

They'd spoken briefly before leaving Kenwood House for the Cyprians' Ball, James explaining to Clarissa how the night should and, more important, *would* play out—or they'd all live to regret it. In a cold, detached tone, he'd made it relentlessly clear that the control lay within his hands. He would brook no arguments, accept nothing less than her complete compliance.

The driver shouted at a conveyance in his path, the colorful oaths he used to encourage the man to move out of the way drawing a giggle from Iris.

"Honestly, Monsieur St. Michelle," Iris said excitedly, "is this not deliciously wicked? Careening about the streets of London in the middle of the night on our way to the most decadent of events?"

James slapped Clarissa on the thigh good-naturedly. "Would you not agree, St. Michelle?" he pressed, then drew his hand back. "Oh, I'm afraid I forgot myself for a moment. Please *pardonnez-moi,* monsieur."

Clarissa rubbed the spot where James's hand had been, her skin stinging from the forceful gesture. "I assure you, Rougier, I thought nothing of it," she replied, knowing she did a poor job of hiding her irritation.

"Come now, you two," Iris coaxed. "The whole point in going to such an event is to forget yourself, is it not?"

Clarissa had hoped that the mere idea of the Cyprians' Ball would be scandalous enough to satisfy Iris's need for excitement. She was beginning to think otherwise, a fear she'd shared with James before they'd departed. He'd listened with marked detachment, then assured her that he'd prepared for all scenarios. Les Moines would have more than James in attendance, a fact that was meant to ease her concerns.

Clarissa simply nodded at Iris and offered a flat *"Oui"* before turning back to the window. Knowledge of the agents' presence had produced little peace. Not that she had any illusions of escaping at the ball. Even if she managed to elude James, where would she go? Who would be able to help her against Les Moines? With her mother across the Channel in France, there was no other choice for Clarissa than to continue with the charade.

The carriage slowed and a pool of firelight from a multitude of torches affixed to a building lit the compartment. Clarissa listened to the two as James whispered across to Iris and she responded with a practiced titter.

Perhaps, as James had suggested, Clarissa should have left well enough alone. If she'd not let her feelings for him get in the way, she'd be in Kenwood House, tucked up in her bed with only her pillows to keep her company. While James . . .

The Argyle Rooms came into view and the carriage pulled into line, drawing to a halt as they waited for the coaches in front of them to deposit their patrons on the steps and move on.

Clarissa breathed deeply. There was no point in thinking on what would have happened had she been capable of controlling herself. There would be no going back . . . or was there a chance still?

"Mademoiselle, are you certain you wish to go in?" Clarissa asked as the carriage rolled forward again before halting directly in front of the steps.

Iris offered James and Clarissa a wide smile, her eyes dancing with anticipation. "I've never been more certain of anything in my life."

A liveried servant let down the carriage steps and opened the door, offering his hand. Clarissa batted it away and jumped down. *"Eh, bien. En avant,"* she muttered to herself, too scared to care if anyone heard her.

"Why are we the only ones in domino?" Iris exlaimed disapointedly, as the three stood just inside the ballroom.

She was beginning to irritate James. "We cannot afford for you to be seen," he answered. "Besides, it makes you all the more mysterious, *non*?" He adjusted his ridiculous mask yet again and looked at the girl. Her dress was Grecian in style, with a bodice that dipped nearly to her navel and an iridescent mask that covered more of her identity than the dress did her body. Clarissa's concern that Iris might want more than mere titillation had been correct—though James could have puzzled it out for himself. The girl's advances when she'd accosted him in his bedchamber had left no room for speculation. He rather thought they'd be lucky to leave with her virginity intact—and that would be, if the rumors concerning the Cyprians' Ball were even half true, a hard-fought war.

Iris smiled teasingly, clearly pleased with James's answer, then looked to the dance floor. James turned to look at the crowd. At first glance, it appeared much like any other ball, civilized, even mundane. The orchestra played the same plodding tunes. The couples performed the familiar tired steps. But as one looked closer, what set the Cyprians' Ball apart from the acceptable ton events began to become clear. The women were uniformly beautiful—no homely wallflowers or beefy grande dames to be found among them. But more than that, they exuded a sexual sophistication that was unique to the courtesan. Prostitutes, though able to complete the job, tended toward mechanical movements—hardly surprising considering the surly lot they served. Wives, on the other hand, from what James had been led to believe, were chaste—something to be worshipped rather than poked.

But the courtesan? She took her art seriously. It was, after all, a means of moving up in the world for the women. Wealth, power, and a certain prestige belonged to the woman who landed the richest of those men who played the game.

James could see the allure and had even sampled their wares, but he preferred his fun without games.

James watched as the music ended and a few couples slipped from the dance floor, disappearing down a number of hallways that extended from the main ballroom.

"Where are they going?" Iris asked, taking her third glass of champagne from a passing servant.

James refused a glass and waved the man off. "You don't want to know," he replied dramatically, hoping that Iris would simply giggle again and let the matter lie.

She threw back the champagne, coughing when the last of it hit her throat. "Monsieur St. Michelle, perhaps you would be so kind as to inform me?"

Clarissa remained calm, though James could see that she was nervous. She'd hardly said a word since they'd arrived and had spent most of her time staring at the floor.

She cleared her throat then addressed Iris. "Mademoiselle Bennett, it is enough that we are here, *oui*?"

"No, it is not," Iris replied sharply as she seductively smoothed the silken skirt of her dress. "We had a bargain, you and I. You'll do well to remember. Now, let us join the party."

She tilted her chin in the air and set sail for the dance floor, with James and Clarissa behind.

"Dance with her," Clarissa furiously whispered to James as she held her mask protectively to her face.

James thought the mask did wonders for her—or perhaps it was the other way around? He couldn't make out her violet eyes, and her delicate winged eyebrows were completely hidden from view. Those eyes, brimming with heat and vulnerability, her brow, gently furrowed as she'd struggled with her words the previous night—well, she'd undone him, that was the truth of it.

"Why should it be me? You're a perfectly acceptable dancer from the little that I recall," he countered, watching as the men in attendance began to notice Iris.

He'd not been completely blameless. Since holding her in his arms on the voyage from France, his resolve had begun to crumble. Putting Pettibone in his place at the lakeside had restored some of the strength that he'd lost to Clarissa. He hadn't even realized it until he'd nearly throttled the man.

He'd stormed into her room intent on showing her who was in charge. And then he'd promptly fallen to his knees and asked—nay, begged—for his heart to be broken yet again.

"But you are accustomed to dancing the man's part. I am not. It only makes sense," Clarissa hissed, slowing as a man approached Iris.

He was tall and elegantly dressed; a man with a title—not, from the looks of it, a second son. His black hair was long and tied back in a queue. Rather old-fashioned to James's way of thinking, but Iris did not seem to mind. She startled at the feel of the man's hand as it wound about her upper arm and pulled her in toward his chest. And then she looked up into his face and smiled, tittering again when he whispered something in her ear. He handed her his glass of champagne and she greedily guzzled it, causing the man to gently applaud.

"I assure you, I will expire if the girl laughs one more time. Mark my words," Clarissa said, her lip curling with disgust.

The man gestured toward the dance floor and pulled

Iris forward. She happily obliged, following the stranger onto the marble flooring, where a waltz had just begun.

"Follow me," James commanded, stalking around a line of potted palms and heading toward the north end of the room. To her credit, Clarissa followed closely behind and said nothing, simply turned when needed and stopped when told.

The two watched as Iris danced with the man, her body becoming more ragdoll and less masquerading courtesan by the second.

"How long do we allow her to dance with him?" Clarissa asked, concern in her voice.

James swore. "It's not as easy as all that. I can't make a scene or someone might recognize me."

"Use me, then. I'm nearly as tall as the man," Clarissa proposed.

Now James found himself dangerously close to laughing. "Yes, you're nearly as tall. But he has four stone on you. It's out of the question."

"Well, what are we meant to do? Allow her to dance the night away with him?" she demanded.

James wished it was that easy. "When you suggested the Cyprians' Ball, did you not know anything of what went on here?"

"Honestly?" Clarissa began, standing tall as she always did when she was readying to admit an error. "No. I overheard Lord Musgrove make mention of it when he visited St. Michelle's studio last spring."

James felt close to roaring now, but for a number of reasons such a demonstrative response would have been inappropriate, the least of which was losing control. He would not lose control when it came to Clarissa, not ever again.

"The purpose of the ball, beyond fulfilling the courtesans' vain need for their own extravagant social event, is to bring the girls to market, if you will."

Clarissa ran a hand over her hair, ruffling the short locks. "I'm afraid I don't understand."

"You're familiar with the horse market Tattersalls?"

"Of course," Clarissa said impatiently. "Go on."

James looked about the room, suddenly struck by the accuracy of his metaphor. "Well, think of the Cyprians' Ball as Tattersalls. The courtesans are the horses, and the men are their potential owners. They'd hardly commit to such an expensive undertaking without taking the horse for a ride. Which they do, in various positions and with some very inventive accoutrements—there." He nodded, indicating the hallways that Iris had inquired about earlier.

Clarissa bit her lip nervously. "But Iris is nearly unconscious from the champagne. Surely he wouldn't dare—"

"He would, and he could," James interrupted, moving quickly as the man put his arm around Iris and walked her toward the hallway on the far left.

Clarissa scurried to catch up and the two walked shoulder to shoulder toward the retreating couple. "What will we do?"

"May I be of service, gentlemen?" A honey-haired woman dressed head to toe in midnight blue stepped directly into their path. "I believe we have a mutual friend—Pettibone?"

James nearly reached for the woman and kissed her full on the mouth, her presence promising to make his task far easier. "Of course. Pettibone. Damned fine fellow." He took her offered hand and brushed his lips across the backs of her gloved fingers. "Follow them into the room. Make sure that the door remains unlocked," he ordered in a smooth murmur.

The woman nodded in agreement and turned toward the hallway, easily reaching Iris and her companion before they disappeared into the last room on the right.

"What should I do?" Clarissa asked, obviously alarmed but still resolute from the looks of it.

"Fetch the carriage at once. Wait for us on the south side of the building, near the servants' entrance."

She nodded solemnly then turned, disappearing into the crowd almost at once.

James set his damned mask right one last time and walked toward the hallway, cracking his knuckles. "This ought to be fun."

Clarissa waited in the darkness of the coach. Finding their driver had taken longer than she had liked. She'd never done such a thing as a woman before, the carriage having magically appeared the moment she'd stepped foot outside an event.

Clarissa was out of her depth in this charade. No matter how she thought on the situation, she always circled back to that one truth. With her painting, she was in complete control. St. Michelle had given her that; his faith in her talent and skill had rebuilt her confidence after James's actions had so brutally torn it down.

James. She'd put him and Iris in harm's way, and for what? To indulge her own feelings? To try to hold on to something that was never hers to begin with? She wanted to cry—she wanted to scream. But she bit her hand and held herself in check. Emotions would be of no use to her now. Indeed, they were a hazard.

The carriage door suddenly opened and Iris's limp body was forcibly lifted onto the seat, next to Clarissa. James climbed in and slammed the door shut behind him, pounding his fist against the ceiling of the coach twice to signal the driver to go.

The coach lurched forward, and Clarissa held Iris in her lap. "Did you reach her in time?"

James tore the mask from his face. "Yes. Seems her companion took to the idea of two women at once with a remarkable amount of enthusiasm. He was too busy unbuttoning his breeches to see me come in."

Clarissa sighed heavily. "Thank God. And what are we to tell Iris?"

"Judging from the amount of champagne she drank, I wouldn't be surprised if she didn't remember a thing," James offered, scratching at his face where the mask had been. "We'll tell her that she had a grand time. End of story."

The lights had grown fewer and farther between, indicating that they were progressing toward the edge of London proper. They'd soon be back within the forested arms of the heath.

"I'm sorry, you know," Clarissa said quietly, looking into James's shadowed face. "I didn't realize."

He settled back into the cushions, his face cast completely in darkness. "Just don't let it ever happen again."

"I promise."

Clarissa didn't miss the double meaning she felt sure James had delivered.

She didn't know how, but she would keep her promise.

10

Sunlight filtered through the mullioned windows onto the bountiful breakfast set out on the buffet. James filled his plate with shirred eggs, six rashers of bacon, an assortment of stewed fruits, and three hot rolls. He took his seat across from Mr. Bennett and accepted a servant's offer of coffee.

He cut into the bacon with enthusiasm and forked a bite into his mouth, looking at Iris, who sat nursing a cup of tea. She looked absolutely awful, though considering the amount of champagne she'd consumed the night before as compared to her diminutive size, James supposed she could have looked worse.

The Cyprians' Ball had not turned out as badly as James had assumed it would. Quite to the contrary, actually. They'd fulfilled Iris's need for excitement before tying herself to a title. In addition, James now knew the identity of another Les Moines agent, which would surely prove useful in his investigation. She'd not revealed her name, but James could hardly forget her face.

He chewed a second bite of bacon then moved on to his eggs. The agent had done just as James had requested, even having the foresight to ensure that Iris's companion stood with his back to the door while removing his breeches. James had found it comical, watching the man attempt to flee with the breeches about his ankles. He'd fallen against the woman in blue and she'd practically had to hold him for James to land the punch. He'd managed to render the man insensible with one strike.

They'd removed the limp Iris from the bed and dropped the unconscious man in her place, ensuring that anyone who came across him would assume he slept, having fallen victim to love's charms, not James's arm. James had scooped Iris up and followed the woman to the entrance where he'd asked Clarissa to wait.

He'd hardly had the opportunity to thank the agent before she was gone.

Wishing he'd had more time to question the woman, James finished his eggs and sat back, savoring his coffee. A name would help, but the face was a start. And a damn sight more than he'd managed since arriving back in England.

Bennett finished perusing the morning paper and folded it crisply in half before setting it on the table. "Well, Iris, I must say that you're a lucky girl to not be allowed out amongst society yet. That Sutter Ball last night was awful."

Iris cringed at the sound of her father's cheerful voice. "Really, Father. How could a ball be anything but grand?"

Bennett looked to James for a show of solidarity. "Rougier, can you think of anything 'grand' about a ball? Honestly, I almost fell asleep while talking with Lord . . . Well, I can't remember his name, which should tell you something."

James smiled. "I'm afraid I've little experience when it comes to balls, monsieur."

"I see you're a lucky one as well," Bennett replied, gesturing for the servant to bring him more coffee. "It's 'deuced' boring—now, did I say that correctly? I heard one of the gardeners use the term and have been looking for the opportunity to trot it out. Tried several times last night but none of the 'bacon-brained' lords and ladies batted an eye."

Iris finished her tea and set the china cup down. "Father," she began, holding her hand over the cup when the servant attempted to refill it. "Surely balls in England are no worse than the assemblies we attend in Halifax, wouldn't you agree?"

"I would not," he replied resolutely. "At least in Canada my money is good for something. Here, it may get me in the door, but—"

"Father," Iris interrupted, "there's no need to shout. It will simply take a bit of time, you'll see," she reassured him, smiling weakly.

Bennett drained his cup and returned it to its saucer. "Not too long, I hope, my girl. You'd best be getting on with catching a suitor—hunting season has started back home, you know," he advised, playfully pinching her cheek. "Though you'll never manage, looking like that," he added, belatedly noticing his daughter's pallid appearance. "Have Daphne help you with some of those pots of rouge that your mother and you seem so fond of. St. Michelle may be the best portrait artist of his time, but you need to look lively for him."

Iris nodded in agreement, though the effort seemed to only rattle her aching head further.

"Perhaps some food would do you good?" James proposed innocently, enjoying Iris's discomfort far more than he should. "A portion of bacon and eggs? Stewed prunes?"

Iris's hand flew to her stomach and she swallowed hard. "No, that's not necessary."

"Then I suggest you employ Daphne's assistance with your . . . ." Mr. Bennett paused, gesturing vaguely in the general vicinity of Iris's ashen face ". . . appearance and quickly. St. Michelle sent word that he'll require your presence directly following breakfast. I do believe he intends to begin painting the portrait today. Let's not keep him waiting."

"*Non,* we do not want to keep St. Michelle waiting," James agreed, finishing off the last of his coffee and standing.

Iris squeezed her eyes shut as the servant pulled her chair back from the table, hesitating before she opened them and stood. "No, we would not want that."

Clarissa arranged Iris's skirts about her and stood back, critically eyeing the scene. "*Mon dieu.* You look dreadful."

Iris surveyed the deep burgundy upholstered settee that had been chosen specifically for the portrait. "Is it the color of my dress? I thought the pale cream would complement the settee perfectly."

"*Non,* it's not the dress—it's you," Clarissa said candidly, moving to smear a bit of the rouge from the girl's cheeks.

Iris rolled her eyes in response. "Yes, everyone seems all too eager to agree on my dreadful appearance."

"Well, the rouge isn't helping. Rougier, hand me that bit of cloth, *s'il vous plaît,*" Clarissa asked, pointing to her table where a clean rag sat.

Clarissa ventured to guess that she herself felt much the same as Iris looked. Though she hadn't taken one sip of champagne last night, she wished she had—the comfort of an incomplete memory would surely be preferable to the ache in her heart and head that still lingered.

James handed her the rag and resumed his seat near the door, not bothering to say a word.

The worst part was that he managed it so easily. It would be one thing if he appeared to struggle with torturing her, even a little. But the man seemed made for the task. The ache worsened. But Clarissa had devised a plan for this very situation while lying in bed last night.

At the first sign of her emotions threatening to get the better of her, she decided to picture herself stomping on James. More specifically, his head. The action would drive him into the ground until nothing was left—not even a hair.

She'd slept very little. She'd read and reread the letters from her mother, a new one having been delivered by Pettibone that very day. And when that had done little to ease her mind, she'd relived every emotional occurrence involving James, from the early days of their blossoming love to the previous evening, when he'd made it clear that they'd come to an end. Each memory was followed by the swift, purposeful image of James being driven into the ground by Clarissa's own feet, until the overwhelming desire to cry turned into a sense of satisfaction.

She'd gone so far as to alter his facial expressions from scene to scene. More often than not he appeared angry, but occasionally terrified, and in more than one scene apologetic. Clarissa felt sure her mother would call such behavior childish. But it was preferable to winding herself about a pillow and crying until she thought she would perish.

Clarissa set to work distractedly scrubbing Iris's face. Childish? Absolutely, she thought guiltily. But it was progress.

"Ow!" Iris squeaked, pulling Clarissa from her thoughts.

"*Pardonnez-moi,*" Clarissa offered, tossing the rouge-soiled rag into a porcelain container near her feet. She walked to her waiting easel and took up a brush, readying to make the first strokes.

"Monsieur St. Michelle," Iris said.

Clarissa dipped the brush into the paint and faced the canvas. "Mademoiselle, it is imperative that you retain the pose." She knew Iris's face well enough by now that, in all honesty, the girl could have sung an aria without it impeding Clarissa's progress. But she preferred silence when working and did not care to argue the point.

"It's just that," the girl continued, clearly ignoring Clarissa's request, "well, the truth is, I remember very little from last night. I was hoping you would be willing to fill in the gaps."

Clarissa glared at James, then nodded toward Iris, indicating that she would not be the one to answer her. She'd learned her lesson and wasn't about to fabricate another story just to please the girl. Besides, it was a bit lazy of James to not have had the discussion with Iris already, wasn't it?

The mental stomping was working. Clarissa felt more annoyance toward James, less heartache.

James uncrossed his legs and laid his book on the table. "I find that hard to believe, Miss Bennett," he said, eyeing her with a wicked grin. "You were, as they say, the toast of the evening. Never have I seen a woman enjoy herself more than you did at the Cyprians' Ball."

He retrieved the book and began to page through it, apparently in search of where he'd left off.

"Really?" Iris asked, a hint of natural color blooming on her skin. "Please, do tell me more."

James abruptly closed the book.

Clarissa hid behind her canvas and stifled a laugh. The stomping was sheer genius, she decided. Really, why had she not thought of it before?

"Well, what *do* you remember?" he countered, drumming his fingers on the volume's heavy leather binding.

Iris relaxed into the settee and cleared her throat. "The champagne, that I'll never forget. And the carriage ride to the ball—sneaking out of Kenwood House was quite thrilling! And a man—tall, dark hair," she murmured, her voice taking on a soft quality. She looked beyond James's shoulder, her eyes unfocused as though she was reliving the bits that her champagne-addled brain was able to remember.

James pushed the book from his lap. It hit the oak floor with a loud thwack, startling Iris.

"Oh," she continued, narrowing her eyes in concentration, "and dancing. I do believe that I danced."

James bent to retrieve the book and returned it to the table. "Oh, *oui,* indeed you danced. And enjoyed three games of Pope Joan—winning every hand, I might add. In fact," he paused, whetting the girl's appetite for the finale, "one of the men in attendance—rumored to be none other than the Duke of Pinehurst—accused you of cheating. We had to run for our lives and very narrowly escaped. The night was everything St. Michelle promised it would be. You couldn't have asked for more."

Iris was discernibly pleased. So was James, who settled back into his chair and retrieved the book for the third time.

Clarissa picked up her brush and dipped it in the turpentine, swishing it back and forth in preparation for fresh paint.

"Oh, but I can."

Clarissa peered around the canvas at Iris, noting with no small measure of displeasure that the girl's foot was tapping. "Whatever do you mean, Miss Bennett?"

"I was promised a night of excitement." Iris focused on adjusting the length of her formal gloves. "And while I do believe you, I cannot recall what are clearly the most adventurous parts. Therefore, I will require a second evening."

James closed the volume with a sharp thud of controlled restraint. "But we had an agreement."

"Precisely. And if I cannot remember the experience, then it's as if it never happened at all."

"It is hardly our fault that you drowned yourself in champagne," Clarissa pointed out, pulling the brush from the pitcher and walking around the canvas to face Iris.

"How dare you take such a tone with me, monsieur," Iris bit back, her indignation rising. "You'll do well to remember that you are here at my request. I could just as easily send you back to France—"

"*Vraiment, mademoiselle?*" Clarissa ground out, raising her brush accusingly.

James strode across the floor and took Clarissa by the elbow in silent warning, restraining her from any further threats. "Miss Bennett, if we were to agree to such terms, what assurances would we have that you would follow through?"

"Ten percent of what my father's paying you for the portrait—paid up front," she replied, adding at the last moment, "and I'll require two outings. Your choice, though I suggest you give it some thought."

Clarissa opened her mouth to vehemently protest but James squeezed her elbow, hard.

"Done, Miss Bennett," he replied, continuing to hold tightly to Clarissa.

Iris gave Clarissa a superior stare then took up her pose.

Clarissa forcibly willed the tension from her body and shrugged her shoulders. James released her elbow and she seized the opportunity, purposefully waving the turpentine-soaked brush closer to Iris as she turned to walk back to the easel.

"Oh," Iris whispered faintly, followed by a strangled "no."

Clarissa looked over her shoulder just as the girl lunged for the rag container and cast up her accounts.

"I see. And you're certain? Because he looks tired, *non*?"

The groom cinched the girth strap on the fine leather

saddle and patted the bay's neck. "Winston here's just come off two days in the pasture. He'll do you just fine."

Clarissa eyed the horse critically, walking around to face him head-on. The gelding startled but quieted under the groom's confident hand. "I wonder, can he see me?"

"Do you ride much back in France, monsieur?" the man asked, gesturing for Clarissa to take two steps to her right.

Clarissa acquiesced. "No, *pourquoi?*"

The groom smiled. "Well, Winston's eyes are here and here," he began, slowly raising his hand in front of one and then the other. "To come at a horse straight on is dangerous, as their eyes can't possibly see there."

"*Oui,*" Clarissa replied quietly, then reached for the reins. "A leg, if you will?"

The groom waited for Clarissa to place her left foot in the iron then took her right foot and hoisted her onto the back of the large Thoroughbred.

"Shall we?" James asked, turning his dappled gray around in the barn aisle.

Clarissa awkwardly negotiated Winston toward the door and nodded.

The groom slapped Winston on the hindquarters and smirked at James. "Enjoy your ride."

James chuckled low in his throat and tipped his hat to the man, then trotted after Clarissa.

Clarissa attempted to slow Winston with a yank on the reins, succeeding in making him come to a complete stop.

"Do not draw the reins to your chin," James suggested as he easily caught up with her. "And an easy tug will do it. Too hard and Winston may well dump you on the ground."

Clarissa nudged Winston into a slow walk, continuing

to clutch the reins as though her life depended on it. "You *know* that I deplore riding."

"You hate riding sidesaddle, Clarissa," James answered as he pointed his gray toward the heath. "This is altogether different. And I needed to guarantee our privacy."

The only place he felt their privacy was completely secure within Kenwood House was Clarissa's room, and he wasn't about to set foot within the chamber again after their heated reunion.

They reached the edge of the Kenwood House property and crossed over onto the heath, the line of willow trees demarcating the two properties. The lush green and wooded expanse afforded the necessary seclusion.

James kneed the gray even with Winston and settled into a slow walk. "Well, aren't you going to ask?"

"Pray, do tell me what I'm meant to be so curious about," Clarissa replied, continuing to fidget with the reins.

James dropped his own and set about arranging the leather properly in her hands, looping each in its place. "To begin with, why I insisted on riding while Iris rested."

"I assumed you wished to torture me," Clarissa answered dryly, her gaze fixed on Winston's ears.

"Hardly," James assured her, "though you should be reprimanded for the turpentine."

Clarissa made a throaty sound of disagreement. "The girl deserved it. Insolent child in search of something bright and shiny, that's our Ms. Bennett. She's no idea what's at stake—"

"Precisely. She's no idea, nor should she. Without her the game is lost—and your mother along with it," James reminded her gravely. "We cannot forget our places, not for one moment."

Clarissa's jaw clenched, the tense muscles just beneath

her ear visible from where James sat. But she remained silent. No outbursts, no arguments. James hesitated, not sure how to proceed.

"Of course you're right. I apologize."

James didn't know what Clarissa was playing at, but he felt sure it was dangerous. "Clarissa, I am deadly serious. You cannot think to—"

"I understand, James. I should not have provoked Iris. It will not happen again," she interrupted, turning to look at him.

Her eyes held no fire, no anger readying to strike. Just calm, cool resignation.

"Good. I'm glad that we understand each other," he replied, nearly asking rather than asserting. "So you see why I agreed to the additional outings? We can hardly afford to lose Iris's cooperation."

Not to mention the fact that he'd hoped to draw more Les Moines agents out with each event, though he wouldn't share such sensitive information with her.

James didn't know why he'd forced the issue at that very moment. Perhaps he needed a glimpse of the Clarissa he remembered.

She leaned over to adjust a stirrup. "There's no need for me to understand, James. My duty is to complete the portrait. Nothing more, nothing less."

James ground his teeth and reached to massage his jaw. "That's not entirely true. I'll need your help with Iris's excursions.

"What on earth for? Surely Pettibone can provide you with whatever it is that you need?"

It was a pity that she knew Pettibone's identity, James thought, but there was nothing that could be done about it now. At least Clarissa assumed that he and James were working closely together, which only strengthened James's tie to Les Moines in her eyes. "Iris trusts you. We do not have time to introduce a third person into our scandalous scheme. She'd suspect something was amiss."

"I induced vomiting in the girl—"

"Don't do it again," James interrupted, cutting Clarissa's excuse short. "And an apology will be needed."

He waited for her to lose her head. Actually physically lose her head—for Clarissa, as he knew all too well, did not apologize when she believed herself to be in the right.

"I'll do so directly." Her words were terse, uttered in a clipped tone. "Now, I believe a canter is in order."

And without a backward glance, she kicked Winston into motion and took off toward an empty field, barely holding on to her seat.

James wondered at the sense of disappointment he felt at receiving exactly what he wanted. Then realized her dead body could hardly paint Iris's portrait, and took off after her.

11

Pettibone heard Daphne's quick, efficient footfalls as she entered the orangery. He didn't bother to look back at her, but instead kept his eyes fixed on the disappearing forms of Lady Clarissa and Marlowe as they rode toward the heath.

"Yes," he said, taking one last look and then turning toward the girl.

Daphne smiled and bobbed a quick curtsy. "I just heard a choice bit of news from my lady—thought that you might like to know. Seems the artist and his friend have agreed to take her on the town twice more."

Pettibone fingered the crisp, green leaf of an orange tree standing in an ornate planter to his right, plucking it loose. "Where, precisely?"

"She doesn't know. Not that I didn't press her—I did, I assure you. Just that they haven't told her yet."

He began to slowly rip the leaf apart, one strip at a time, wishing it was the maid's squat neck. "And what will they receive for their efforts?"

"Coin, though she didn't say how much," Daphne replied, reaching for the bits of leaf as Pettibone sent them sailing to the ground.

He let loose the remaining pieces of shredded leaf and turned back toward the arched windows. The two had disappeared from sight, but he continued to gaze as he pondered. Two more outings should provide ample opportunity to kill Marlowe, leaving Lady Clarissa in his own capable hands. He would have to act quickly to arrange the necessary help, but it could be done—he'd waited long enough.

Daphne cleared her throat behind him.

"Thank you," he said dismissively, then reached into his pocket and pulled out three half-crowns. He turned to her, the sight of her round, homely face making the bile rise in the back of his throat. "For your trouble," he added, then dropped them into her eagerly outstretched hand.

She wrapped her stubby fingers about the coins and hid them away in the folds of her skirt.

She disgusted Pettibone for the very reason that she was useful: Greed. Plain and simple. He wondered how far she would go for money, then stopped. He'd not sully himself with the likes of Daphne. After all, he would be moving up in the world soon enough, once he had Marlowe out of the way. His father would finally understand how valuable he was to the organization and give him the position he deserved. Or he would simply take it, years of being underestimated having left him with very little patience or humanity.

"Anything else?" Daphne asked, her Shropshire accent suddenly even more grating to Pettibone's ears than before.

"You may go," he replied, "but do let me know if you hear anything more."

The maid executed a crude curtsy and hastily left the room, the coins jingling in her pocket.

The room still smelled slightly of vomit.

Clarissa held the jug of turpentine to her nose and breathed deeply. She supposed the lingering aroma was her fault.

She'd dismissed Iris nearly an hour before, the effects

of last night proving more powerful than the poor girl could stand.

"Poor girl," Clarissa said, out loud this time, hardly believing that she'd even referred to Iris as such. Miss Bennett was neither poor nor a girl, with machinations and drive for such untamed adventures surely worthy of wanton women twice her age.

Clarissa reached for her brush and dabbed at the paint on her pallette. Perhaps she was being too harsh with Iris.

She applied the paint in one short stroke and stood back, surveying the line. She coveted Iris's diamond and ruby earbobs just a tad too much. She had to admit that coveting, in any degree, was unacceptable, at least according to the Almighty.

Clarissa looked up to the ceiling and sighed. "Can you blame me?" she asked, then looked down at her painting smock and the drab, male clothing hidden beneath it. The little tailor in Paris had done an admirable job, but Clarissa was tired of the same colors and lines, day after day. She longed for a printed muslin gown or perhaps a satin pair of ball slippers. At this point she'd make do with a bonnet festooned with feathers, her mother's preferred style. Something—anything that reminded her of who she really was.

She stepped back toward the painting and dipped the brush into the turpentine again. She was becoming someone else. She'd watched her mother transform overnight when her father had betrayed them. And now, it appeared, it was Clarissa's turn.

It was all due to James. Les Moines terrified her; her mother's imprisonment, for lack of a better term, chilled her to the bone. But it was James's reappearance in her life that had shaken Clarissa's very foundation. Her outrage at his reappearance had turned into manageable unease with their alliance. Lust and a long unanswered longing had turned to hurt and confusion. Even for an emotional creature such as herself, Clarissa knew that she could not keep up such a pace, nor was there anything to be gained from doing so.

She squinted at the canvas, seeing exactly where each line and shadow, shade and texture would shape the finished portrait. Clarissa understood that she needed to do the very same thing with herself. Look to the day when she would be reunited with her mother and figure out just who she needed to be in order to get there.

The ride with James had proven successful. Clarissa had been horrified at the thought of venturing out yet again with Iris, but she had agreed and kept her mouth shut. His insistence that she apologize to the silly, spoiled girl nearly found Clarissa using her crop on James rather than Winston. But she'd kept her wits about her, Clarissa thought, rubbing distractedly at her aching jaw. She'd even enjoyed the horseback ride, though she wasn't about to tell James that. The dreary breeches did provide at least one convenience that a gown could not.

She swished the brush back and forth in the turpentine and considered her palette. The Clarissa she'd been on the ship was too fiery a character for the remainder of her stay at Kenwood House. Such high emotion and underlying anger, while keeping her heart safe from James, would prove confusing at best to the Bennetts. And at worst? Suspicion, as James had made clear on their ride, was something they could not afford to induce.

She dipped the sable brush into a muted tone. St. Michelle thought such a practice wasteful, most artists choosing one utilitarian shade for their first sketch of the subject upon the linen canvas. Clarissa needed the portrait to be whole, from beginning to end. She undertook a broad stroke that outlined the edges of Iris's background, the snap of the bristles as she broke the contact between brush and canvas satisfying.

No, she mused, the Clarissa from their Channel crossing would not do. "Very well," she said to herself. The Clarissa who had ridden out onto the heath it would be. Surely self-restraint would come more easily to one the more it was practiced. And she would grow used to her impersonal interactions with James. After all, she didn't have a choice. If she expected to keep her emotions contained enough so that she would survive this ordeal, she could not—would not—engage him in such a manner again. His ability to turn from her with such ease was terrifying.

Perhaps St. Michelle had been right all along. She needn't completely quench her fiery personality in order to achieve some measure of success in the art world. Perhaps she simply required an equal measure of pragmatism—something she'd always feared she couldn't wish into existence. On the contrary, if her experience thus far had proven anything, it was that she did possess the necessary skills. It was simply going to be a matter of taking control of the situation—something Clarissa felt sure she'd master in a relatively short amount of time.

"Am I interrupting?"

Clarissa startled at the low voice, dropping her brush to the floor. She discovered Pettibone had entered the room and now stood no more than half the room's length from her easel.

"I apologize," Pettibone began, strolling toward Clarissa and turning his head to view the canvas. "I did not mean to frighten you."

Clarissa wanted to tell the man if that were the case, he should not have embroiled himself within a murderous organization bent on threatening both her and her mother, but bit the inside of her cheek instead. "Startled, yes. Frightened, not in the least," she said confidently, sensing that she needed to establish a firm footing with Pettibone from the start.

He smiled as if it pained him to do so. "Good. I see you've begun."

Clarissa knelt to retrieve the brush, using the edge of her smock to wipe at the drops of paint. "Well, yes, in a sense. Of course, the sketches took some time."

It was an odd sensation, standing there with him. He was dressed as a footman, and his appearance gave no indication whatsoever that he was anything but a servant. As an artist, she was a footman's superior. To the Bennetts, Pettibone existed to serve St. Michelle's needs. Therefore, the prick of irritation his comment inspired in her was not at all unusual.

But Pettibone was not a footman—a fact Clarissa would be wise to remember.

"Naturally," he concurred, looking about the room. "He's told you there is very little time?"

"Marlowe? Yes, of course. But paint dries only so quickly, Pettibone."

He chuckled. It was a thin, uninspired sound that made the hair on Clarissa's neck stand up.

"And Marlowe. Tell me, what do you think of him?"

Clarissa could not fathom what the man was playing at, but she didn't like it one bit. Still, she'd only moments before decided upon a course of action that precluded clouting the man with her tools. She wiped the brush one last time across her smock before setting it in the jug of turpentine. "I don't think of Marlowe," she replied in a controlled, even tone, turning to face Pettibone. "He is one of your kind. That is all I need to know."

Pettibone looked at the canvas one last time then turned to meet Clarissa's gaze. "I am sorry for all of this," he began, gesturing about him. "When I received news of St. Michelle's unfortunate fall, I insisted that we abandon the scheme. But Marlowe, well, he convinced our superiors that you—and your mother—were our only hope."

"My mother?" Clarissa asked, careful to control her breathing. "What do you mean?"

Pettibone's face fell. "You did not know? It was Marlowe who suggested that we take your mother to ensure your cooperation."

Clarissa abruptly turned her back to Pettibone and plucked the brush from the jug. "No, I did not know— until now."

"This must be upsetting for you. I apologize," Pettibone offered in a low tone. "But it is why I asked after Marlowe. You see, I do not entirely trust the man."

Clarissa bit the inside of her cheek until she tasted blood. "Isn't that the nature of your work, Pettibone? I wouldn't think that it would be wise to trust anyone."

"Touché," Pettibone replied, his fetid breath brushing hot against her ear. He'd moved markedly closer. "Though there is truth in what you suggest, men in my vocation find it necessary—essential, even—to rely on others."

"And Marlowe does not inspire such confidence?" she managed evenly.

"In a word?" Pettibone asked, "No. He is rather new to the organization. This assignment is meant to be his final test before being given more substantial responsibilities."

Clarissa couldn't endure the man's nearness one more moment. She suddenly twisted about, catching Pettibone by surprise. "I'm not sure that I understand. He wants to prove himself and ascend to a higher rank. Surely this makes perfect sense to men of your ilk. It is the reason that you do what you do—out of loyalty to Napoleon, yes?"

"I suppose so," Pettibone said, his reptilian smile surfacing once more. "But a woman masquerading as a world-famous painter? It seems a bit reckless, as though he wishes to fail."

Clarissa's mind was spinning. She desperately wished Pettibone would leave so she might have a moment's peace to try to unravel the gravity of all that he'd shared.

"I assure you, Pettibone, I haven't the faintest idea—nor interest, to be quite honest. I am here to paint a portrait, that is all. I'll leave the nefarious goings-on to you and Marlowe." She smiled with as much charm as she could muster and gestured toward the door.

Pettibone bowed low, his obviously rigorous study of English customs perhaps the only thing Clarissa could find to recommend him. "Good day, Lady Clarissa."

"Oh, one more thing, Pettibone," she added.

He rose and waited patiently for her to continue.

"I require a cat."

"Is that all of them?"

James, Clarissa, and the poor groom who'd had the misfortune of assisting Clarissa with Winston the Thoroughbred the day prior stood in the small room just off the north end of the barn. Normally used to store oats, the room had been taken over by three cats.

At least, that was as many as James could see at the moment, though he suspected there were a number more lurking out of sight.

"Yes, Monsieur St. Michelle—at least all that we could catch," the groom answered apologetically.

"*Excusez-moi,* but why, exactly, are we here?" James asked, watching as a large male marked the leg of a rickety wooden stool.

He'd not seen Clarissa since their ride yesterday, which had suited him perfectly. Her demeanor had thrown him, though it had been exactly what he'd needed. Leave it to Clarissa to do the unexpected, he thought dryly.

Clarissa eyed the tabby with obvious disappointment and approached a gray female perched on top of a barrel, her back arched in the most impossible of poses. "I require a cat."

The gray hissed vehemently and Clarissa stepped back. "Though not that one."

"If it's mice you're worried over, Chester here's your boy. Best mouser in the barn." The groom pointed to the corpulent orange cat now napping in a bit of stray hay. "Don't let his size fool you. He's quite the springer—but with it being morning and all, he's a bit tired, I suspect."

Clarissa assessed the big tomcat with little enthusiasm. "*Oui*, well, he's handsome enough, but hardly looks to be a good companion."

James gave the groom an apologetic look.

Clarissa saw him and glared. "Are you not aware of the long tradition of studio cats, monsieur?" She paused, trying to remember the groom's name.

"It's Thomkins, monsieur, and no, I'm afraid I know very little of art."

"Is that so?" Clarissa asked, feigning disbelief. "Well, Thomkins, cats are prized by artists for many reasons. Their calming presence, their intelligence—many have become their master's muse."

All three looked again at Chester, his long fur sticking out at impossile angles while his sizeable stomach gently expanded and contracted as he breathed.

"And the mice," Clarissa added, aware that Chester had done little to help her cause. "What of this one?" she asked, squatting down to peer into the opposite corner.

The groom stepped over and squinted into the dark. "Oh, that's Ink."

"Ink?" Clarissa repeated, her displeasure evident.

"Well, we'll find you a more suitable name, of that you can be sure," she addressed the cat as she pulled him from his hiding spot.

James couldn't understand just what she'd found so disagreeable about the cat's name. He truly was as dark as ink, his black coat glossy despite the layer of dust settled upon it.

"And what is your story?" she inquired of the cat as she held him in her arms.

The groom hesitated, then looked to James for reassurance.

James sighed resignedly. "Though it is entirely possible that St. Michelle expects the cat to answer, I do not. *S'il vous plaît,* regale us with Ink's history."

"He's a bit long in the tooth, this one. Got into a scrap with a badger, oh, couple years past now, and still has the limp to prove it. And he's skinny, seeing as he's not the mouser he once was, but he gets by."

The tomcat looked far from comfortable in Clarissa's arms, his tail twitching back and forth with serpentine speed. But he did not hiss nor scratch her arms, so James couldn't see why he wasn't the perfect cat for her.

"I think he likes you," he assured Clarissa, anxious to be done with the matter.

Clarissa stroked the feline between his flattened ears. "He doesn't—but he will. *Oui,* I'll take him."

James clapped Thomkins on the back. "Excellent. We'll let you get on with your day, then."

"Here," Clarissa said firmly, then handed the cat to James. "He'll require a bath. I will see you and," she paused, looking at the cat thoughtfully, "Cinder?" she asked, looking at the groom.

"Bit frilly if you ask me," he answered honestly.

"Exactement," Clarissa agreed. "Well, I'll expect you and the cat who's yet to be properly named in the studio this afternoon."

She opened the door and walked out, the remaining cat stealthily escaping while Chester continued to sleep.

"Have you ever bathed a cat?" James asked Thomkins as Ink's claws dug into his coat sleeve.

"Never even heard of it being done. Can't imagine why you would. Cats hate water."

"Is that so?" James growled with annoyance.

"More than anything," the groom replied, nudging the orange lump with his foot. "Chester here found himself in the middle of the water trough a few days back. Sulked like a woman left at the altar, he did."

Thomkins laughed at the memory, finally giving up on Chester moving of his own accord and bending down to retrieve him. "I almost wish I had a bit of time to help."

"I'd happily postpone Ink's baptism until you've a spare moment," James offered. "I wouldn't want to deprive you of the opportunity to do what surely no one before has done."

Thomkins smiled and allowed James to walk through the door first. "Quite kind of you, but no. I'm afraid my work won't wait. I'll get you set up, though. Let me see if Cook has a bowl she could spare."

James watched the groom stroll down the aisle, Chester's tail bobbing with each of the man's steps.

"*Parfait.*"

12

The sound of footsteps reached Clarissa's ears long before James appeared. She arched her back, relieving the ache that had developed after sitting too long upon a leather-topped bench.

"Looking for inspiration?"

She turned her attention from the portrait hung on the wall directly in front of her and fixed him with an indifferent stare. "Perhaps I could simply paint over the face of Lady Wentworth here with Iris's features. Do you think anyone would notice?"

"I fear that you've set a verbal trap," he answered, placing the black cat on the floor and joining Clarissa on the bench.

The cat limped toward Clarissa and sat, his tail twitching about her ankle. "How so?"

James stared up at the portrait then looked at the many more that surrounded it. "If I agree, you'll question my faith in your work. If I disagree—well, you'll question my faith in your work."

Clarissa could feel the beginning of a small smile on her lips despite her desire to remain unaffected. "I'd not even thought to catch you so, but I cannot deny that your logic is . . ." She dropped her palms to the leather seat and leaned back, her eyes looking up at the gilt border just where the walls met the ceiling as she searched for the right word.

"Logical?" James offered helpfully.

"Yes, actually," Clarissa agreed, continuing to examine the decorative touch.

James's low laugh held amusement. "You needn't sound so surprised. I can be rather clever when it's absolutely necessary."

Clarissa's gaze drifted back to James. This felt altogether too comfortable. Too familiar. Too dangerous. Especially with a man who'd insisted her mother be taken hostage. Pettibone's revelation concerning her mother had hurt far worse than Clarissa could have imagined. James was keeping more from her than she'd realized. Well, two could play at that game.

"Thank you for seeing to Pharaoh's bath," she said politely, cutting short the flirtatious moment.

James only nodded in response. "Pharaoh, is it?"

The cat jumped awkwardly into Clarissa's lap, settling himself down upon her fawn breeches. "Looks as if he already knows his name. Then Pharaoh it is. Now, I suppose I should return to my work."

"There is something I need to speak with you about—beyond Pharaoh," James replied, his tone turning serious.

Clarissa began to stroke the cat, her mind working furiously. Did he know of Pettibone's visit to the studio? And if he did, what was she going to tell him? She'd not yet decided. She'd come to the portrait gallery for that very reason; critically examining the work of others was a way of freeing her mind to think on other things. But she'd only begun the process, the last hour hardly sufficient time to complete such a task. She hated him for treating her mother so inexcusably. But did she hate him enough to endanger his life? For Pettibone inspired in Clarissa an intense mistrust that she felt sure was warranted.

"I've decided on Iris's next outing."

Clarissa nearly let out an audible sigh of relief. "Is that so?"

"Yes. A boxing match—not far from here. It shouldn't draw many members of polite society, but enough that Iris will be pleased."

Pharaoh growled in irritation and swatted at Clarissa's hand. "How on earth will you explain the presence of a lady at such an event?" Clarissa asked.

"Really, St. Michelle?" He lifted a brow, lips quirking in a small smile.

Clarissa resumed stroking the cat at a more leisurely pace while she mulled over James's response. Suddenly, it occurred to her that the man just might be fool enough to repeat his daring use of disguise. "You cannot mean to—"

"But why wouldn't I?" he interrupted, examining Clarissa from head to toe. "It has worked well, wouldn't you agree?"

"First of all," Clarissa said matter-of-factly, "the girl is far more endowed than I. Where do you think to put those?"

James's critical gaze rested on Clarissa's bound breasts. "True enough. Hers are roughly three times the size of yours. But this is for one night only. Don't you think an additional binding or two would suffice?"

Clarissa folded her arms across her chest and fought the urge to tell James just what she thought he should do with his "additional bindings."

"As for the rest of her far-more-feminine form," he continued, "we'll just have to do the best we can. The majority of the men at the match will be foxed, which should aid our efforts."

Clarissa crossed her legs, sending Pharaoh jumping for the space between herself and James. "Yes, I believe it was my grandmother who said, in a pinch, public drunkenness is always helpful."

"We've no choice in the matter. Better to accept that now," James replied, standing. "I'll fetch Iris and meet you at the servants' entrance tonight at one o'clock. Agreed?"

"Will Pettibone be joining us for the outing?" Clarissa inquired, attempting to keep her tone disinterested, though she was eager for information on the man.

"No," James replied. "Why do you ask?"

She shouldn't have mentioned Pettibone, that much was clear. James was readying to leave and now here he sat, asking a question that Clarissa couldn't begin to answer.

"Why do I ask?" she countered, attempting to secure a bit of additional time.

James picked up Pharaoh and set him gently on the floor, then slid the distance between the two on the bench until his leg brushed up against Clarissa's. "Pettibone is mine to deal with, not yours," he said firmly.

"Of course," Clarissa agreed, running her fingers through the short hair at the nape of her neck. "Really, there's no need to turn so serious. It was a simple question."

James reached out and caught her chin between his forefinger and thumb, staring hard into Clarissa's eyes. "There is nothing simple about Pettibone—nor the men that we work for. This is a matter of life and death, Clarissa. I need to know you understand that."

The feel of his warm, strong fingers on her skin made Clarissa tense, as did his words. He had no idea just how right he was. Pettibone was up to something, Clarissa could feel it in her bones.

She searched James's eyes, finding nothing beyond a cool, calculated concern. If it was true that the eyes were the windows to the soul, Clarissa believed she'd found her answer.

She nodded, then pulled away, needing to be free of his touch.

"We'll be one step closer to our goal by the end of the evening. Just keep that in mind." James stood and strode from the gallery, leaving Clarissa with only Pharaoh and her thoughts for comfort.

Clarissa listened until she could no longer hear his boots upon the oaken floors. She lifted Pharaoh from beneath the leather bench and buried her face in his soft fur, his small, warm body comforting her sore heart.

"It's so dark! I can't see anything."

James gripped Iris's hand harder and continued on down the hall. "It's meant to be dark, mademoiselle. How else would we make our way through Kenwood House undetected?"

"Oh," she said conspiratorially, then added, "Still, would one candle have ruined everything?"

James wanted to say that she'd already ruined everything, but held his tongue. The silly girl had tried his patience time and time again. And James was not a patient man to begin with.

He'd waited nearly an hour outside her chamber door while her maid fussed with the preparations. Iris had asked after a modiste to adjust the cuffs of her shirt—requiring that James explain the ridiculousness of such a request at the late hour. Daphne needed two explanations of how to properly button the breeches, ending in James demonstrating on his own. Then Daphne had nearly fainted at the indecency of it all—a malady cured quickly by the addition of funds to what she'd already been promised by Pettibone. James had wanted to tear down Iris's door and dress the woman himself, but even he could understand why such an act would be disastrous.

When she'd finally stepped from her room, the

pleased look on her face only irritated James further. He'd straightened and rebuttoned her coat as best he could until he felt she could pass for a man—at least for one night.

Agreeing to more "adventures"—as Iris had been so fond of calling them—would hopefully prove fruitful. Pettibone was so tight-lipped about Les Moines that James felt sure he'd hardly get anything useful out of the man.

And James wanted information. It wasn't enough to intercept the funds. He wanted to destroy every last one of the conspirators, from Durand and Pettibone to the woman at the Cyprians' Ball and all the way up the ranks to the person who pulled the strings. James was a loyal Young Corinthian, and that had been enough to convince him to accept the task in the beginning.

But now? Now he wanted someone to pay. His time at Kenwood House had only served to remind him what he'd learned so long ago: Anything beyond physical lust was pointless. He mentally slammed his fist into the wall for allowing thoughts of Clarissa to enter his mind. What James would not give if she'd never seen fit to reappear in his life.

But the neckless twin, in all of his infinite wisdom, had broken St. Michelle's arm. And if Les Moines had not employed the neckless twin? Well, James would probably still be scurrying down a dark hallway with Iris in tow, but he certainly would not be scurrying toward Clarissa.

"Ouch," Iris squeaked as she struggled to keep pace. "You're about to break my wrist."

"My apologies, Mademoiselle Bennett," James murmured, though he could hardly find it in himself to feel anything but irritated.

He knew that Clarissa was as much to blame for his situation as anyone—including himself. When they'd parted years ago, he'd told her she was weak for not trusting in him. And he'd believed it. But he hadn't blamed her. She was, after all, a woman.

So he could hardly hold her accountable now. She was, despite appearances, the same feminine creature who had drawn him to her like a moth to the flame. As of late, though, something had come over Clarissa. He could not quite put his finger on it, but she'd altered her demeanor—and purposefully. *Purposefully.* Such a word in relation to Clarissa was unthinkable. She was anything but purposeful. Headstrong. Emotional. Mercurial. Those were descriptions suitable for the woman he'd known.

James stopped abruptly at the end of the hallway. "*Attendez.* There's a light up ahead," he whispered into Iris's ear. There was no one about, but he thought it best to embellish a bit while the woman was fully aware.

"How utterly exciting!" Iris whispered urgently, peeking around James's shoulder. "I feel as though I'm a spy in His Majesty's service!"

Iris's words were akin to being brained by a cricket bat. James pulled the girl toward the stairs and made haste for the main floor.

And suddenly realized that Clarissa was turning into a spy. Before his very eyes, no less. He'd hardly thought of her in such a way, but it was true. He'd come to rely on her—through no fault of his own, of course; the utter lack of Corinthian support made it completely necessary. But she was becoming his partner.

Where were he and Iris off to at that very moment? To meet Clarissa. Who was needed to part Bennett from his money? Clarissa. James missed the last step, stumbled, and almost pulled Iris down with him.

"Now where?" she whispered eagerly.

Clearly, the near fall had only heightened the sense of danger for her. "This way."

They continued silently toward the rear of Kenwood House, reaching the servants' stairs quickly.

It was difficult to accept that his fate lay, in part, in the hands of a woman—even more disturbing that the woman was Clarissa. But more than that, he'd somehow robbed her of what made Clarissa Clarissa. And he wasn't sure he could ever forgive himself for that.

"Careful on the stairs," James hissed to Iris as they descended, a faint glow of candlelight dimly illuminating the hall as they approached the bottom.

He guided her through the servants' dining room, toward the large kitchen, the light growing steadily brighter.

"*Mes petits,* I was afraid you'd decided against going," Clarissa remarked upon their entry, her perfect French accent both seductive and startling to James.

She was St. Michelle. From her shorn glossy black locks down to her perfectly polished Hessian boots, she'd become what he'd wanted her to be.

"I would not miss this for all the world," Iris answered teasingly.

"*Non,* I suppose you would not," Clarissa answered, then threw the lock on the sturdy wooden door. "*Allons-y!*"

"You cannot mean for me to ride *astride.*"

Clarissa ducked down below Winston's side and fiddled with his saddle pad in an attempt to hide her relief. "I suppose that we will not be able to go? *Dommage.*"

Iris let out a huff of irritation. "Why is it necessary for us to travel by horse when we possess perfectly serviceable carriages?"

James smoothed out the saddle pad on the dappled gray before setting the saddle atop the horse. "This is not the Cyprians' Ball, mademoiselle. There we had the advantage of masks."

"But I am wearing the costume, just as you re-quested," she replied, gesturing to her hastily tailored clothing.

Clarissa stood and looked at Iris. All the bindings in the world would not make the woman look like a man. Her curves were somewhat hidden, though recognizable if one bothered to look closely. Her hair, the fair com-plexion, the ridiculously pert cupid's bow of a mouth. The disguise was lunacy. Clarissa bit the inside of her cheek to keep from laughing and walked to the tack room, eyeing the saddle she'd used on her first ride.

"*Oui,* the costume is a start. But we cannot arrive in an expensive carriage and expect to go unnoticed. This is a completely different clientele, Mademoiselle Ben-nett," James replied, cinching the saddle of the chestnut intended for the girl. "*Très* dangerous, on that you can be sure."

Clarissa knew that what James was keeping from Iris had everything to do with the two of them and nothing to do with the girl. It would be the end of everything if they were recognized at the boxing match by an ac-quaintance. From what Pettibone had suggested, James had only been involved with Les Moines for a year and a half—hardly enough time for the ton to forget his ap-pearance.

And if they were recognized? Clarissa couldn't bear to think on what would happen then. Everything that meant anything to her would be lost—perhaps even her own life.

"But there will be ton in attendance, yes?" Iris pressed, the sound of her voice grating on Clarissa's nerves.

James had done everything but assure the woman that they would be dead by sunrise, and all she could think to do was inquire after polite society? Clarissa hefted the saddle into her arms and returned to Winston.

"*Oui*, but you'll not be able to speak with them. Remember, Iris," James paused, coming to Clarissa and taking the saddle from her, his face filled with exasperation, "you're not the daughter of a wealthy Canadian banker. Tonight, you're someone else altogether."

Both Clarissa and James looked at Iris. Her eyes reflected something akin to frenzy, and her foot tapped furiously on the earthen floor of the barn. "Yes, of course," she said, breaking the trance with a wicked grin. "I'm someone else."

Clarissa wished with all her heart that the girl was, in fact, someone else. Someone who lived a good distance from here and rarely left her home. She turned to watch James put the saddle on Winston and glanced back at Iris, severely disappointed when she discovered her wish had not come true.

"Right, then," Iris said firmly, taking the chestnut's reins in her hand and pulling the mare toward a barrel. She scrambled up on top of the barrel and threw one leg over the mare's back, her second coming quickly behind—and before she'd managed to secure the first stirrup. She instantly slipped from the saddle in one swift movement, almost as though she'd intended to do so.

James rushed to where the girl had landed somewhat unceremoniously on her backside. "Are you quite all right, mademoiselle?"

"That is harder than it looks," she replied, waving off James's offer of help to collect her from the ground and getting her feet beneath her all on her own. She stood, wiped the dust from her breeches, and looked at James. "Now, give a man a foot up, won't you?"

James held the mare's reins with one hand and cupped Iris's foot with the other, supporting her until the boot was firmly settled in the stirrup and her other leg had cleared the mare's back. She hooked her second foot into the iron and beamed triumphantly.

James turned to Clarissa but she pinned him with a warning glare as she took up Winston's reins. She'd been masquerading as a man far longer than Iris. If she couldn't mount her own horse . . . Well, she wasn't quite sure why it was important at that very moment, but it was, and that was enough.

"Do prepare for a long night, won't you, Winston?" Clarissa whispered to the Thoroughbred. He snorted in reply. She lifted her foot and placed it securely in the stirrup, offering a prayer before firmly gripping the saddle and pulling herself up while pushing down hard on the stirrup. She hastily threw the other leg over Winston's back, then slid into the saddle and willed herself to stop. "Rougier, *dépêchez-vous*," she said reproachfully, then caught the second iron with her booted foot.

13

The servant had only been able to supply James with the farmer's name and a general idea of the location of the match. But they'd ridden toward Cricklewood, where the light from the torches glowed ahead of them.

It was meant to be an inconsequential match between two promising, but by no means important, pugilists. The growing din of human voices as the three continued down the dirt road toward the light made James wonder whether the servant had been correct.

"Oy. Out of the way," a driver yelled from behind. James gestured for Clarissa and Iris to follow him onto the grass.

The carriage navigated the rutted road and made to pass them. "Plenty of people for such a small match, yes?" he asked of the driver.

"Seems Percy was released today. Came straight here to fight," the man replied, clucking to the bay to keep moving.

James slowed his gray and allowed the carriage to move on before reclaiming the road.

"Percy?" Clarissa asked, appearing at his side.

James clenched the leather reins between his fingers. "Thomas Percy. Best boxer in London—some say all of Europe and beyond too. He most recently resided in Newgate Prison."

"Why?"

James turned to Clarissa. "You do not want to know."

"Well," Clarissa began pragmatically, "at least none of us is his opponent. What do you know," she added, low enough so that Iris could not hear, "there is a silver lining of sorts."

"What are you two discussing?" Iris asked, awkwardly urging her mare up alongside James's gray.

Being detained between two beautiful women was normally something that James would have enjoyed. But their incessant questions were making it very difficult to do so. "Apparently, one of the boxers has been replaced by a much more notable pugilist."

"You say this as if it's a bad thing," Iris replied disbelievingly. "Wouldn't you rather watch a famous fighter ply his trade?"

"Although," Clarissa answered, "an accomplished fighter against one who is not as skilled could become quite messy—"

"Do you mean physically? I've never had much of a stomach for bloo—"

"The problem," James interrupted, needing the two to stop talking, "is not the quality of the fight. It is Percy and the crowd he has drawn."

"Oh," the two women said in unison, then fell silent, Clarissa clearing her throat in what she hoped was a manly way. The sound of the crowd was growing louder, and they were passed a second time by a carriage, the men contained within shouting in delight at having finally arrived to watch the great Percy fight.

"We must turn back," James said. He tugged the reins gently and the gray came to a halt. Looking toward the crowd then at the farmland surrounding them, James knew there were Les Moines agents out there, somewhere. Pettibone had made it clear that he would send a handful, though he'd refused James's request that they be made known to him beforehand.

"We cannot!" Iris replied vehemently, continuing on toward where the match was to be held. "I've ridden—astride, no less!—nearly an hour to attend. And attend I will."

James was torn. The appearance of Percy would mean far more members of polite society in attendance—perhaps even Young Corinthians, though he could not say for sure. But by the same token, identifying additional Les Moines agents was part of his assignment, something he could not accomplish without giving Pettibone cause to send the agents out in the first place.

"As you said this afternoon, with the completion of this evening—or early morning, as the case is—we will be one step closer to our goal."

James could hardly believe that the words—so defeated and willingly so—could have come from Clarissa's lips. If it were not for the fact that she'd followed the statement by urging Winston on toward the fight, he would have assumed a fourth rider had joined their party.

He urged the gray into a trot and drew even with the two women. "It will be necessary for us to be even more careful than I'd first thought necessary," he warned Iris.

"Monsieur Rougier, you are beginning to bore me," the girl replied teasingly, then took off at a canter toward the crowd.

Clarissa watched Iris as she bounced and barely hung on to her seat atop the chestnut, her hat nearly flying off every time a hoof connected with the ground. "This was all your idea—you'd do well to remember that fact."

"You've no need to remind me," James said gruffly. "Come, we best catch up with her before she rides directly into the bout."

James allowed Clarissa to go first, realizing he would

have to watch both women carefully. He wasn't an agent who found adapting difficult—quite to the contrary, actually. James had lived his life since Clarissa's betrayal with little concern for what should happen and an eye toward what might.

But even James found the current state of his assignment challenging, "Devil take both the bothersome wenches."

"It's completely barbaric!" Iris exclaimed, her eyes glowing with excitement.

Clarissa flinched as a spattering of blood from Percy's opponent's lip hit her on the cheek. She swiped at the spray and continued to watch as one man beat the life out of the other. "I suppose to a woman, such a sport makes no sense."

It certainly made no sense to Clarissa. Iris had insisted that they edge their way quite near the ropes outlining the ring. James was doing his best to protect the two, wedging his body between the taunting crowd and herself and Iris, but he could do nothing regarding the roaring noise. Nor the scent of sweat and inhumanity laid bare. It was as if every man in attendance had forgotten to bring his sense of decency.

A particularly vile individual spat into the ring at that very moment. Clarissa's stomach churned. Perhaps she had been too accommodating when she'd assumed the men had simply forgotten their decency—she was more inclined to believe they'd had none to begin with.

Iris let out a high-pitched scream of delight when Percy landed a particularly nasty blow to the man's stomach. "It's so male—so different from anything we women are allowed to enjoy. But you'd not understand such a thing."

Clarissa couldn't help herself. Her eyes widened in complete and utter confusion. She watched as an umpire called the end of the round and sent the two to their respective corners. Percy didn't make use of his knee man but did accept some water and an orange slice from his bottle man. His opponent was finding it difficult to remain upright, his knee man literally gripping the man's arms in an effort to keep him conscious. Blood flowed from several cuts upon his face, and Clarissa could swear that bruises were already forming angry black and blue marks across his chest and stomach.

Iris had been correct about at least one point: It was barbaric. The umpire brought his fingers to his lips and whistled, signaling the beginning of the next round.

Clarissa turned her head toward James, went up on her toes, and brought her lips close to his ear. "Just how many rounds are there?" she asked, not sure if he'd heard her over the cacophony of jeers and yelling all around them.

"They fight until one or the other falls," he yelled into her ear, his warm lips brushing her lobe.

"Or one dies," she answered distractedly, turning her attention back to the ring in order to stop the sudden tingling of her skin.

Percy led with a swift right hit to the man's jaw, much to the approval of the crowd, who yelled with glee. His opponent teetered for a moment as though he would fall, then gathered his strength and lifted his fists. The crowd turned on him even more aggressively, one man next to the rope suggesting that he give in and die. Clarissa looked closely at the man. He was attired in expensive clothing and held a brass eagle–topped walking stick in his hand, which he enthusiastically raised high each time Percy landed a blow. He was clearly a member of the aristocracy, though his behavior hardly alluded to such.

Clarissa continued on, noting with rather unpleasant interest just how many of the ton's males were present.

She didn't recognize anyone, per se, but their clothing and demeanor set them apart. James had been correct in his assumption that Percy would draw a larger number of the ton. Clearly the chance to witness complete and utter annihilation was more than these men could refuse.

"Marlowe!"

The sound of James's name, barely audible above the din of the crowd, made Clarissa look back to where a man held his arm aloft in salutation. He shouted again then began to make his way from the back of the crowd to where they stood.

"Look away now," James whispered urgently. "Appear as though you know nothing of this 'Marlowe.'"

Clarissa did as James had asked and turned her attention back to the ring.

Percy slammed a savage blow to his opponent's chest, sending the fighter buckling to his knees.

The man with the walking stick bellowed at him anew as the crowd pressed against the rope barrier.

James caught Clarissa's arm in an iron grip and strengthened his hold on Iris. But it was too late. The crush of spectators knocked her down. James physically threw men off of the girl in his attempt to lift her from the now muddy field.

Iris recovered her smashed hat and quickly returned it to her head before taking James's offered hand and rising.

And then she planted a none-too-delicate punch directly on the nose of the man who'd brought her down. "For your trouble," she said caustically, then cradled her fist against her heart.

The man, as short as Iris but four times her width, brought his fingers to his nose and examined it gingerly. "You broke my nose, boy," he muttered, wiping the blood on his coat sleeve. "And that'll not do at all."

James released Clarissa's arm and pushed her to her knees. "Stay low to the ground. Go directly to the horses and wait."

"What on earth—"

But Clarissa didn't have the chance to finish her sentence. A large man with a ruddy complexion yelled out something about a fight and then all hell broke loose. James grabbed Iris and threw her to the ground next to Clarissa. Then he began to punch whomever came into his line of sight.

"Follow me," Clarissa yelled to Iris, pointing toward the ring.

The crowd surged forward, apparently anxious to participate in the brawl. Clarissa looked once more to where James stood, his head down and his arms swinging as he worked his way in the opposite direction from where the man who'd uttered his name had last been seen. There was no point in thinking on just who the man may have been—at least not now.

She looked at Iris then pointed toward the ring, crawling as fast as she could for the rope. Iris quickly caught up and matched Clarissa's speed.

"Where are we going?" she urgently asked, barely avoiding a man as he fell to the ground just in front of her. She screamed and scrambled toward Clarissa, knocking the two off course.

Clarissa righted herself and pushed Iris back into a crawling position. "To the horses. Keep low to the ground and you'll be safe. *Comprenez-vous?*"

"Low to the ground," Iris repeated to herself, then repeated it again.

Suddenly her backside rose up in a most unnatural position. She let out a second scream and flailed her arms.

Clarissa wheeled about and discovered a man had grabbed Iris's breeches and pulled, picking her up off the ground. In order to do what, Clarissa could hardly imagine.

She beat at the man's feet with her fists and he only laughed, clearly amused with Clarissa's lack of strength.

Iris continued to flail, adding her legs to the mix and nearly knocking Clarissa unconscious with her foot.

She'd had enough. Clarissa reached for one of the stakes that had held the rope around the ring. It had been stepped on in the fray and loosened from the ground. She wrapped her arms and legs around it and pulled with all her might, falling backward when it came free.

She took the stake in hand and stood, the crazed crowd about her nearly jostling her down again. It took a moment to find the two, the man having made fairly good progress by employing Iris as a sort of battering ram. Though the girl's limbs were slim, she was quick and her flailing almost timed perfectly.

Clarissa waded toward the middle of the ring, ducking to miss a punch intended for another before reaching her intended target. She tapped the man on the back and waited for him to turn, then she swung with all her might, hitting him squarely across the cheek with the wooden stake. His head snapped to one side and he faltered, his grip on Iris loosening.

Suddenly a fist flew from out of nowhere, the sound of bones crunching reaching Clarissa's ears as the man staggered back from the force of the blow. He listed first to the right, and then to the left, before falling backward, taking Iris with him.

Iris rolled off the man onto all fours and began to crawl furiously toward the edge of the ring where, just beyond the torches and down a grassy hill, the horses waited.

Clarissa turned to thank the owner of the fist, only to be pushed down to the ground once again.

"I told you to stay down." It was a familiar voice that delivered the rebuke and Clarissa hazarded a glance up the length of his body to find an incredibly unhappy James looking down on her. "Go!" he demanded, then quickly bobbed to elude a new opponent.

Clarissa dropped to her hands and knees and resumed her desperate attempt to escape. She scrabbled toward the edge of the ring, weaving as best she could on all fours as men dropped around her.

Finally reaching the rope, she pushed herself under it then stood to run toward the darkness, stopping only when she sensed she was far enough away from the battling crowd to be safe. She looked about frantically for Iris, finding her not far off from where she stood.

"Iris," she called, running toward the girl. "Come, quickly. We must fetch the horses."

Iris simply stood stock-still, her eyes focused on the crowd. "He's amazing."

Clarissa looked back to the ring. James was moving ever closer, plowing through men as if they weighed nothing at all. She paused for a moment, understanding what had captured Iris's awe. The moment passed as quickly as it had come.

She jerked Iris by the arm and set off toward the horses. "Amazing or not, it will be the end of us if he discovers we're waiting here in the dark. Now, *dépêchez-vous, idiote!*"

14

"Such an early start after a rather late evening?"

Pettibone's appearance in the studio did not frighten Clarissa this time. Pharaoh had alerted her to the man's approach, the cat's willingness to leave his comfortable station atop the chair her first clue. His low growl of displeasure was the second and had told her it was the Frenchman.

Clarissa eyed the man with cool acknowledgment. "Are you all knowing, then, monsieur?"

"In a way," he confirmed, coming around to stand directly behind her left shoulder before holding out a letter. "My, you've been busy," he commented as he looked at the canvas.

The boxing match had upset Clarissa. So much so that sleep had proven elusive. She'd tossed and turned for more than two hours before dressing and traversing the silent wing to the studio.

"Yes, well, inspiration seems to have struck," she replied, taking her mother's letter and swallowing her irritation with Pettibone as he continued to watch over her shoulder.

She couldn't really say what one thing about last night she'd found so distressing. The match itself, with the blood and jeering crowd had made her stomach turn. Iris's surprise punch and general lack of maturity had been irritating at best, worrisome at worst. And then there was James. Clarissa understood that she and Iris were no more than commodities to him. But as she'd watched him bring down man after man to ensure that they made it safely to the horses, well, she'd been impressed. And a tad curious. She felt sure there had been fear in his eyes when he'd bested the man who'd taken Iris. Not over the task—no, his methodical dismembering of all who strayed across his path had proven him more than capable of the fight. No, it had been a different fear altogether, as though Iris's safety had meant more than just a means to an end.

"How much longer will it take?"

Pettibone's question pulled Clarissa from her thoughts and she focused on the canvas once again. "Three weeks?" she ventured to guess. She'd completed the preliminary work and was now moving toward the multiple applications of color for shading and effect.

"And your third outing with Miss Bennett?"

"Oh, there will be no third outing, on that you can depend," Clarissa answered quickly, turning to face Pettibone with a resolute stare. "The boxing match was absolute chaos. Even Iris could not have found it enjoyable. I'm sure the girl will see the sense in forgoing her final 'adventure,' though I can't imagine what she could have found adventurous about last night."

Pettibone nodded, though he looked skeptical as he walked to where Pharaoh was sunning himself near the windows. "Miss Bennett is quite headstrong, and desperate for excitement. What you found to be chaos— well, one has to wonder whether she didn't find it that much more thrilling. Do you think she'll agree to let loose of the last?"

"With all due respect, Pettibone—or whatever your true name may be," Clarissa began, walking around the easel to address him, "if not for Marlowe, we would have been pummeled into the ground, and very likely still stuck in that field right now. As far as I'm concerned, it's for the sake of Miss Bennett's own safety that we must put an end to the outings. I would think you would agree."

Pettibone reached down to pet Pharaoh, eliciting a low hiss from the cat. "Yes, of course."

"After all, without Miss Bennett, there is no money. And without the money . . ." She paused, looking at him knowingly. "Well, I would think that your superiors would be quite displeased."

Pharaoh swiped at Pettibone's hand, his needlelike claws slashing into the skin. The man examined the wound then grasped Pharaoh by the scruff of the neck and tossed him to the floor. "And you would be right in your assumption."

Clarissa hurried to where Pharaoh sat, dazed by Pettibone's casually cruel move. She gently picked him up and held him in her arms, stroking her hand slowly across his bristling back.

She didn't like Pettibone—she never had. Nor did she trust him. But there was something else, something far more sinister about the man than she'd first realized. She turned back to the easel and slowly walked toward it. What was it, exactly? He was, after all, a criminal, which implied a certain level of natural debasement. She narrowed her eyes and thought back on all that she knew of the man. What did she find so troublesome? What was pricking at her mind even now as she attempted to puzzle out Pettibone's secret?

"You've done an admirable job, by the way. Most in your situation would not have been able to perform so well."

Clarissa's skin crawled at the compliment. Was that it, then? His attempts at flattery? There was simply no way that the man actually cared for her. She saw it in his eyes. In his superior air. Felt it in the tension that sang between them every time they spoke.

Even James had done her the courtesy of resisting such an approach to motivate her to work faster.

James? Clarissa continued to stroke Pharaoh, the act seeming to help her think. Pettibone's revelation that James had insisted on her mother being held had been excruciatingly painful. His proposal that James was perhaps not trustworthy, that had seemed odd, but not beyond the bounds of sense.

Pharaoh let out a low growl and Clarissa realized she'd begun to stroke him too hard. She offered a kiss between his ears as amends, then bit her tongue. Pettibone had played her, and played her well. She felt sure that the man was not privy to her past relationship with James, but clearly he'd deduced enough to realize that she felt some sort of attachment to him.

She mentally pictured Pettibone buried up to his chin in freshly dug dirt, while she pounced upon his head over and over. And over again.

Clarissa did not know precisely what was going on, but she was going to find out.

"Am I interrupting?" James closed the door behind him, carefully keeping his expression blank.

Pettibone stood by the windows, looking as though he was awaiting a response from Clarissa. For her part, Clarissa appeared unaware that she'd been addressed. Her back was to Pettibone and she held Pharaoh in her arms, a look of concentration on her face.

She started at the sound of James's voice and adopted an amiable if somewhat remote smile. "No, not in the slightest."

James turned to Pettibone in search of a reply.

"Lady Clarissa and I were discussing the events of last night," he began, his face neutral. "I thought reviewing the information might be helpful. Would you agree?"

James nodded and walked to a Windsor chair, settling into the seat with nonchalance. "Of course," he concurred.

Pettibone took the seat opposite and crossed his long, spindly legs one over the other. Clarissa joined them as well, arranging Pharaoh in her lap.

"I've already told Pettibone my thoughts on the boxing match," Clarissa told James, her tone direct, but not discourteous. "It was far too dangerous—for all of us. We cannot allow Miss Bennett's final adventure to take place."

James rubbed at his tired eyes. He'd spent most of the night thinking on the match and all that had taken place. Clarissa was right; the evening had proven entirely too dangerous, though she only knew the half of it. James wished he could say that Iris's behavior had shocked him. But it had not. The woman's devious delight in breaking every rule of propriety was seemingly endless.

Though he did have to admit that her skillful jab was surprising in both force and aim. He shuddered at the thought of whom she may have practiced that punch on.

No, Iris had not been the worrisome bit last night. It had been the Young Corinthian in attendance. He'd not known Michael Sterling well, never having worked a case with him, but they'd crossed paths socially and he'd heard Carmichael mention him now and again.

Clearly, Sterling had known enough of James to remember his name—but not enough to have heard that he'd turned traitor and then died in the sea off the

Dorset coast. It was entirely possible that the man had simply come for the match. But James could not help but wonder at his presence.

"Never mind the fact that someone recognized you," Clarissa added.

James gritted his teeth but remained calm.

"Recognized?" Pettibone asked as he examined a scratch on his hand. "By whom?"

"I'm not sure," James answered, hopeful that the man would drop his inquiry, at least for the time being.

Pettibone's eyebrows furrowed as if he'd encountered something distasteful. "Not by a Young Corinthian?"

It was all James could do to keep from throwing himself at the man and breaking his neck in two.

"Young Corinthian?" Clarissa asked, clearly confused and, much to James's annoyance, curious.

Pettibone appeared thoroughly surprised. "Has he not told you?"

"Why on earth would I?" James asked him, holding on to his restraint by a thread.

Pettibone offered James an apologetic look. "I suppose I'd just assumed that you had. After all, you two have been working closely together."

"Well, he somehow failed to inform me," Clarissa replied testily. "On that point we can be sure. Now, would one of you please tell me what's going on?"

Pettibone feigned offense. "I would not presume to divulge Marlowe's secrets."

James gripped the armrests with punishing force. "How kind of you."

"I've had enough of niceties, gentlemen," Clarissa interjected, exasperated.

James's mind quickly cataloged his options. Unfortunately, there were none that would safeguard his relationship with Pettibone and also keep Clarissa from thinking him a traitor. Obviously, the assignment was more important than her opinion of him.

And yet, he paused. The very awareness of this fact made him even more committed to his decision.

"For a time, before joining Les Moines, I served within another organization."

Clarissa mulled over the information with little obvious concern. "And this other organization, was it French or English?"

James cleared his throat. "English."

Clarissa's facial expression changed instantly. She'd put the pieces together—and was clearly not happy with the result. "And did your affiliation with this English organization end before you took up with Les Moines?"

"Oh, no, that was the brilliant part," Pettibone replied with malicious relish. "Marlowe remained with the Young Corinthians long after he'd begun working for our organization."

Clarissa's quick intake of breath was accompanied by a look of shock and horror that settled over her troubled face. "So you were spying on your own country while pretending to serve?"

"Well, that is generally the job of a turncoat—" Pettibone began.

But James raised his hand and silenced the agent. "This has nothing to do with the assignment."

Clarissa captured him with an icy glare. "But it does. It speaks to your very nature. What kind of man could turn on his own country? And for what? Money?" she ground out, her voice quivering. "I thought your involvement with Les Moines was despicable. But to know that you're capable of such . . ." Her voice trailed off and she turned to look at Pettibone as though for support.

James wanted to tell her that she was wrong. That he

was playing this deadly game all in the interest of England. He craved nothing more than to convince her of his worth. Of the truth. But he could do no such thing. And now she believed him to be even worse than she'd first thought. This would actually work to his advantage, and in the end prove to be a good thing. So why did her look of utter revulsion slay him so?

"As I said, this has no bearing whatsoever on our current situation," he repeated, a cold emptiness filling his chest.

"Marlowe is right," Pettibone agreed, though the look of pretend sympathy he offered Clarissa said otherwise. "You must concentrate on finishing the portrait."

"Of course," she agreed, her haste to do so needling James.

"I'll inform Iris that the final outing has been canceled." James saw no point in pushing the conversation further. It was already apparent that Pettibone's information regarding the Young Corinthians had swayed Clarissa and there was nothing that he could do—or should do—to convince her otherwise.

Clarissa lifted Pharaoh from her lap and stood, depositing the cat back on the warm seat of the chair. "I've work to do. If you both would please leave?" She didn't look at James, but walked to the easel. From the sounds of it, she immediately began to beat a paintbrush back and forth in the turpentine-filled jug.

The emptiness in James's chest had turned to something far more disturbing—something more akin to the ache of regret.

"Rougier!" Iris called, pulling away from the dance master and running across the polished floor of the Kenwood House ballroom as though she were flying. "I have the most amazing news."

James braced himself as she came to a sudden halt in front of him, then bobbed a serviceable curtsy. "Mademoiselle Bennett, may we speak—"

"Quite rude of you, Rougier. Never interrupt a lady," she admonished before smiling brightly. "Besides, my news is far too important to wait."

James wanted to shake the girl until her head, clearly filled with nothing more than nonsense, came loose and spun across the room like a top. Instead, he gritted his teeth and indulged her, managing a small, polite smile. "Of course, Mademoiselle Bennett. Please, do tell me this 'most amazing news.'"

"Oh, there's no need for me to tell you, Rougier, when I've the invitation right here." She fished a letter from her pocket and handed it to him. "You simply won't believe your eyes."

James looked at the invitation, noting the wax seal on the outer piece of paper. It bore the royal imprint. James himself had never received correspondence from anyone within the royal family. But as a Corinthian he was expected to know everything there was to know about each member of the family, down to how they took their tea and who was cavorting with whom. The royal seal was, by far, much easier to keep track of.

He slid his finger under the wax and cracked it anew.

"Can you believe my good fortune?" Iris clasped her hands as if in prayer, her elation barely contained.

There was no need for James to read the invitation, but he did so anyway, taking care to raise his eyebrows with enthusiasm at regular intervals. It would hardly do for someone with Lucien's status to know anything of the queen's drawing rooms. "Am I to understand that you are going to be—"

"Presented to the queen?" Iris interrupted, completing a pirouette around James. "Indeed you are!" she answered, affecting a British accent.

He couldn't help but laugh, his amusement encouraging Iris into a second pirouette. It was a ridiculous ritual, as far as James was concerned, this debut business. So much time and money spent on readying a girl—and for what? Trussing oneself up in yards of silk and fripperies, only to spend hours in an antechamber awaiting a summons to the throne room. And when one is finally summoned? You curtsy, and if you're lucky, the queen acknowledges you with a word or two.

He remembered Clarissa claiming that the only worthwhile moment of the whole ordeal was seeing herself for the first time in her dress. It had been a pale shade of violet—to accent her eyes—and encrusted with some sort of crystals whose name James could not recall. And then, she'd recounted with some dismay, she'd had to walk in the formal gown, hoopskirts and all, and her enjoyment had sputtered, her four-hour respite in the antechamber before being allowed near the queen having dowsed it for good.

He looked at Iris's beaming face, her glow of happiness undeniable. Despite all that she'd put him through, he found he could not ruin this for her. Besides, it might just make the impact of his news less disappointing.

"Well, Mademoiselle Bennett, this is *très* exciting news. And in one week's time?"

She faltered slightly at this, though she quickly regained her composure. "Yes, well, I'm told that normally one would be given three weeks to prepare. I'm sure that it was merely a mistake—but I can hardly point out such an oversight to the queen."

She said this as if the queen herself had sat down at her writing desk, thought long and hard over just the right words, then set to work. In actuality, girls such as Iris, without English blood or nobility to her name, were admitted to the drawing rooms for one reason only:

blunt. Such a debut required sponsorship by a lady of the peerage. And there were plenty of noble widows in need of money.

"And who is your patroness?" he asked, curiosity getting the better of him.

"Lady Druesly," she answered, pleased that he'd inquired.

Lady Druesly, from what James could recall, had been a saint for enduring her marriage to Lord Druesly. The man, according to ton gossip, had successfully drunk, gambled, and rutted away his family's immense fortune, then promptly died. Apparently leaving Lady Druesly . . . to sponsor Canadian heiresses in order to keep herself in silks and plumage, James thought.

James nodded appreciatively.

Iris looked at the musician seated at the pianoforte in the corner. "A waltz, if you please."

The music began. The sound hardly filled the monstrous space, but then, James doubted that even a full orchestra could.

Iris cleared her throat and looked at James expectantly. "This is the part where you ask my permission to dance."

He still needed to tell her that there would be no third outing. He could attempt to put a stop to the dance, or he could save himself the time and simply tell her while twirling her about the room.

"Mademoiselle Bennett, would you be so kind as to do me the great honor of dancing with me?"

"Well done, Rougier," she praised, then curtsied and held out her hand.

James placed her hand in his, gently rested his other at the small of her back, and swung her smoothly into the waltz.

"There is very little time to prepare," Iris chattered,

clearly still focused on the invitation while following each step with ease. "But I feel confident I'll represent the Bennett family in a most satisfactory manner."

James allowed her to complete a turn then reeled her back in. "Actually, what I need to discuss with you will be affected by this as well."

"Really? How so?" she asked, cocking her head slightly.

They executed a perfect turn past the dance master, who smiled approvingly. "Lovely, Miss Bennett. Absolutely lovely," he called after them. "Though, if I might, do remember your elbows."

Iris dropped the offending points ever so slightly. "I have a tendency to hold them too high—like poultry," she explained matter-of-factly. "Now, you were saying?"

"St. Michelle and I have discussed the matter. We feel it's best to cancel our third outing."

Iris slowed and her elbows rose. "But why?"

"Elbows, Miss Bennett," the man admonished.

She abruptly lowered them once again and smiled brightly at the dance master. "We have an agreement."

"Last night was exciting enough to count for two, *oui*?" James replied grimly. "You could have been killed."

"But I wasn't."

"Elbows," the dance master called again.

She was beginning to lose her temper. Iris adjusted her elbows with a jerk, then looked again to James. "Everything was fine before—"

"Before you attacked that man," James interrupted, wanting to be done with the conversation.

"And if I promise not to attack another?"

James couldn't help but admire the girl's tenacity. Still, it made very little difference. "I believe that would be, in general, a good rule to follow, Mademoiselle Bennett.

But St. Michelle and I will not budge. There will not be a third adventure."

"Miss Bennett—"

"Yes, Mr. Mills, I know—*elbows!*" she shrilled, then defiantly raised them even higher.

15

Miss Bennett glanced dejectedly at the gentleman's clothing laid out upon her bed. "Daphne, I've no need for the suit anymore. Please see that it's given to one of the male servants."

Daphne continued to pull the pins from her lady's hair, the weight of Pettibone's coin in her pocket urging her to speak despite the fear she felt. "My lady, whatever do you mean?"

"There will be no outing this evening. My adventures are at an end."

The maid knew better than to encourage a young woman to venture out on her own. It was dangerous, never mind highly inappropriate. And dressed as a man? Daphne had grown up one of ten children in Shropshire, her house little more than a hovel and her parents forced to work themselves to the bone just to scrape by. She may have been poor with no place in polite society, but she'd been raised with morals and manners. Every coin in her pocket would be sent straightaway to her family, where all the rest of Pettibone's blunt had gone.

She hesitated, carefully pulling the final pin from Miss Bennett's golden hair and placing the lot of them on the dressing table. Either she took advantage of this moment to do as Pettibone had instructed or she did not and the money would be lost. How would her parents feed her brothers and sisters? How would Daphne live with her decision?

"Really, my lady, it's not like you to give up so easily." Daphne took a deep breath, the worst part over. She picked up the tortoiseshell-handled brush and began to pull it through her mistress's hair.

"Daphne, I have no choice in the matter," Miss Bennett replied, her shoulders slumping. "Rougier offered very little information on the outing. All I do know is that we were to patronize a gaming hell of some sort—and that's very little in the way of particulars. I've no idea of the establishment's name nor any way of finding it."

Daphne willed her hand to continue drawing the brush through the smooth fall of blond hair. "I know someone who might."

Miss Bennett caught Daphne's hand and pulled her around to face her. "Really? Are you certain?"

"I've heard one of the footmen speak of the Eagle's Nest—the very place St. Michelle's man inquired about. Before coming to Kenwood, this footman worked for a gentleman who frequented the establishment." It was more difficult to get the words out while Miss Bennett was looking right at her, but Daphne pressed on. "It's not for the faint of heart, mind you. According to this man, the Eagle's Nest attracts a desperate crowd."

Miss Bennett's eyes blazed with sudden excitement, and Daphne's heart fell. She didn't want any harm to come to her lady, truly she didn't. But Pettibone frightened Daphne. And the thought of her family starving or freezing to death frightened her even more. She turned back to her duty and began again to pull the brush through Miss Bennett's hair.

"Daphne, what on earth are you doing?" Miss Bennett rose abruptly from her beechwood chair. "You must go at once and speak with this footman. We don't have time to waste. It's nearly night!"

"This moment, my lady?" Daphne asked hesitantly.

Miss Bennett rolled her eyes. "Well, of course. I'll be

far too engaged the rest of the week preparing for my presentation at court. If I do not go to the Eagle's Nest tonight, I will not have the opportunity to go at all."

Daphne had hoped to put off Miss Bennett's trip to the gaming hell for at least one night, in the hopes that the passage of time would give her lady pause. Daphne's conscience would have felt less guilty if Miss Bennett had thrown caution to the wind after having time to think things through. Then her own reckless nature would have been to blame, rather than Daphne's conniving.

"But we've no time to arrange for an escort, or carriage," Daphne began, stepping closer to Miss Bennett to begin brushing her hair yet again.

"Please, Daphne," Miss Bennett replied with exasperation, ducking to avoid the maid. She hurried to a rosewood chest of drawers and rifled through countless chemises and stockings, finally pulling a silk embroidered purse from the drawer. "There is always enough time when one is wealthy. This man, the footman who knows of the Eagle's Nest, bring him this." She untied the corded drawstring and reached into the purse, the coins within tinkling against one another. She withdrew five guineas and held them out. "Bring him this and tell him there will be more if he cooperates."

Daphne looked at the coins in her palm and sighed. Of course the footman—whom she knew through Pettibone—would say yes. No one would say no to such a fortune, especially when he'd wanted the silly chit to go all along.

"Go now! And return at once. I'll need help with my clothing and hair," Miss Bennett ordered, peeling off her fine silk dressing gown then shooing at Daphne with both hands. "Really, Daphne, you're as slow as treacle."

Daphne bobbed a polite curtsy and turned slowly, opening the door and stepping out into the dark hallway with nothing more than a single candlestick to light her way. *Rather handy that,* Daphne thought to herself as she headed for the stairs. The darker the hall, the slower the going, which would suit her conscience just fine.

Carrying his boots, James strolled slowly across the lush grounds of Kenwood House, his clothing soaked from his midnight swim in the lake. He'd taken to swimming nearly every night when possible, the endless starry sky easing his frayed nerves, as though somewhere, beneath a separate part of the sky, he could be different. He supposed that it was hope he craved. But for what, he couldn't be certain.

Or he knew and he simply did not want to admit it.

His boots suddenly became too heavy. He pitched one and then the other toward the looming dark bulk of Kenwood House, the release of anger he experienced somewhat satisfying.

But not nearly enough. "You had to go and think, didn't you, James?" he asked himself, annoyed that he'd ruined the calming effects of the water.

It had taken every last ounce of his control to keep from flying across the room and attacking Pettibone that afternoon. He'd neither trusted nor liked the man. But now he hated him—and with good cause. Pettibone was playing a deeper game with an unknown agenda, and James didn't like it one bit. He sensed it was more than merely that the man loathed him. No, it was clearly far more nefarious than that.

But that wasn't what had sent him off to the lake. James reached the spot where the first boot had landed. He picked it up and hurled it yet again. Clarissa's reaction to the news that he was a turncoat had torn him in two.

"Goddammit," he shouted, coming across the second boot and hurling it toward the house. "Of course she thinks you're a bloody traitor. But you can't tell her, you lout."

James didn't want to care. He'd found it so easy not to in the years since Clarissa. Letting go of emotion for the sake of his sanity had come so naturally. He'd even found himself wondering, shortly after their parting, how she'd managed to live so open to the storms and showers of her highly emotional life.

No, James didn't want to care. But he did. He'd built the fortress around his heart so carefully, only to have Clarissa begin the slow, torturous process of tumbling it down one stone after another, until he was left talking to himself. In the dark. On a lawn at Kenwood House.

It was lunacy. James smiled reluctantly. "Naturally, it's Clarissa. Could it be any other way?"

Something in his gut shifted. Then the pressure rose, moving through his lungs, past his heart, settling momentarily in his throat, then seemingly escaping through his skull.

He looked up at the night sky as though he might see the thing flying off in the darkness. But all his eyes found were the stars. Countless stars, shifting and shimmering with hope.

He smiled again, thinking on how Clarissa would have interpreted the moment. Surely a number of large, flowery adjectives would have been put to use and a few long descriptions of the precise nature of the pressure and its journey.

With a sudden flash of insight, James realized what he was feeling—it was relief. In that moment, he'd finally let go of the burden he'd so stupidly held onto for so long. He no longer cared whose fault it was. It did not matter. At least not to him—and he prayed that it didn't matter to Clarissa. He wanted her. She gave him hope. She gave him life. And he needed her more than he'd ever needed anyone or anything in his life.

"You stupid, stupid man," he said aloud, tripping over a boot. He picked it up and held on to it as he searched for the other.

How could he have stayed away once he'd tasted her again? The feel of her lips on his had shaken him to the core. That he'd been able to leave her five years ago was beyond comprehension. And now? James could not think of a suitable excuse.

He located the second boot and jogged toward the house, intent on wasting no more time.

A candle flame bobbing in the dark caught his eye as he approached, Iris's maid quickly coming into focus.

"Daphne?" he asked, slowing to a walk and stopping in front of her.

"I'm sorry, Mr. Rougier, it's Miss Bennett, sir," she began in a nervous tone.

The last thing James wanted to discuss was Miss Bennett. "*S'il vous plaît,* tell your lady I'll be happy to speak with her in the morning." He nodded politely and moved to take his leave.

But Daphne clutched his arm and held tight. "You misunderstand, sir. She's gone."

"Where?" James asked, a sudden sense of dread threatening to settle on his shoulders.

Daphne released his arm and looked mournfully at the ground. "I oughtn't have done it, I know that now. But Mr. Pettibone, he pays so well. And my family, Mr. Rougier, sir. My family needs the money."

"Where has she gone?" he said pointedly, yanking one boot on with difficulty.

"The Eagle's Nest, sir."

James bit off a curse. There would be no use shouting at Daphne. Pettibone would be persuasive—and his purse, James imagined, would be even more so. No, there was no point in upsetting the maid. But he certainly could use her.

"Did she go alone?" he asked, pulling the second boot on.

The girl looked as though she were about to cry.

"Daphne," James repeated softly, sensing he needed to proceed carefully. "I can see you regret your part in all of this. So please, help me. Did Mademoiselle Bennett travel alone?"

"No," she whispered, choking back a sob. "One of the grooms accompanied her. I don't know his name, but he seemed familiar enough with Pettibone."

James swore under his breath. What was Pettibone up to? Endangering Iris would only threaten his plan. But perhaps it wasn't Iris he was after at all. Perhaps it was James—or worse, Clarissa. None of it made any sense at the moment, but James felt certain that securing Iris's safety must come first.

"Daphne, I need your help. Go to my chamber and retrieve a change of clothing. There's a small wooden chest just inside the doorway of the dressing room. Collect that as well. I'll send Thomkins to the kitchens in a quarter of an hour to fetch these things. *Comprenez-vous?*"

The maid nodded quickly, then stopped, her brow furrowing. "Don't you want me to fetch Monsieur St. Michelle as well?"

"Absolutely not," James answered more firmly than he'd intended. He composed himself and began again. "Do not speak with anyone—not St. Michelle and especially not Pettibone."

Her eyes widened and she stood stock-still. "You're frightening me, sir," Daphne said quietly, her voice quivering.

James thought for a moment, suddenly realizing he'd forgotten something. "Daphne, I apologize, but there's not enough time for me to reassure you. Go to my chamber, continue to the dressing room, and retrieve my clothing and chest, as I asked—and one more item. You'll find a pair of boots. Within one of the pair is a small leather pouch. The contents of the pouch—enough, I would wager, to keep your family comfortable for many years—is yours. My only requirement is that you leave Kenwood House this very night and never return."

Daphne stared at James as though she couldn't understand what he had just said. "There's no time to waste, mademoiselle."

"I'm sorry, sir. I knew what I was doing was wrong. I don't deserve anything—least of all your money."

James tried to understand that the girl was terrified, but his patience was wearing thin. "If you don't do as I ask, I fear that you'll have Pettibone to answer to. Do you want that, Daphne?"

She turned ghostly white as his words sank in. "No, sir. No, I don't. I'll fetch your things, as you asked."

"Good. I'll have Thomkins ready a cart and ask that he drive you directly to the Fireside Inn. In the morning you can catch the first coach for home."

"Thomkins, sir?" she asked hesitantly. "It's just that Pettibone seems to have a fair number of friends in the household."

James was all too aware of this fact. Still, his gut told him that the groom was trustworthy. He only hoped he was right. "I trust him. That should be enough for you. Now go. And hurry."

Daphne swallowed hard. Her expression became more resolute as she nodded in agreement. "I will. I'll go fetch your things then make haste for the barn. I'll not stop for no one, sir. I promise."

James watched as the girl disappeared back into Kenwood House, then turned for the barn. He prayed her word was good.

* * *

The excitement of her resolution had somewhat cooled, Clarissa admitted to herself as she lay in the darkness of James's chamber, her head propped against one of the feather pillows.

Following her conversation with Pettibone and James, she'd gone for a ride on Winston. James had been right in his assumption that she would enjoy riding astride much more than sidesaddle. She'd let Winston carry her across the open fields of the heath and back again, so immersed in her thoughts that every picturesque hollow, bit of fall foliage, and breathtaking vista barely caught her eye. Pettibone's revelation of James's involvement with a second spy organization was damning. It confirmed her suspicions that the man wished to use her in some way against James.

Clarissa would rather never paint again than allow someone as deceitful and dangerous as Pettibone to use her in any way.

Especially against James.

It had been the cantering that had brought Clarissa to the most important conclusion of all: She still loved James. Even now, after convincing herself that she needed to tamp down her emotions and embrace the order and safety to be found in acting according to one's mind without thought for one's heart, she realized that it didn't make one whit of difference. No matter which organ she employed, she loved the man. Despite what had happened before—and since.

She stared up at the ceiling and sighed. He took far too much pleasure in being right. And he'd been cool to the point of cruel during their time at Kenwood. Yet Clarissa realized with a pang that, essentially, the same could be said of her.

She couldn't fathom how he'd found himself in the employ of Les Moines, but she felt sure that together they'd figure something out. They had to. The only remaining question was whether he'd accept her belated apology.

She'd watched him burn with emotion when he'd realized she still blamed him for what had happened five years before. Could she convince him to let go of the pain and suspicions that had kept them apart for far too long?

A sliver of light cut its way across the ceiling and Clarissa froze. It was all well and good to plan a grand gesture: an overdue apology and lovers' reunion. But to follow through with said plan? Clarissa was suddenly stricken with shyness as she raised her head and peered through the darkness at the moving lantern.

Odd, that, she thought, squeezing her eyes shut then opening them again. James had either shrunk since that afternoon, or it was not James who was tiptoeing across the deeply piled carpet toward the dressing chamber.

Clarissa swung one leg over the edge of the bed, carefully setting her foot on the floor before lowering her other foot and standing. She waited until the form had disappeared into the dressing chamber before following on tiptoe.

She stopped just outside the partially open dressing chamber door and listened, the sound of rustling clothing reaching her ears. She took a deep breath and pushed hard against the door, sending it slamming against the inside wall. "What do you think you're doing?" she demanded of the person facing away from her.

The figure squeaked and nearly dropped the lantern in her haste to turn around.

"Daphne?" Clarissa asked, surprised to see it was Iris's maid.

The frightened woman burst into muffled sobs. Clarissa nearly took the poor girl in her arms to comfort her, but she was still in St. Michelle's clothing. The last thing Daphne needed was to be embraced by a French-man right now.

"Beg your pardon, sir."

"*Non,* please, allow me to apologize. I didn't mean to upset you so," Clarissa began, looking about the shad-owed room for something to dry Daphne's tears. She snatched up a discarded cravat and handed it to the maid. "But, mademoiselle, what are you doing in Rou-gier's dressing chamber? If it's money you need—"

Daphne let out a wail of protest. "I might have done some bad things this evening, sir, but stealing isn't one of them."

"Then help me understand why you're here," Clarissa replied, gesturing to the small room, "in the middle of the night."

"I can't."

"You must," Clarissa said simply, though her tone was earnest and firm.

Daphne let out a second wail and handed the lantern to Clarissa so that she could blow her nose. "He said I mustn't tell you—not you or Pettibone. I promised. Please, don't make me break my promise."

Clarissa's stomach rolled at the mention of Pettibone's name. "Is 'he' Rougier? *S'il vous plaît,* Daphne, you can tell me at least this."

Daphne began to frantically pull together what ap-peared to be a complete suit of clothing from James's things, beginning with a shirt. "I told you. I made a promise."

She was frightened, that much Clarissa could deduce on her own. This fact, and the inclusion of Pettibone in whatever was going on, filled Clarissa's heart with dread. "Daphne, what if there was a way to get us both what we want—me, information, and you to keep your promise?"

Daphne paused, looking at Clarissa as if she'd suddenly sprouted a third eye. "How would we do that, then?"

"You made a promise that you wouldn't 'tell.' Nodding yes or no when asked a question is not telling—not in the strictest sense, *oui?*"

The maid pondered Clarissa's words, clearly wanting to unburden herself but unsure whether she should. She continued on with her search for clothing, pulling at a pair of breeches in the wardrobe.

"Daphne, Monsieur Rougier is a dear friend of mine. And I suspect you would agree that the man is deserving of our help—if he was to find himself in need of it. Help me, Daphne."

Daphne stopped and clutched the breeches to her chest. "I want to do the right thing, sir."

Clarissa squeezed Daphne's shoulder reassuringly and gave her a kind smile. "Is it Monsieur Rougier who asked you not to speak with either Pettibone or myself?"

Daphne hesitated, then jerked her head up and down.

"Good girl," Clarissa praised the young maid. "Now, has he gone somewhere?"

Daphne nodded in the affirmative, the look of relief on her face assuring Clarissa that she'd done the right thing.

"Do you know where, exactly?"

She shook her head from left to right emphatically.

Clarissa paused to consider the possibilities. Why was Daphne involved? Of course! "Does this involve Mademoiselle Bennett?"

Daphne's head moved up and down so strenuously Clarissa feared it would fall off.

"It's the gaming hell, *oui?*" Clarissa asserted triumphantly.

Another enthusiastic head nod told her that she was correct.

But such knowledge would do very little good if

Clarissa didn't know the name or location of the establishment. She'd not been privy to the planning of their outings—but Pettibone surely had.

"Does Pettibone know the location of the gaming hell?"

Daphne's eyes flashed with fear at the mention of the man's name as she nodded yes.

Clarissa frowned. She could hardly go ask the man, that much was clear.

Daphne collected a pair of boots then reached for a small wooden chest in the corner.

Clarissa stared at the chest, then the boots, and finally the clothing—and something clicked. "Daphne, did Rougier send you to fetch these things for him?"

This last question drew the most fervent nod of all.

"Why didn't you say so in the first place?" Clarissa ground out, belatedly remembering their agreement. "Of course. I apologize. I should have put the clues together sooner."

Daphne gestured toward the door of the dressing chamber, her arms laden with James's things.

"You cannot carry a lantern in addition to all of that," Clarissa told her firmly. "Therefore, I will. And if that means it's necessary for me to follow you wherever you may be going, then it is entirely on me—a fact that I'll make sure Rougier understands."

Daphne nodded and hurried toward the door, stopping short at the sound of voices in the hall.

Clarissa listened as Pettibone and a man stood just outside James's chamber, whispering low enough that she couldn't understand their words.

She turned to look at Daphne, who was trembling from head to toe and had turned unnaturally pale. Clarissa pointed to herself, then to the door, indicating that she would continue. She then gestured for Daphne to return to the dressing chamber until it was safe to come out.

The maid didn't waste a moment, but turned around immediately and hurried for the safety of the other room.

Clarissa steeled her nerves then turned the handle, opening the door just wide enough to allow herself through but no more. "Pettibone, what are you doing?"

"I need to speak with Marlowe. Is he abed?"

"No," Clarissa replied simply, her tone hiding her racing heartbeat. "I've need to speak with him as well. Come," she urged, beginning to walk down the hall, "he often visits the library when he is unable to sleep."

Clarissa glanced over her shoulder to make sure the two men were following. The footman hesitated, looking to Pettibone. The agent began to walk after Clarissa, and the footman followed.

"How fortuitous that we crossed paths, St. Michelle."

Clarissa's skinned crawled. "Yes indeed."

James had chosen the Eagle's Nest for a variety of reasons. Its location, within a mile of Kenwood House, was beneficial in its easy access. He could reach the gaming hell either directly through the busy warren of nearby streets or more covertly through the heath. Its distance from the more popular gambling establishments also meant, in theory, that fewer of the ton would bother patronizing it. The quality looked to a gaming hell for cards, women, and drink. For these gentlemen, going to the hell itself was dangerous enough. They didn't require any further thrills from their fellow patrons.

The Eagle's Nest was, according to those in the know, a viper's den that attracted only the most serious of customers. Seasoned criminals, gamblers, and drunkards made up the lion's share of the patronage, which, when James had set about conceiving of Iris's adventures, had actually made sense. It afforded him the greatest amount of anonymity, which was a primary concern at the time.

And now? James fingered the mustache that he'd hastily affixed just above his upper lip in the barn before riding off at breakneck speed across the heath. He required anonymity even more now, the Corinthian's sighting of him at the boxing match making his nerves burn.

As for Iris's proclivity for getting herself into the greatest amount of trouble she could possibly find? Well, he'd hardly known that when he'd chosen the Eagle's Nest. He settled his top hat more firmly in an effort to assure his wig stayed in place. The Eagle's Nest was the last establishment a risk taker such as Iris should ever enter. But there was little that could be done about that now.

He reined the gray down Wessex Street, the smell of rotten produce and the stench of all sorts of iniquities being undertaken burned his nostrils as he neared the Nest. A man roughly the same size as the plain, painted door that he guarded glared at James as he pulled up his mount and jumped down.

"You'll see to my horse?" James asked the mountain of a man, in a slightly superior tone, aware that he needed to take the upper hand here.

The doorman grunted, his beefy arms folding across his massive chest. "Now, why would I do that?"

"The Bishop of Canterbury wishes it so," James recited the sentence he'd memorized from Pettibone's contact.

The man nodded reluctantly at the secret password and snapped his sausage fingers loudly.

A scrawny boy, no more than ten, came running from across the street. "Yes, sir," he said anxiously in a high-pitched tone, cowering in front of the giant.

"Take his horse, Squeak, and be quick about it," the

man ordered, making to cuff the boy with the back of his hand.

But the boy was quicker, his meager form doing him a service. He slid out of the way, closer to James. Taking the reins, he looked up through a mess of tangled brown hair. "He's a beauty, your horse."

James reached into his waistcoat and retrieved a few shillings, depositing them in the boy's waiting hand. "He is indeed. Make sure to take good care of him and there will be more where that came from."

"Off with ya," the man growled, tiring of the boy's dallying.

Squeak trotted away with the gray in tow, toward the back of the establishment.

"Come along, then," the man said impatiently, turning to the door and banging hard on it with one closed fist. A panel instantly slid open to reveal a pair of eyes.

"Open up," he demanded.

The sound of locks being thrown followed and the door creaked open, revealing a man of similar build to the first.

"Step inside, then," the first grunted, moving aside to let James pass.

James stepped over the threshold into a small antechamber. The room contained nothing more than the second waiting man and a second door.

The first door slammed behind him, leaving James, the second guard, and one lone candle. "Not much of a job you have here," James commented, looking about the sparse room.

"Even less so when I'm expected to chitchat with the customers," he grunted, clearly as charming as his counterpart. "Password, please."

"Fair enough," James replied. "Nelson's short pants."

The man nodded in the same manner as the first then

beat on the door. A panel opened, revealing not only another set of eyes, but the sounds of drunken revelry.

"Open up," the man commanded, then turned his back on James and resumed his station.

This door featured nearly double the locks of the first but an equally burly man behind it was revealed when he slowly opened the plain wooden entryway and gazed critically at James.

"Are you all related, then?" James asked, gaining a smirk from the brute.

He gestured for James to enter and closed the door behind him, sliding the bolts home as soon as James passed. "Such humor will get you good and killed here, sir," the brute warned.

James pulled two guineas from his vest and handed them to the man. "It would do to have a friend."

The brute grunted knowingly and took the coins in his meaty hand. "Just ask for Harry."

"I'll do that," James replied, then turned to take in the Eagle's Nest. It wasn't much to look at, though James hadn't expected it to be. A low haze of smoke hung in the air, making the already dark environs even more so. He was standing in one of what he assumed to be several card rooms, this one hosting All-fours, Loo, Faro, and Ecarte. The large, round tables were full, each rickety chair occupied by a man resembling Harry in demeanor, though their clothing told a different story. Only one or two men of quality were present, their exquisite coats, obviously the work of Weston, and starched cravats making them stand out.

A number of those a few rungs further down the social ladder occupied several of the tables. Business owners, if James was right in his assessment, their clothing noticeably poorer in quality to those of the ton, but vastly superior to the rest of the men who made up the crowd. These were the working class and lower. Their ragged appearance and complete lack of polish immediately identified them as such. The one fact that unified all the men was their utter seriousness toward the task at hand. Their faces told one another and James that tonight was not for frivolity and a bit of muslin. No, tonight was for winning.

An old, scarred bar ran the length of the south wall, with several men behind it, serving rum punch. A serving wench approached, her rouged cheeks and lips practically glowing in the gloomy lighting, her round hips swinging seductively from side to side. "Welcome to the Eagle's Nest, love. You can call me Rosie. What's your pleasure tonight?"

James smiled down at the woman as she caressed his lapel. "Well, I don't rightly know. It's my first time here. What would you suggest?"

She quirked an eyebrow knowingly, her other hand playing with the ribbon at the neck of her low-cut bodice. "Me."

"I believe I've need of some sport—to whet my appetite, Rosie, before moving on to more intimate pursuits," James answered, reaching for the ribbon and pulling it loose.

Rosie shivered at his touch and smiled widely. "Well now, if that's the case, I'd suggest a bit of Loo here, in the main gaming room. Or if you're feeling more adventurous, Commerce just back there." She paused and gestured to an archway just beyond where they stood.

James looked about, surveying the room for any more possible hallways. He felt sure that Iris would not have been content with Vingt-et-un or Loo.

"Don't worry, love. Go on back and I'll bring you a drink. Anything you'd like."

James gently tugged on the ribbon, coaxing Rosie closer. "And if I required something a bit more challenging, then?"

"Come now, you're too sweet to go looking for trouble," she replied, her breath heavy with gin.

James skimmed a finger along her jaw then down her neck to her substantial bosom. "Don't let appearances fool you, Rosie. I'm a man with a considerable appetite for many things," he said, "a decent card game with skilled players being only one."

She shivered again, clearly understanding his meaning. "Oh, I know what you're looking for, then. Through there," she gestured toward the archway a second time. "Only, take a sharp right and ask for Bramble."

"Thank you, my dear," James said, drawing his finger over her heart and tapping once gently. "Do save some time for me later, won't you?"

"I wouldn't dream otherwise," Rosie answered, then turned back toward the bar.

16

James wondered, not for the first time that evening, whether the proprietor of the Eagle's Nest had been offered a discount by organized cutthroats if he employed every last man of ursine frame, frighteningly ugly visage, and unremittingly surly nature. Bramble, a match for the men who'd allowed James into the hell, was even less helpful—if that were possible.

He'd only stared at James for a moment as though he meant to refuse him entry into the room. "You can't afford it," he'd spat out, daring James to reply.

"You really are all becoming quite predictable," James growled, drawing yet more guineas from his pocket and tossing them in the air.

The man, surprisingly agile for his size, caught the coins and tucked them away in his homespun waistcoat. "Right this way, then."

James followed Bramble through the door and stood for a moment, then leaned lazily against the wall, surveying the scene. The room, though smaller, looked very much the same as the one in which James had just been standing. Nothing about the furniture nor embellishments communicated that this one held the presence of "deep punters." There was only one table, as opposed to the ten or so in the main room. But it was the same version of scarred oak covered with serviceable table linen as all the others. It sat squarely in the middle of the room, with six men seated on six rickety chairs about it.

The windowless walls possessed a few worthless paintings scattered about haphazardly, as though some-one had thought to pretty up the place then abandoned their efforts altogether. Two ancient carpets lined the floors. It was impossible to tell what color they'd once been, years of footfalls having worn down their surely once vibrant hues to a sort of mishmash of creams, dull browns, and what James could only describe as a scrubby bracken green.

There were more candles here, lining the walls in sconces. One large candelabra was placed in the middle of the table, illuminating each and every player. James supposed this was done on purpose, the likelihood of someone cheating amongst this lot—and in a much more skilled manner—more of a threat than what the punters in the front room represented.

There was no bar, but James watched as various and assorted serving wenches sailed in and out of the room, taking orders for spirits from the men, then re-turning with glasses, and occasionally entire bottles, in hand.

At first, it appeared there was only one way in and out of the deep punters' room—namely, the door through which James had just arrived. But the wall directly across gave him pause. There was something off in the line of the chipped wainscoting, and he decided a closer look was in order.

Before making his move, he studied all six of the men at the table, aware that it was actually five men and one woman. Seated conveniently enough with her back clos-est to the troubling wainscoting was Iris, her elbows on the table and her head nearly touching her cards in a protective manner. If he'd not ordered the clothing himself and witnessed the woman in them before, James didn't think he would have recognized her.

She'd donned a different hat from the one she'd worn to the boxing match: probably nicked it from the Les Moines agent Daphne had assured him had accompanied Iris to the Eagle's Nest this evening. It hid the length of her hair easily. The rest of her costume was the same, though it did look far more rumpled than it had before and there appeared to be a smear of mud just near the left shoulder.

James stifled a smile at the thought of what could have caused the wrinkling and mud. His coin was on Iris having taken a tumble during her hasty ride to the gaming hell. He'd have to remember to ask once he'd removed her from the Nest and restored her to safety within the walls of Kenwood House.

But first, he had to do just that. James strolled to a chair and carried it to the table. "Might I join in?" he asked, his movements making it clear that he intended on playing no matter what the answer might be.

"Did you have a chat then with Bramble?" one of the men countered, the rest of the table turning their attention toward James.

"In a manner of speaking, yes," James replied, noting the bit of wainscoting that had caught his attention from across the room. It was a hinged door, painted to match the wall and devoid of any sort of handle.

The man, as old as the carpet but in much worse repair, nodded. "If Bramble let you pass, then yes, we've room for one more.

James nodded and set his chair next to Iris, who hazarded a look at James while she scraped her chair to the right to make room. Her eyes darted back to her cards just as quickly. He couldn't tell if she'd recognized him or not.

James looked at his fellow players and offered a friendly smile. "And what are we playing this evening, gentlemen?"

"Vingt-et-un," the old man answered. James could see now that he was the dealer in what was, for all intents and purposes, a fairly straightforward game. Vingt-et-un, or Twenty-one, involved each man playing his hand independently against the dealer. At the beginning of each round, players were required to place bets, after which they were dealt two cards. The object of the game was to achieve a higher card total than that of the dealer without going over twenty-one.

James emptied the contents of his waistcoat pocket onto the table, a small fortune in coin clinking as it hit. "Don't let me waste any more time, my good man. Please, on with the game."

James had played Vingt-et-un while inebriated. He'd played it while naked. He'd played it blindfolded. He'd even played it while foxed, naked, and blindfolded at the same time, though admittedly, he'd not fared well that time.

He casually looked over the group of men gathered at the table, certain that he'd easily win. There were two who appeared to still have their wits about them— seasoned card players who more than likely played for a living. A few were merchants or gentry of some sort or another, who might have had some skill if they weren't in their cups, having obviously partaken of the Eagle's Nest's rum punch. As it stood now, these men were able to keep their heads up, but James didn't know how much longer that would be true. That left himself and Iris.

The dealer instructed the table to contribute their coin to the pool. James tossed his three crowns into the center of the table and watched as the others did the same.

Each player was dealt three cards face-side down, the dealer finishing by placing three cards face up on the table to form the widow. James picked up his cards, taking note of the four of clubs and the jack of hearts before turning his attention to the dealer. The old man exchanged the five of diamonds from the widow for a new card, his thin lips spreading into a smug smile when it landed faceup and revealed the ace of spades. The dealer looked to one of the inebriated merchants and awaited his move. This continued on, with each player attempting to make his hand first. James was keeping even, which was surprising for him. But even more surprising was Iris's run of good luck.

James began to watch Iris in earnest, careful not to draw attention to her. She followed each player's cards with alarming intensity despite the growing tension at the table. And then he noticed the smallest of movements. Her bottom lip would twitch every time the dealer dealt a card. James continued to watch, mentally recording every time her lips reacted in such a way.

God Almighty, she was cheating. Where on earth had the woman—really, more of a girl if one was being completely honest—learned to count cards? She was audacious—ridiculously so—he'd give her that. Even James hadn't mastered the art of counting cards, though he preferred to blame this on his own laziness rather than any mental shortcomings. What he did understand was that it was a form of cheating in which the player kept track of the cards dealt, then used this to his—or her, as the case may be—advantage in one of two ways. Either the player placed larger bets when she had the advantage. Or . . . James could not remember precisely what the second strategy involved. But it was neither here nor there.

Iris was employing the first strategy and doing a damn fine job of it. James was torn between admiration for her and a growing sense of dread—for if he'd detected her cheating, then surely it was only a matter of time before the others did.

How could she be so intelligent, yet so wantonly reckless?

"Just hold on a bloody minute."

James's question would have to wait. He looked up at the player on Iris's right who'd uttered the demand. "Is there a problem?"

"He's fuzzed the cards," the man replied, gesturing toward Iris.

Iris peered up from her cards and turned to take the man in. "Prove it," she said in a low, menacing tone.

Not again.

The disgruntled player knocked Iris's cards from her hand and eyed her pile of coins with disgust. "There's no way you've won all that fairly. I've seen you. You're counting cards."

Iris put her hands over her winnings and sneered at the rest of the men at the table. "As I said, prove it."

"Bramble," the dealer shouted over his shoulder.

The large man left his place at the entry and plodded toward the table. "What is it?"

"Seems this gent here," the old man began, pointing at the menacing gamester, "thinks that gent there is counting cards. See if he is, will you?"

Iris guffawed at the dealer's words. "Though I'm not intimately aware of the particulars of cheating at cards, I do know that it's something one does with one's brain. How do you propose, Mr. Bramble, to prove such a thing?"

"Simple, really. I'll break your neck if you don't tell me the truth."

And with that, the giant moved toward Iris and made to pluck her by her head from her seat, hat and all.

God Almighty. James jumped to his feet, pushed Iris forward, then grasped the edge of the table, tipping it up and over onto the remaining players. The feel of Bramble's thick fingers as they curled around his neck wasn't unexpected, but still painful as the man took hold of him with a viselike grip and pulled him back away from the table.

Unable to break Bramble's hold on his neck, James shoved backward with all of his weight and smashed Bramble into the wall, pitching forward and repeating the movement a second time and a third. Bramble's fingers loosened. James grabbed an overturned chair and smashed it against the wall, breaking a leg free. By then Bramble seemed to have recovered some strength, his grip tightening yet again.

James gripped the chair leg and swung it over his shoulder, the sound of it connecting with Bramble's face both gruesome and gratifying. James took several more whacks before Bramble fell away from him and landed on the floor with a deafening thud. James turned to make sure that the hulk had been knocked clean out then surveyed the room. All of the men were fighting now, save for the dealer, who was desperately trying to retrieve every last coin and pocket it for himself.

James found Iris tucked up in the corner, the upturned table a barrier between herself and the offended player. The maneuver had been quick thinking, but it was obvious she had little time left before the man captured her.

James quickly closed the distance to the gamester and then tapped him on the shoulder. When the man turned his angry face to see who had summoned him, James let loose with the chair leg, striking the man squarely across the cheek.

He dropped hard to his knees, looking as if he might say something, then his eyes rolled back and he fell flat on his face.

"Come, Iris, there's no time to waste."

Iris looked utterly surprised at the sound of her name, her eyes narrowing as she looked closely at James's face. "Do I know you, sir?"

"It's Rougier, mademoiselle. Now, come with me."

17

The hidden door within the room at the Eagle's Nest proved not to be the most direct escape route. James thumped on the door hard and it gave way, revealing a dank, dark hallway. He'd yanked a chair in one hand and Iris in the other through the opening, slamming the door shut and wedging the chair up against it in the hopes that the obstacle would hold the men off for a trifle longer.

He pulled Iris down the hallway, reaching a hot, cramped kitchen where a number of women looked up from preparing an assortment of meats and side dishes. James adopted a superior stare and continued on through the steaming, smoke-filled room as if he knew exactly where he was going. He spied what appeared to be a door to the outside and strode confidently toward it, Iris following behind him.

He turned the handle and shoved the door open, yanking Iris clear of the threshold before slamming it shut.

They emerged in the alley that ran behind the Eagle's Nest. James heard and smelled the presence of horses. He looked across the alley and could just make out what he assumed were the Nest's stables.

"Well, that's a bit of luck anyway," he said under his breath, tightening his grip on Iris's arm as he prepared to go in search of their horses.

Suddenly Bramble burst through the door behind

them, with the dealer following. "You weren't thinking of leaving now, not when everything's gettin' interesting?"

James shoved Iris behind him and gave the two men a sardonic smile. "Bramble, it wasn't sporting of you to attack the gentleman, especially when he was correct. One can hardly prove that a player is cheating."

Bramble rolled up his sleeves and spit into his hands, rubbing them together with a bit too much glee. "I believe I'm going to enjoy this."

"Leave him to us," someone shouted from down the alley. James turned to his right and found three men coming their way.

"Go to the stables, Mademoiselle Bennett." He gestured across the lane. "Find your horse and return to Kenwood House."

"I cannot in good conscience leave you here—"

James hardly had the time to argue with the woman. "Go. Now."

Iris's terrified gaze flicked to Bramble, then to the approaching men, and finally back to James, before she spun on her heels and ran for the stables.

James sneered at Bramble, who'd taken notice of the men as well and was backing toward the door.

"Afraid, are you?" James asked, more out of curiosity than anything else.

Bramble pushed the dealer back through the door. "Not afraid. Just know when to leave well enough alone." He stepped over the threshold and pulled the door shut.

The moment the door closed on the two, James focused his attention on the men in the alley. "Come now, gentlemen. Doesn't this seem a tad excessive?"

"We'll be the judge of that," the apparent leader spat out as he toyed with the length of wood in his hand.

As a general rule, James quite liked fighting. He was naturally good at it and often started arguments with the full intent of finishing them by blackening someone's eye. Carmichael claimed James could do with some boxing lessons, since his style was more underhanded than a gentleman's should be. But that was, in part, what made James so good. He held no qualms about fighting dirty, especially when it came to opponents such as those he was about to face.

He glanced about and quickly assessed what there was to be found close at hand, reaching for a discarded broken bridle and reins. "If you insist."

"Oh, we do," the leader snarled, then ran at James. His club cut through the air at eye height and James instantly ducked, narrowly missing being brained before he could throw a punch.

The other two jeered at the man's miss, which only angered him more. "Be a good boy and stand still now."

James yanked the reins from the bridle and wound one end of the supple leather about his right hand. He swung the loose end until it whipped in the air, then flicked it at the length of wood, ripping it from his attacker's hand.

The brute reacted with pure rage, running full tilt for James with his hands outstretched. James watched the man's footsteps closely, counting down until his attacker had at most only three more paces before he reached James. At that exact moment, James lunged for the man's gut and knocked him over, forcing him down to the ground, where he landed on his right side. James planted his foot against the brute's ribs, pulled a knife from his own boot, and sank the blade in just below his armpit.

Blood began to run from the wound and the man's body stilled. James looked up as the two remaining attackers moved closer, both with knives drawn. He slid his blade back into his boot and grabbed a discarded gig wheel. Gripping it to his chest with both hands, he braced himself for the impact as the two charged. The men split off from each other, one remaining directly in front of James while the other ran in a wide path around him. As the man in front attacked, James absorbed the force with the wheel then spun to meet the second man behind. He continued to twist, the two stabbing James three times before he flipped the wheel on its side and drove it into one of the men with a quick lunge forward. James spun and kicked the second man's legs out from under him. The man hit the ground hard. James turned back to the first. He dropped the wheel on top of him and leapt on it, landing hard. The sound of cracking ribs echoed in the alley. The attacker's face grew more flushed until his eyes bulged and he ceased to breathe altogether.

Without warning, James was shoved forward. He landed hard on the packed earth in front of the stables. Instantly, he rolled from his stomach to his back just as the third attacker's knife sliced through the air to narrowly miss James. The man dropped to his knees on top of him. His left hand grabbed at James's neck and squeezed while his right hand raised to plunge a knife into James's heart.

James reached for the knife and desperately attempted to pry it from his attacker's hand. His chest was on fire, as was his throat, but he fought on, knowing he had mere seconds before the attacker robbed him of his last breath.

The man's grip loosened slightly as he focused his strength on the knife. The blade was slowly moving closer and closer to James's flesh, threatening to pierce his heart. He dragged a ragged breath into his lungs and willed every last ounce of strength into his hands, the knife finally dropping from the attacker's hand.

The man scrambled for the knife, letting go of James's throat. James punched him in the gut, then landed a second blow to his chin, knocking the brute to sprawl on the dirty cobblestones. James retrieved the knife, shoving upright and turning swiftly to find the man already rising.

"I must say, I'm surprised at the lack of loyalty within Les Moines," James ground out breathlessly, pulling his elbow back, then thrusting it forward, the knife savagely coming to land in the attacker's stomach.

"I don't know what the bloody hell you're talking about," the man replied, holding his stomach as bubbles of blood spilled from his lips.

James released the knife and stood, quickly moving his injured body toward the stable doors. He opened one roughly and limped inside, noticing a growing spot of blood on his breeches just below his hip.

He ignored the groom who appeared from out of the first stall and continued down the aisle, searching for the gray.

Squeak stepped from the last stall, eyeing James with horror. "He's here, sir," the boy called.

James walked to Squeak, reaching awkwardly into his waistcoat pocket and producing a handful of coins. "Did you do as I asked, boy?"

"Yes, sir. He's been fed, watered, and treated like a king, he has. I wanted to help—when I heard the row and all," the boy answered apologetically. "But Smith there told me to stay put."

"Then you wouldn't have done the job that I asked you to do, now would you?" James reassured the boy. He dropped the coins into the lad's waiting hands then walked into the stall. "Now, do me a favor and give me a boot up, would you?"

The boy did as James asked, then stood back and watched James maneuver the gray out of the stall and down the barn aisle. "And if anyone asks after me, Squeak?"

"I never heard of ya, nor seen ya neither, sir."

"Well done, boy."

She should have brought a lantern, that much was clear. Clarissa tripped over a molehill for what seemed the thirtieth time as she ran toward the barn. The moon in the dark night sky afforded some light—sufficient enough for Clarissa to have picked her way through the cutting garden's neat rows and hedges. But the lawn that stood between Kenwood House and the barn was proving more problematic.

Pettibone had detained Clarissa until she'd nearly screamed with frustration. Their search of the library had proven fruitless, as Clarissa had known it would be. Pettibone had mentioned he needed to speak with Daphne, setting Clarissa's mind racing. She'd insisted he accompany her to the kitchens where, in all likelihood, James would be discovered enjoying a light supper. When they'd not found James there either, Pettibone had suggested they partake of the cook's secret supply of port. Clarissa had reluctantly agreed, the few sips that she'd taken of the strong drink doing little to settle her already jangling nerves.

She saw a growing light in the distance. Certain it could only be the stables, Clarissa ran toward it. Pettibone had refrained from accusing Clarissa of withholding James's location, but just barely. The truth was that she didn't know where James was—not precisely anyway. Her opportunity to follow him to the gaming hell had vanished the moment she'd heard Pettibone's voice outside James's chamber. She only prayed that Daphne had made it safely to the stables in time.

Worry made her run faster until her lungs threatened to burst. She hit the pebbled path to the stables with a satisfying crunch and sprinted the remaining distance.

She reached the large double doors and pried one open. The light emanated from the left. She carefully closed the door behind her then hurried to the tack room.

"*Merde,* Thomkins," James yelled from inside the room.

Clarissa pushed open the door and found a chaotic scene. James, shirtless and bleeding, sat on a wooden chair in the corner. Iris was holding a clean length of gauzy fabric and a bottle of brandy. Thomkins stood over James, a crude needle and thread in his hand as he stitched up what looked to be one of three fresh cuts that Clarissa could see.

"What is going on here?" Clarissa demanded, shutting the door behind her and rushing to where the three worked.

James flinched as Thomkins set the last stitch and bit off the thread with his teeth. "How did you know where I was?"

"Daphne," Clarissa replied tightly, the sight of James in pain making her blood run cold. "Is she safe?"

"I drove Daphne to the Fireside Inn myself, sir," Thomkins answered, tying off the thread.

Clarissa sighed, thankful at least for the maid's escape.

"Monsieur St. Michelle, please accompany Mademoiselle Bennett back to the house," James pressed, his hands gripping the sides of the chair as Thomkins readied the needle. "And be sure that no one sees you." He implored Clarissa with his eyes that she simply do what he asked.

And she knew why. If this had anything to do with

Pettibone, then Iris was in just as much danger as they were.

"I should stay and help," Iris argued, gripping the fabric tightly. "After all, you risked your life for me. The least I can do is see to your treatment."

Clarissa couldn't think straight, the strength it was taking just to remain calm nearly draining her. "Mademoiselle, why, after Rougier informed you of our decision, did you venture out? And alone, no less."

"I wasn't alone," Iris said defensively, looking at all three with desperation in her eyes and voice. "There was a servant—Smith, I believe. He escorted me to the Eagle's Nest. Once I'd paid my way into the punters' room, he went in search of rum punch. He never returned."

Clarissa looked meaningfully at James. If this Smith was indeed a member of Les Moines, wouldn't he have been given strict orders to stay with Iris, no matter what may have arisen?

Perhaps the issue wasn't whether Smith was a member of the organization, but rather just what his orders had been—and who gave them to him. It was Pettibone, of course. It had to be.

Clarissa could feel her head growing light as fear and anger bubbled up inside her. She'd suspected that Pettibone could not be trusted. She should have gone to James sooner. If she had, there was every possibility that he would not have been harmed this evening.

"It's of no concern now, *je vous assure,*" James said reassuringly to Iris, even attempting a small smile though he was clearly in a great deal of pain.

"I've put plenty of horses back together, Mademoiselle Bennett. At least Monsieur Rougier here won't kick me," Thomkins said, then smiled. "That is, I hope not."

"Come, mademoiselle, you look exhausted," Clarissa

urged, taking the girl's hand and all but dragging her to the door. "I'll see you to your room and find a maid to assist you to bed."

Iris set the fabric down on a grain barrel and looked back at James. "Not that I am doubting your skills, Thomkins, but I would be more than happy to call in a proper surgeon."

"That will not be necessary, Mademoiselle Bennett, but thank you for your kindness," James replied, his voice resolute.

Iris looked as though she would continue to argue, so Clarissa pulled her out as quickly as she could. The darkness, save for the small sliver of light from beneath the stable doors, greeted them as they began their short journey back to Kenwood House.

"Was it worth it?" Clarissa knew that she shouldn't have asked. She sensed that even Iris, such a formidable, headstrong, obstinate girl, could not bear the question. It was spiteful, asked out of pain and guilt. But she asked it all the same. The shock of seeing James injured and the realization that Pettibone presented a far more urgent threat than she'd thought had been too much.

"I could have died in that gaming hell—should have, really," Iris responded, her voice oddly distant. "If not for Monsieur Rougier . . ."

The moon was enough to dimly illuminate Iris's face. She wasn't crying. No, she was staring straight ahead as if she could only see the gaming hell and nothing else.

"I don't know why I do the things I do, St. Michelle," she continued as she pulled the hat from her head. "Do you ever feel that way?"

Clarissa's problem was the exact opposite of Iris's. She knew far too much about why she did the things she did. It presented its own set of challenges, but she didn't see the point in saying so. "What do you mean?" she countered, the girl's demeanor softening Clarissa's anger.

Iris unwound her heavy braid of hair and let it drop against her back, her fingers combing through a few tendrils that had escaped to curl about her face. "I'm driven to do these things as though they mean something. But they don't. Not really. All my life I've perfected whatever it was that someone told me I ought to do. And then I grew bored and went looking to hone my skills at something stupid and dangerous. It makes me sound ridiculously shallow, does it not?"

"Not at all," Clarissa assured her in a softer tone than she'd intended. She'd been there once, a daughter with certain expectations and responsibilities. She'd been lucky, though, to have possessed a personality that could endure. And she'd had her painting.

And then James.

Clarissa wanted to reassure the girl with a motherly arm about her shoulders, but refrained, offering the crook of her arm instead as any man would. "I cannot imagine the pressure placed upon a girl in your situation, mademoiselle," Clarissa continued, the outline of Kenwood House coming into view. "It would be difficult for the most agreeable of girls. But you? You have spirit, which, in my opinion, is a good thing. But it makes it harder for you—not impossible, but definitely more challenging."

"He could have died," Iris whispered, the weight of her words not lost on Clarissa.

"But he did not, nor did you. Take what you've learned from tonight and never forget it, Mademoiselle Bennett," Clarissa urged, knowing that whatever they faced in the coming week, it would not be easy.

"I will, monsieur. I promise."

Clarissa smiled, though she hardly felt like doing so. "I'll keep you to it."

"He's alive," Brun said flatly, his mouth a grim set line.

Pettibone folded his arms over his eyes as his already minuscule quarters seemed to shrink even further. Marlowe had done him the service of going after the foolish girl just as he'd hoped, then failed to die. Hate burned in Pettibone's belly.

He hated the feel of the cheap woolen blanket at his back upon the rough, lowly cot that served as his bed. He hated the pillow upon which he'd placed his head for the last several weeks, the stink of whomever had used it before him still lingering in the molding feathers. He hated the clothes he was forced to wear every single day, the cut inferior, the fabric coarse and badly dyed. He hated the wretched English food he was given to eat. He hated the chattering, stupid servants that he had to pretend to like. He hated the Canadian girl and her money. He hated the English woman and her painting. He hated the English man and his ability to stay alive.

But most of all, he hated his father. For it was his father who was responsible for all that was wrong in his life. Without his father, all of it would simply have been a bad dream. He would be the leader of Les Moines, and he never would have been foolish enough to accept Napoleon's plea for help.

And for that, he would make the man pay.

"Thank you, Brun. Your services are no longer needed," Pettibone replied, sighing deeply.

"What will you do now?"

Pettibone stiffened with annoyance. He'd grown weary of the caliber of men that his father had supplied him with for this mission, Brun being particularly irritating. Oh, the man had readily agreed to do as he'd asked as far as Marlowe was concerned. Even agreed to cooperate for much less money than Pettibone had been willing to offer. But still, he grated on the nerves.

"That's hardly your concern," Pettibone answered, not even bothering to address the man with a direct gaze. "I suggest you leave the grounds at once—while there's still time."

"What do you mean, 'still time'?"

Pettibone would have killed the man for his insolence right there, in the tiny, ill-appointed room, but he couldn't be bothered. "Miss Bennett will surely ask where you took yourself off to while you were supposed to be protecting her—as will Marlowe. How do you plan on explaining your absence?"

"I'll return to Paris, then," Brun replied, his voice confident.

Pettibone unfolded his arms and turned to look at the man. "Will you? And what will you tell Durand?"

Brun looked hard at Pettibone, clearly offended. "I'll tell him that you sent me home."

"No," Pettibone said simply. "You see, that would suggest that I'd deviated from Durand's very specific plan—and we both know what he'd think of such a move."

"Where would you suggest I go, then?" Brun pressed, his temper rising.

Pettibone sat up and swung his legs over the side of the cot. "I don't really care. You're not my problem. But I would suggest steering clear of Les Moines."

"I could go directly to Durand and tell him about you, you know."

Pettibone sneered at Brun's attempt to threaten him. "Please, we both know what the old man would say to such a thing. You'd be dead within an hour. At least making a run for it buys you a bit more time than that."

Brun could not argue, a fact that made Pettibone smile. "Now go. The rest of the household will be up and about soon enough."

Brun raised his fist as if to punch Pettibone, then lowered it. "You're not worth it," he lashed out, adding, "Durand will discover what you've been up to—and then you'll pay." He walked to the flimsy door and opened it, the wood floor creaking as he stepped across the threshold. He looked back at Pettibone and scowled, then closed the door silently.

"Now," Pettibone said to himself, drumming his fingers on his knee. "What am I to do?"

This was a golden opportunity that he wasn't willing to forgo. His father had not trusted him. Therefore, he needed to be shown that his son could—and had—proven himself worthy. His attempt to kill Marlowe had not worked. And he'd hardly be able to blackmail the man into leaving as he'd essentially just done with Brun. If he could not remove Marlowe and complete the mission himself, then perhaps foiling the plan altogether would be worthwhile.

He stood abruptly from the rickety cot and crossed to the dilapidated trunk he'd brought with him from Paris. He lifted the hinged lid and let it rest against the wall. Mr. Bennett had made use of him some weeks before in relation to the money that would be paid to St. Michelle for the portrait. A letter had been sent to an Edinburgh bank with whom Bennett did business. Funds were to be withdrawn from his account and sent to the Banque de France in Paris. It had seemed simple enough, though Bennett had added an interesting requirement: The funds would be deposited in a safe. The combination to the safe would be locked in a strongbox. And the key to that box would be sent to Bennett.

He'd actually thought Bennett quite clever when he'd forced open the letter and read the contents before re-sealing it and handing it off to a messenger.

But when the envoy had arrived at Kenwood House and turned over the key, Pettibone had not been privy to the exact location of its hiding place. He'd searched the house every night since but had no luck.

He fingered the extra clothing he'd brought along, lifting a second pair of boots then a pair of breeches before deciding there was nothing here he needed.

Bennett would present the key to Clarissa when the portrait was finished. All Pettibone had to do was wait for the woman to complete her work, then the key could be his.

And with the key, he'd secure not only the fortune, but his father's long-awaited fall from power. It would be easy enough to concoct a story that proved Marlowe's ties to the Corinthians had not been cut as he'd led everyone within Les Moines to believe—something Pettibone thought might even be true.

The money and a turncoat captured, all by his hands. His father's position would be his. And the first order of business would be to kill Durand for all he'd made his own son endure over the years.

Pettibone closed the trunk and reached for his coat, which hung on the back of the only chair in the room. Then he swept some spare coins from the lone night table and pocketed them.

He'd steal away, the hope being that Marlowe and Lady Clarissa would assume he'd given up and retreated back to Paris. If he was lucky, they'd let down their guard a bit. And when the time was right, he'd retrieve the key, then leave this godforsaken country, never to return.

He lifted the candlestick and opened the door, turning

to look back at the rat hole of a room one last time. *"Bon débarras,"* he said under his breath, sure that such accommodations were nearly in his past. He could feel victory in his bones—and this time he'd not allow anyone to stand in his way.

18

James could not wait any longer. He'd endured Thomkins's ministrations, no less than three knife wounds sewn back together by the skilled and thankfully incurious man. Afterward, he made his way as quickly as possible to Kenwood House, the pain in his gut and thigh stabbing him with each step.

And he'd waited for Clarissa. He'd moved a comfortable upholstered chair closer to his door and sat, listening for her footfalls in the hall. Then he'd taken to standing just outside her door.

When that proved fruitless, he'd let himself into her chamber and sat on her bed, needing to rest for only a moment. The night had been, by far, one of the most exhausting of his life. It seemed so long ago that he'd marched across the lawn, soaking wet and suddenly far smarter than he'd been before diving into the lake. It was at that very moment he'd decided to say to hell with the past and his long-held grudge against God and everyone else—especially Clarissa—for love. *Love*. Love had sent his heart soaring, dropped it like a boulder in the deepest sea, and finally forced him to realize that there was nothing more important in life. Love was a demanding master, but every last trial was worth it if it meant Clarissa could be his.

He'd laid his head on the pillow, the unique scent that was only Clarissa's filling his nostrils and tightening his groin. He needed to tell her exactly how he felt, the sooner the better. The men who had attacked him behind the Eagle's Nest had claimed to know nothing of Les Moines. He supposed that the dying man could have been lying, but after years of service within the Corinthians, James had become a good judge of such things. Besides, they'd fought like common ruffians, their base moves hardly the polished and honed fighting techniques James would have expected from seasoned French agents. He felt sure that the man had told him the truth. In which case, Pettibone had reached outside Les Moines for hired help. Why would he do such a thing? Daphne's information only served to complicate the already tangled truths and half-truths that James faced now. Pettibone had wanted Iris to go to the gaming hell. Had he assumed James would discover the girl gone? And if so, was James Pettibone's end target?

He knew Pettibone disliked him, that fact was crystal clear. But threatening James put the entire operation in jeopardy. Perhaps Pettibone was not as devoted to Napoleon's cause as Les Moines believed him to be.

James closed his tired eyes and savored the feel of the smooth silk coverlet against his bruised face and torn body. He and Clarissa could not stay at Kenwood House much longer. Pettibone was becoming too menacing of a threat. And without Corinthian support, James would have a difficult time protecting Clarissa and Iris—not to mention Mr. and Mrs. Bennett and the rest of the household. Well, James was never one to back down from a challenge, that was for sure.

But for now he allowed himself to sink farther into the soft bed, the pain in his battered body melting away as he did so. Pettibone. What was he up to? Pettibone. Pettibone . . .

"James?"

The voice, so sweet, was startlingly close to his ear. James came fully awake in a flash and instinctively grabbed the person around his upper arms and threw him down onto the bed. James rolled on top and anchored the intruder's hands to the soft surface with his own, the muted light from a lone candle on the nightstand illuminating Clarissa's face.

"James!" Clarissa hissed angrily. "Why are you attacking me? And more important, what are you doing in my bed?"

This was not at all how James had hoped to begin his apology. He released her hands and rose to his knees, turning rather inelegantly and landing where he'd begun his hasty attack. "I'm sorry, Clarissa. I didn't know it was you."

"Who else would it be, James?" she asked as she sat up and frowned at him. "And you still haven't told me what, exactly, you're doing here."

James rolled on his side and grimaced, the twisting motion sending a flash of pain from the knife slash at his side.

"Is it very painful?" she asked in a much softer tone, concern on her face.

Well, sympathy is a start, James told himself. This had all seemed much easier in his mind. But now, with Clarissa next to him, the only thing between them a man's dressing gown—"You're dressed for bed."

"Of course I'm dressed for bed. That is typically what I do before . . .well, before going to bed. Did you hit your head this evening, James?"

"I was attacked, Clarissa. By no less than four men," James answered.

"Four?" she cried, her leg brushing his as she shifted closer. "How on earth did you manage—"

"My point," James interrupted, trying to ignore the distraction of her slim, warm, soft leg pressed against his, "is that clearly you've been in the room long enough to discover my presence. That it came as such a surprise is hardly my fault."

Clarissa's eyes widened and her mouth opened and closed twice. "Are you suggesting I'm to blame for your frightening me nearly to death?"

Dammit, he'd gone and lost her sympathy. This was not going according to plan at all.

"Because I'll tell you right now, Mr. James Marlowe, under normal circumstances, no one in his right mind would find your argument in any way logical. This evening, while it may have been normal for you, was not for me. In fact, my experiences within the last twenty-four hours were as far from normal as I dare say—"

"I'm sorry."

Clarissa's jaw dropped and hung there as if it would never close again. James reached up and gently prodded it back into its charming home just below her top lip.

"Oh," she finally uttered, her hands twisting nervously in her lap. "For what, exactly? That is . . ." Her voice trailed off and she dropped her head. "I should not have asked. It's just that—"

"You're speechless," James said, relief flooding through his body at having finally uttered the apology he'd owed her for five long years.

Her head snapped up and she glared at him. "What is that to mean? It's not as if I absolutely *never* pause to draw breath. Does my chatter trouble you so?"

James sat up though it pained him to do so, crossed his legs and drew them up, then turned to face her. He pulled her into a mirroring position and took her hands in his. "That's not it at all. The point that I was so poorly attempting to make was that you were surprised at my apology—as well you should be. It's been far too long in coming."

She gripped his hands tightly and leaned in. "Do you mean you're sorry for what happened with my father?"

"To begin with, yes. But understand me, Clarissa," James replied, his heart achingly wide open, "it's more than regret. I take responsibility for my actions. I made my choice, and I've struggled ever since with my decision."

"Stop," she begged, pressing their joined hands to rest on her heart. "Please. Do not say such things. I am the one to blame. I expected far too much—more than any human being could have managed. I accused you of knowing nothing when it came to love. Yet I'm the one who betrayed our love by not accepting your choice."

She dipped her head and placed a loving, gentle kiss on his fingers. "And then you returned, out of nowhere. And I couldn't let you hurt me, not a second time. So I tried to be strong and control my emotions—I did, honestly. But in the end, it was you who were hurt. If not for my foolish pride—" Her voice cracked and she closed her eyes as if she was in pain. "James, you could have been killed. And it would have been my fault." The stark words held an agony of terror and remorse.

James closed the small distance between them and freed his hands from hers, embracing her with the new-found strength that her words had inspired. "No, it wouldn't. It wasn't like that at all. I called you weak, claimed that you failed me for feeling betrayed when I sided with your father. Emotion is not a weakness, Clarissa, it's a strength—one of the strongest you possess. You are a very strong woman. Never let anyone tell you otherwise."

He loosened his hold on her and pulled back so that they were face-to-face. "I'd only just decided to ask you to marry me. But I had to side with your father—and it made me angry. So angry, in fact, that I needed someone to blame. When you accused me of never having really loved you . . ." He paused, the memory of her words still painful to this day. "Well, I had someone to blame."

"Oh, James, a proposal?" she asked, her soft, comforting hands coming to rest on his shoulders. "But I don't understand. Why did you have no choice?"

"Pettibone mentioned my being employed by an English organization before I met up with Les Moines," he began. He'd held the Corinthians' secret for so long . . . much to the detriment of his own heart. If, when the mission was complete, Carmichael was to find fault with his decision to reveal his connection, even after all that Clarissa had endured on behalf of the Corinthians, then James did not want to be an agent any longer. "He was telling the truth. I work for the same group as your father. That is how we met."

Clarissa's brow furrowed. "My father? A spy?"

"Yes, one of the best, actually. The woman he'd been rumored to be having an affair with worked within the group." James was almost sorry to have to tell Clarissa the details. But if she was to believe him, she needed to know. "Mind you, many of the agents dallied with women—the majority of Corinthians are not married, one reason being the dangers we face on a daily basis. I had too much respect for the man to ask, and he never broached the topic with me. If I had told you the reason why I supported your father—well, I couldn't. I did my duty because that's what I'd been trained to do. All I had, all I cared about, were the Corinthians and your family. When your father refused to address the rumors and your mother moved away, I—"

"You lost me too," she whispered, placing her hands on his face. "We've both been such fools."

James couldn't help but smile at her simple, yet undeniably correct statement.

"Oh, I must tell you," she started, her face becoming animated. "I suspect that Pettibone is up to something beyond Les Moines's interest in the portrait. And I fear it has to do with you."

James's smile grew wider with delight in the way her face lit up when she shared information she deemed particularly important. "I know. I've suspected as much myself. And tonight proved my suspicions. Don't think on it. I'll take care of you. You have my word."

"So you are still a turncoat?" she asked, reaching to toy with her short locks.

"Yes, but I serve the king, not Napoleon. Why?"

"I love you, James Marlowe. And I would still love you if you were a dastardly, no-good, gallows bird. But this makes things far less complicated."

She returned her hands to his face and closed the space between them. "Tell me you love me."

"I love you."

There he was. The James who'd stolen her heart so long ago. Only he was a man now, his life as he'd lived it having honed his character, crafted his soul, and brought him back to her.

Clarissa had never expected him to be the one to apologize first. For five years, she'd dreamed of him walking back into her life, dropping down on his knees, and begging for her forgiveness. She realized now how selfish and wrong such a desire had been. Her experience with Les Moines had tested Clarissa in every way. But it had forced her to learn a lesson she'd been unable to master for far too long. It was a strength, as James had assured her, to allow one's emotions space to breathe, to color, to grow. It was a strength, made even stronger when partnered with practicality and pragmatism, for then one could truly see people for who they were—what they felt, and what they needed. Clarissa's emotions had allowed her to judge Iris without knowing her, but the practical need of continuing on as St. Michelle tonight had cleared the way for a deeper understanding of the girl—and, in turn, herself.

She'd done the same to James, her outrage over his involvement with Les Moines blinding her to anything else.

But no longer.

"Show me," Clarissa begged, placing her lips on his. It was achingly beautiful. His warm mouth, seemingly made for hers, met her tentative touch with gentle enthusiasm, pressing lightly as his arms encircled her waist. The crush of her breasts against his chest started a fire burning in her belly that snaked its way to her arms and legs, the pooling heat at the apex of her thighs urging her on.

Intoxicated by his presence overwhelming her entire being, body and soul, Clarissa reached for his cravat, unknotted the linen, and began to unwind it slowly, torturously. "At last, it is me doing the dressing—or undressing, as the case may be. Not that I failed to appreciate your aid in any way, mind you," Clarissa teased, her breath beginning to quicken. "I wouldn't want you to think that I wasn't appreciative."

"I suspect that by the end of this evening, there'll be no mistaking the level of appreciation we share for each other, Clarissa," James answered, reaching for the silken sash at her waist and pulling gently. It slipped free and the dressing gown fell open to reveal her perfect body. "Shocking, Lady Clarissa," he remarked on her lack of a chemise.

Clarissa set to work on his shirt buttons, pausing for a moment when he cupped her left breast in his large, warm, strong hand. She caught her breath when the pad of his thumb stroked over her nipple until it pebbled. "That is only the beginning, Mr. Marlowe."

She pushed the shirt off his shoulders and untangled it from his arms, gasping when she saw the raw, fresh wounds. Instinctively, she placed her palm over one, as if she could provide some measure of healing. "Are you quite sure that you're up for this, James? I do not want to hurt you any further."

He removed her palm from the wound and placed it on the bulging firmness of his penis, the rock-hard firmness making Clarissa shiver in anticipation. "Yes, Clarissa, I am 'up' for this, have no doubt."

She smiled devilishly, then licked her lips. "Well, if you insist, though I will demand that you take a slightly less physically demanding role." She began to unfasten his breeches, abandoning the smooth, torturous pace of earlier and taking a decidedly more frantic tempo that matched the heat now threatening to consume her from within.

"Clarissa, I assure you, I could have been attacked by twelve men and mauled by a bear as I returned to Kenwood House and I would still be able—wait, that is not the right word. What word am I looking for?"

"Masterfully prepared," Clarissa offered helpfully, noticing the unintended husky tone her voice had taken on.

James's breath caught as she gently pushed him to lie back, then moved to his boots. "Yes, precisely. Even if I'd been accosted by eighteen men and mauled by a pack of wild dogs—"

"Is it eighteen now? James, if you're attempting to seduce me, you've no need. I'm wet," she whispered, catching his hand and placing it precisely where he could feel for himself.

"Masterfully prepared, Clarissa," he repeated, his voice raw. "God, you feel so good, so right." He rubbed slowly, stroking one finger into the slick folds between her legs every now and again, then returning to the maddening massage.

Clarissa shrugged free of her wrapper then dropped to

all fours on the bed, arching her back. Her breath came in quick, hard pants as he continued to rub, the pressure building with each touch.

He shifted closer and stroked his other hand over her bottom, squeezing it, then walked his fingers slowly up to the mid-point of her back, taking hold of where her hip met her thigh.

Clarissa could have given in right there, exploded into a million pieces, overwhelmed by the powerful, exquisite emotions pulsing through her. But she slipped away from his clever, warm, arousing touch to reach his boots. "Not just yet."

She pried one glossy boot loose and then the other, stripping his stockings off quickly then tugging at his breeches. He lifted his hips in assistance and they slid toward Clarissa, revealing his smalls—all that was left between their skin.

She loosened the fabric tie and removed them, twirling them above her head before tossing them to the floor.

James started to rise, but she pushed him back again. "I warned you."

He almost looked disappointed, though the sight of her naked body as she straddled his bare midsection seemed to help if the flush of blood to his face was any indication. "Christ, Clarissa, you're torturing me."

She smiled and placed a finger in her mouth, sucking on it lightly before running the damp tip of it the length of James's fully erect penis. "We can't have that, now can we?" Her murmur was throaty, seductive, as she caressed the head. She luxuriated in the sight of his body, familiar yet different since they'd last made love, skin to skin and utterly bare to each other over five years ago. He'd been barely a man, his physique markedly sleeker than the broad shoulders and thickly muscled chest that met her eyes now. Her gaze moved lower. Beneath the ugly wounds lay a taut and trim stomach that tapered to his hips and groin. She lovingly stroked his penis again then tucked him against her, the exquisite fullness as she slowly sank taking her breath away.

"You are beautiful, James," she whispered, lowering herself until her breasts skimmed his chest. "And you're mine."

"Promise me that you'll always love me just as you do right here, right now." His voice was thick with emotion.

She rocked back and forth, her breasts bouncing against his chest and creating the most delicious friction. "I promise."

He cupped her breasts in his hands and kneaded roughly, coaxing a moan of pleasure from Clarissa. He tugged at her nipples and she cried out, the sensation both shocking and stimulating.

"More?" he murmured.

Clarissa licked her lips, the haze of pleasure threatening to pull her under. "More," she demanded as his arms wrapped around her.

He took one breast into his mouth and sucked, whirling his tongue around the nipple then biting gently.

When he released her, Clarissa gripped his shoulder with frustration. "More! Now!"

"Patience," he murmured before taking the other breast in his mouth and repeating the sweet agony.

"You torture me on purpose," she groaned, a second moan of ecstasy escaping from her lips.

James bit down on the nipple then swirled his tongue around the sensitive nub. "Turnabout is fair play, Clarissa," he replied as he stroked his palm over her backside.

She caught her breath and sat up. "Really?" She continued to ride him but gently increased her speed.

"Is that the best you can do?" James teased. His voice was rougher, and the accelerated rhythm had his fingers flexing against Clarissa's hips.

"You know me better than that." She threw her head back and exposed her long, elegant neck, then ran her fingers from her throat to her breasts, caressing them lavishly. James grunted with approval as she drew her hands lower across her stomach then below to where he ended and she began, stroking her swollen folds slowly.

"All right. You win," he insisted, his breath ragged and his voice full of need. "Please, come to me."

Clarissa dropped her head and looked into his eyes. "As you wish."

She reached behind and grasped his testicles, watching as his mouth contorted. She squeezed gently and he let out a hoarse moan. She squeezed again and he bucked, then sat up and dragged her back with him until he slammed into the headboard.

"Widen your legs," he commanded, his hands encircling her calves and helping her. "Now hold on."

Clarissa threw her arms around his shoulders as James's hips lifted and fell, taking her with him. She matched his passion thrust for thrust. He dug his hands into the bed at his sides, supporting their weight as he drove her closer and closer to climax.

He took her mouth with his, his tongue roughly claiming hers. She let the pleasure take her over, the smell of his skin, the taste of his mouth, the feel of him inside her too much to deny.

Clarissa broke the kiss and tucked her head against his shoulder, holding on as if her life depended on it. "James, I cannot. I cannot hold on. Please," she panted, her lips touching the shell of his ear.

"Then let go."

And she did. Clarissa squeezed her eyes shut as she

gave in to the driving need, her skin suddenly sensitive to the very air in the room. She wrapped her legs tightly about James's waist and cried out over and over again, sure that she would never recover.

James wrapped her in his arms and rolled, his arms supporting him as he drove deep inside of her again and again.

Clarissa raked her nails across his back possessively. "Come to me. Now."

James shuddered hard and let out a muffled groan as sweet release took control of him. He shifted sideways, taking Clarissa with him, wrapped in his arms. "I love you, Clarissa. I always have. And I always will."

Clarissa stroked his hair and intertwined her fingers in his soft locks. "You have my heart, James. Truly, deeply, madly, forever, you have my heart."

19

"Well, I now see why your services are in such demand," Mr. Bennett said as he stood in the studio and admired the finished portrait.

Completing the painting had required continuous work. Clarissa rose in the morning, stopping to eat only enough to keep her strength up, then retreated to the studio, where she would paint until she could no longer keep her eyes open.

James arrived every day with a tray of food, once for lunch, and again for dinner. Clarissa had begged him to keep his visits brief, his presence in the studio hardly conducive to work. He'd obliged—though his nightly demands for attention more than made up for any time lost during the day. They'd made love more times than Clarissa's exhausted mind could count, his need for her rivaling hers for him.

Clarissa suspected their heated coupling was only intensified by James's worry over the disappearance of Pettibone. The footman hadn't been seen since that evening at the Eagle's Nest and none of the servants nor grooms or gardeners knew where the man had gone.

Of course, James and Clarissa felt certain he'd vanished after learning James and Iris had emerged from their attack alive. But knowing why Pettibone had gone offered little consolation. He would return, it was only a matter of when.

"Your daughter is *très* beautiful, Monsieur Bennett,

which makes my work a true pleasure," Clarissa replied, joining Bennett before the painting.

The man was right. The portrait had turned out magnificently—in fact, Clarissa felt sure it was her best work to date. Iris's choice in dress and backdrop had been perfect. The pale pink of her silk gown, the warm, wholesome hue of her youthful skin, the deep, fiery red of her ruby earbobs, the glistening gold in her blond hair. But it was more than the marriage of color and light. Clarissa had captured the essence of Iris, subtly emphasizing her features and personality for a portrait that was both natural and flattering. Her eyes held the intelligence and danger that made Iris sparkle, her gently upturned chin conveyed the will of iron that she possessed, and the slight hint of a smile spoke volumes of the girl's insatiable desire for life.

Clarissa widened her stance to match Bennett's. "She's quite a girl, *c'est vrai,* Monsieur Bennett," she added, realizing that every detail she'd just made a mental note of could be either positive or negative, depending on how one looked at it.

Mr. Bennett turned to Clarissa and let out a hearty chuckle. "Now, that is an understatement, monsieur."

"Perhaps," Clarissa replied, smiling though her tone was serious. "But I would not want to be the one to underestimate the young lady, monsieur. Would you?"

For the first time in their acquaintance, Clarissa witnessed Mr. Bennett's countenance fall. His amiable nature turned to disappointment. "Have you any children?"

"No, Monsieur Bennett—at least, not yet."

"I've two—Iris and her older sister, Rose," Mr. Bennett began, turning to look at the painting again. "It's a gift, monsieur, do not misunderstand me for one moment. But it's difficult, even when you have all the money in the world at your disposal. Children need more than toys and fancy dresses. They need one's time. I'm afraid that Mrs. Bennett and I managed Rose properly, but Iris? There just was not enough time."

Clarissa wondered at the man's use of the word "managed" in relation to his daughters, sure that it perfectly illustrated much of what was wrong within the father's relationship with his child. But Mr. Bennett did not need to be told what he'd done wrong. He needed to know that there was so much he could do right, even still.

"Monsieur, let me tell you of a person. This person," Clarissa began, picturing James in her mind's eye, "was attentive, encouraging, interested in who I was and what captured my imagination—this person was everything to me. And then this person deeply hurt me, and left. I was angry and bitter. Devastated. For a time I blamed all of life's woes on this person. But do you know what?"

"What?" Mr. Bennett asked hesitantly, keeping his gaze firmly affixed to the painting.

Clarissa reached out and put her hand on the man's shoulder. "If this person were to walk back into my life this very day, I would forgive. There is nothing that can be done about the past, but the future? Well, that is up to you. Do not waste any more time, Monsieur Bennett."

He heaved a deep, mournful sigh and finally looked Clarissa in the eye. "Thank you, Monsieur St. Michelle—for everything."

She had no way of knowing whether the man would take her advice to heart. But Clarissa could, at the very least, be thankful for the ability to not only articulate such words, but mean them. Her time at Kenwood House, though rife with danger and emotional trials, had given her a gift she'd quite likely never have found otherwise: peace of mind.

For five long years she'd blamed her father and James for everything that was wrong with her life, thinking that doing so managed, in some small way, to make her feel better. Opening her heart and taking responsibility for all that she was, both good and bad, had forced her to realize the truth and brought her to this valuable moment in time.

"You're welcome, Monsieur Bennett. And thank you for this opportunity. My days spent at Kenwood House are ones I will think back on often, I assure you," Clarissa replied sincerely, holding out her hand.

Bennett took it in his and shook it vigorously, his jovial demeanor slowly returning. "Oh," he said suddenly, reaching into the inner pocket of his bottle-green waistcoat. "I nearly forgot." He retrieved a key and handed it to Clarissa. "You earned every last shilling, and more."

Clarissa took the small silver key and looked at it with keen curiosity. "I'm afraid I don't understand."

"I'm a banker, monsieur," Bennett teased, elbowing Clarissa in the ribs. "I'd hardly expect you to travel with such a vast sum in your possession. The moment I secured your services I withdrew funds from an account I have in Edinburgh and had it sent to Paris."

Clarissa forced a smile, her stomach turning at the news. "The key is to a safe, I presume?"

He elbowed her again, clearly amused. "Hardly. Safes are opened with combinations, St. Michelle. No, the key is to a strongbox at the Banque de France. Within the box you will find the combination to a safe located at the bank that holds your payment. It always pays to be *safe*," he finished, winking at his banker's wit.

"Thank you for such forethought, Monsieur Bennett," Clarissa replied in what she hoped was a sincere tone. "Now, I fear we must be off for France. The Comte de Claudel awaits me in Paris."

"Yes, Iris mentioned that you had to leave immediately," he replied. "Nasty stuff, crossing open waters. I bid you a safe journey, monsieur—oh, and do say goodbye to Iris before you go. She's grown fond of you, I believe."

Clarissa nodded smoothly in agreement, her concern over the complication growing, though she kept it to herself.

"Will it present a problem?" Clarissa asked.

James eyed the key from Bennett. "I hope not," he answered as the two made their way down the grand staircase.

He'd disclosed his connection with the Young Corinthians, but little else beyond that, hoping to keep Clarissa as safe as possible. The less she knew, the safer she'd be. "Though the sooner we return to Paris, the better."

They approached a maid who was busily dusting one of the wall sconces in the foyer. "Mademoiselle Bennett?" James inquired.

"The library, in the east wing," she replied, gesturing toward a corridor on their right.

James moved down the hall with Clarissa struggling to keep up with his long strides. Pettibone's disappearance had troubled James for many reasons, chief among them being he preferred to have his enemy in his sights at all times.

Pettibone's disappearance had made it nearly impossible to ensure that the household was safe. James's inability to identify the Les Moines agents within the staff was maddening. He'd almost hoped at least one of them would come forward with questions concerning Pettibone. After all, if James was correct in his assumptions, Pettibone had disappeared and left his agents without any indication of what to do next. But none had made an attempt to contact James. Not surprising, he supposed, as Pettibone had more than likely spread rumors concerning James's place within the organization. If it were him, James would have kept his mouth shut, just as they were doing now.

He and Clarissa passed through the portrait gallery and continued on. "Remember, we've very little time, so be quick," James reminded her.

"I believe it's you who will need to be brief," she replied teasingly. "Iris has formed quite an attachment to you," she continued.

James grunted as they approached the library.

"James," Clarissa pleaded, grabbing his arm and forcing him to stop. "All humor aside, I would ask that you be sensitive to the girl's feelings. You saved her life—she's not soon to forget that fact, nor how it's made her think about her own life. Please . . ." She paused, looking deeply into his eyes. "James, be kind," she finished in a hushed whisper.

He couldn't refuse Clarissa—especially when he knew she was right. Over the last week Iris had demonstrated a marked change in her demeanor. She'd become a gracious, sympathetic, and sensitive young lady. She was thoughtful in her actions, considerate with her requests, and accommodating with not only Clarissa and James, but the household as a whole.

"I promise," James agreed, then pulled her quickly toward the library. "But we must return as soon as poss—"

"I'm well aware of this," Clarissa interrupted, gripping his arm to make her point.

"Your mother's life depends on our actions," he seethed in a strangled breath.

James couldn't know if Pettibone had been in communication with his agency, but he felt sure that if he had not, the remaining agents had. Isabelle's life was of little consequence to the organization, even less so once Durand suspected his loyalty. He had to return to Paris in order to bargain for Clarissa's mother before it was too late.

"I know that," Clarissa countered, a flicker of fear in her eyes. "No one knows it more than I—I've not had a letter in nearly a week. All I'm asking is that you simply listen. And be kind. Promise me."

James grunted in agreement, noting that the large library doors were closed. He pushed Clarissa behind him as he opened one of the heavy panels and slowly entered the library. "Mademoiselle Bennett?" he called out.

"I'm here," Iris's voice responded from somewhere beyond the rows of leather-bound books.

Clarissa attempted to walk on in the direction of Iris's voice, but James gestured for her to fall back behind him. She thought to protest until James glared at her with deadly seriousness. She hesitated briefly, then did as he'd asked.

James reached into his boot and withdrew his knife. Then the two walked slowly down the main aisle, the plush Kidderminster carpet absorbing the sound of their footfalls. James surveyed each row they encountered, first the one on his left, then the one on his right. There were only three rows remaining when he caught sight of something unusual.

He held his hand up in front of Clarissa then pointed to the floor, indicating that she must wait. She nodded in silent understanding and James turned down the row, inching his way toward what he'd seen. As he came closer, the shape of a slim hand came into focus. He reached the end of the row and peered around the corner, discovering the unconscious body of Maggie, the maid who'd taken up Daphne's duties.

He knelt down and pressed his hand to her chest. Her heartbeat thudded slowly under his fingers and he sighed with relief. Standing again, he returned to Clarissa and gestured for her to continue on with him toward where he believed Iris to be. James hated the thought that he was dragging Clarissa into an ambush, but leaving her in the aisle could prove equally dangerous.

"St. Michelle, Rougier. Where are you?" Iris called out, the noticeably higher pitch of her voice confirming her fear and the impending danger.

Clarissa reached for James's shoulder and gripped it tightly with trembling fingers.

He patted her hand with his and took a step forward. "So you've returned, Pettibone."

"You had to know that I would."

James reached the final row and stepped into the open space beyond, turning toward where he now saw Pettibone held a knife to Iris's neck. *"Naturellement."*

Clarissa gasped. "Let her go!" she demanded, making to push off from James then retreating back behind him when his outstretched arm blocked the way.

"I'm pleased to see that you've finally convinced Monsieur St. Michelle who is the boss," Pettibone leered, pressing the knife against Iris's neck. "It does give me hope that our negotiations will run smoothly."

"Rougier, what does he want?" Iris croaked, terror dancing in her wide eyes.

"We'll hardly 'negotiate' with the likes of you, monsieur," Clarissa snapped, her body tense against James's.

"If it's money, please, my father will pay what you require," Iris begged.

Pettibone tightened his hold around her waist, a venomous smile settling on his lips. "Oh, my little pigeon, if only it were that simple."

James could not afford for Iris to be drawn any further into the grasp of Les Moines. As far as she knew, Pettibone was nothing more than a former servant turned violent would-be thief. If he allowed Pettibone to continue, he risked much more of the assignment being revealed.

"Let me be perfectly clear: You deal with me, Pettibone, and me alone. Now, what are your demands?"

The man sneered, clearly frustrated by James's taking command of the situation. "First, drop your knife and kick it over to me."

James obeyed reluctantly, shoving the weapon with his boot and sending it clattering in Pettibone's direction.

The man adroitly kicked the knife with the side of his foot and sent it spinning even farther away from James and Clarissa, its final resting place against the woodwork along the opposite wall. "What is the girl worth? Hmmm?" Pettibone wondered aloud, turning his face toward Iris's and eyeing her critically. "Nothing more than a spoiled Canadian heiress," he asserted, his dismissive tone having its desired effect as Iris visibly paled.

James itched to wrestle the knife away from the cretin and cut his throat, but he waited, needing to be certain before acting. "I've no time for your theatrics, Pettibone. Tell me your terms."

"You disappoint me. I'd hoped for a much longer siege—"

"Your. Terms," James ground out, his control slipping.

Pettibone flinched. "Oh," he replied, "*d'accord*. There is a bit of a ticking clock, isn't there? I wonder, does the marchioness suspect that the end is near?"

A choked cry tore from Clarissa's throat and she attempted to lunge again.

"Enough," James insisted.

Pettibone captured James with a demented stare. "Very well, then. The key, *s'il vous plaît*."

"How did you know of the key?"

Pettibone huffed with marked frustration. "Really, have you so very little faith in me? Who do you think mailed the missive to Edinburgh requesting the transfer of the funds?"

James clenched his teeth. "And in return you'll release Iris?" he pressed, hardly willing to give Pettibone an ounce of recognition.

"Without another word," Pettibone replied.

James had no choice. He knew it, and so did Pettibone. "On the count of three," he instructed, giving Iris a fortifying glance.

"Une—"

"You get ahead of yourself, Lucien," Pettibone cut in. "You will set the key down there," he instructed, pointing his knife at a marble bust stand that held a likeness of Diana, Goddess of the Hunt.

James acquiesced, too busy judging the distance between himself and Iris to allow the man's brusqueness to shake his concentration. "So be it."

He pulled the key from his waistcoat pocket and walked to the stand, setting the small silver object down on the smooth surface. "Now hand over Mademoiselle Bennett."

Pettibone forced Iris to walk with him to the stand, where he quickly pocketed the key. "Oh, come now, let us end with a flourish. On my count. One," Pettibone began, lowering the knife from Iris's neck. "Two—"

James widened his stance.

"And," Pettibone continued.

Iris was breathing hard, her eyes wild with fright.

Suddenly Pettibone yanked her backward by the hair, slamming her head into a library ladder that stood at the end of the aisle. He shoved her forward, sending her flying into James, the force of her body knocking the two against the opposite bookcase.

Clarissa screamed and rushed forward, pulling Iris off

of James and into her arms. "Iris!" she called, but the girl only laid limply against Clarissa's chest, her eyes closed and a trickle of blood beginning to pool at the back of her head.

James lunged at Pettibone just as the man ducked behind a Trafalgar chair.

"Think, first," Pettibone began. "If you do not let me go, everything—and I do mean everything—will be brought to light. And how will Durand respond to such attention? Lady Westbridge, Clarissa, you—all dead. But he won't stop there. St. Michelle and the Bennetts will be next."

James gripped the arms of the chair, enraged. Pettibone was right. To apprehend him would all but guarantee a bloody and deadly retaliation from Les Moines.

"And what of your beloved Young Corinthians?"

James willed his face to show no surprise.

"Oh, yes. Your continued allegiance to the Corinthians was simple enough for me to puzzle out—unlike the rest of Les Moines. But this key will finally convince Durand of my worth."

"So, this is it, then?" James asked, desperate to buy a few minutes' time, as if that would solve this impossible predicament.

Pettibone smiled triumphantly. "Hardly. You still have a chance at beating me back to France. But if I were you, I would not hold my breath."

He backed away from the chair, watching to be sure that James did not follow. Reaching the French windows, he turned the knob of one and pushed it open, offering James an elegant bow before he turned and disappeared.

James threw the chair against the wall and stalked to the open door, just catching sight of Pettibone as he climbed aboard a waiting horse and galloped off across the lush lawns.

* * *

Iris had regained consciousness by the time James returned from the terrace.

"Did he escape?" Iris asked, her voice hoarse.

Clarissa supported the girl's head in her lap, dabbing at her wound with a handkerchief. "*Oui.* But do not think on such things now, Mademoiselle Bennett."

"But the key. Did he make off with the key?" she pressed, ever the banker's daughter.

Clarissa looked to James for direction.

"*Non,* Mademoiselle Bennett. Have a bit of faith in us," he answered.

Iris smiled in response but her body continued to shake all over.

"I'll alert Monsieur Bennett and send for the doctor," James announced, the grim set of his features as he strode from the room only making Clarissa more desperate to cry.

But she bit the inside of her cheek instead, fighting off the tears until she had the liberty to let them loose.

"It's all right, *mon petit chou.* Everything will be all right," she murmured, saying this for herself as much as Iris—even if she didn't believe it for a moment.

"Iris! Iris!" Mr. Bennett's terrified shouts reached the back of the library shortly before he came running down the aisle. "Dear God, my girl," he moaned in disbelief as he dropped to his knees at her side. "Who did this to you?"

Mrs. Bennett followed quickly behind, her face pale with shock and worry. "Iris, can you hear me?" she asked, inelegantly lifting her umber skirts, settling in beside her husband and clutching her daughter's hand in hers.

"Yes, Mother, I can hear you," Iris answered weakly. "Father, it was Pettibone."

"The servant who disappeared last week?" he asked.

Iris nodded.

Mr. Bennett stood and strode toward the open door. "He can't have gotten far. I'll go in search of him myself."

"No!" Clarissa argued, desperate to keep the Bennetts safe from harm. "You're needed here, monsieur. With your family."

Bennett turned back and looked at his wife and daughter.

"Come, my dear," Mrs. Bennett implored as she reached out for her husband. "Monsieur St. Michelle speaks the truth. We need you here, not out chasing after this dangerous man."

Mr. Bennett once more looked out the windows at the expansive lawn of Kenwood House and beyond to the heath, the realization that Pettibone had slipped from his grasp clearly settling in.

"You're right, of course," he replied, then walked back and took his wife's offered hand. "Never fear, my girls. The doctor is on his way."

20

James reined the gray gelding around a cart carrying cabbages as he and Clarissa rode through the southern end of the city of Dover. It was early evening yet still light, a salty breeze wafting in from the Channel. The cry of gulls overhead alerted him that they were nearing the harbor. He squinted into the distance, the telltale sight of masts bobbing into view just beyond a hodge-podge row of buildings giving him at least a bit of relief.

He offered Clarissa a small, encouraging smile. "We're nearly to the port," he assured her, hopeful that the news would cheer her. She'd been unusually quiet for most of their long journey from London to the coastal town, which had been just as well, James thought. They'd pushed their horses at a staggering pace, stopping only to sleep at the posting inn before returning to the road.

Clarissa had done as well as any Corinthian agent would have, not complaining once nor asking for stops along the way. On more than one occasion, James had noticed her standing in her stirrups to relieve what must have been sore muscles in her inner thighs and backside, but she'd pushed on, her commitment to her mother clearly strengthening her resolve.

James had been thankful that Clarissa hadn't inquired as to whether or not he felt they could catch up to Petti-bone. By the time they'd seen to Iris and accepted Mr.

Bennett's offer of the horses, it had taken over an hour to extricate themselves from Kenwood House and set out on the road toward Dover. With more than an hour's lead, capturing Pettibone was not completely beyond the realm of possibility, but it was hardly helpful.

Clarissa pointed ahead. The road split off, one track leading toward the outskirts of the city while the other dipped gradually and disappeared between a hulking pair of warehouses. James nodded toward the first one and she frowned, looking ready to argue.

"Cooper's Livery Stables is this way," James said in quick explanation. "We'll have word sent to Bennett that the horses will be waiting for him there."

Clarissa's brow cleared and she nodded without comment. They continued on at a trot for a short ways before reaching Cooper's. James stepped out of the saddle and handed the reins to the stable boy who'd come running the moment they arrived. Clarissa dismounted and stood at Winston's head, cooing softly in his ear while James went to make the necessary arrangements. She talked to the horse till James returned, then kissed Winston gently on the nose and turned over the reins.

He pointed at the coastline. The port was straight across from where they stood, separated only by the shipbuilders that marked the line between the merchant area of Dover and the wharf. "We'll walk from here. It shouldn't take long.

Clarissa nodded and followed as James led them down a walkway that ran between two businesses.

They reached the usually bustling port within minutes, the working day nearly at an end and the piers largely deserted.

He pointed down the docks, past the naval frigates and ships of the line, to where the privateers anchored. "There," he said. "We'll inquire after suitable transport there. I'll do all of the talking, agreed?"

"Agreed," Clarissa replied, eyeing the ships in the dimming light. "Are those privateers?"

James quickened his pace. "Yes."

"Pirates, then?"

James turned and looked at Clarissa, noting her apprehension. "They've no interest in you or me beyond money," he reassured her, adding, "and do not refer to them as pirates. Actually, do not refer to them at all."

"Then we'll follow the original plan," Clarissa answered sarcastically.

The small spark of her spirit returning pleased James more than he could say. "Precisely. Come along, now. I've pirates to parley with."

Their footfalls on the wooden pier alerted three men who stood just at the end of the gangway to their approach. The men, who'd looked to be deep in conversation, stopped talking and turned to eye James and Clarissa with suspicion as they made their way nearer.

"Gentlemen," James began with confidence. "Might I have a word?"

He'd made use of pirates in the past. Their knowledge of the comings and goings—both legal and otherwise—of the ships in port had proved invaluable to him on many previous occasions. Even still, he knew to trust them no more than was necessary.

"Depends," one of the men answered, his full black mustache and beard obscuring his mouth as he spoke.

"On?"

"On who you are," the man replied, his companions staring stonily at James and Clarissa.

"It makes no matter who I am," James began, reaching into his waistcoat for a number of coins. "I've need of transport."

The three listened intently as James shifted the money from one hand to the other, the satisfying sound of coins clinking capturing their interest. "Is that so? And what sort of transport will you be needing?" the black-bearded man asked.

"Something fast, with a knowledgeable captain adept at navigating around large obstacles," James replied, purposefully dropping a two-guinea piece on the pier.

All three watched as the coin spun then slowed to drop flat, ringing on the planking. "It's McGary you'll be wanting, then," the bearded one answered. "As old as the good Lord himself, but he'll get you where you need to go."

James watched as the man bent down and picked up the coin, then gestured for James to hand over the rest.

James ignored the man's request. "And where might I find McGary?"

"Just past the powder hulk—McGary is the only one fool enough to moor there, but you'll hardly be bothered."

James looked farther down the wharf to where he could just make out the dismantled ship. It was large enough that even if the men were telling the truth, he'd not be able to see another vessel beyond it. But he had no other choice but to believe them. "Thank you, gentlemen," he said, then handed over the remaining coins.

"You best be off now," the bearded one grunted, looking at the placement of the disappearing sun. "Filch'll be on duty soon enough and you don't want nothing to do with that one. Gives right hospitable excisemen a bad name—don't he, boys?"

The other two smiled, revealing no more than ten blackened teeth between them.

James returned the friendly gesture, always aware that a well-made acquaintance today could prove even more useful in the future. "Thank you again, gents. I'm much obliged."

He turned to the gangway and James gestured for

Clarissa to follow him back up the pier. "What did I tell you? Pirates are just as polite as you and I."

"Let's hope the same is true of McGary."

The pirates had lied. McGary was not just old—he was ancient. Clarissa would go so far as to say he was the oldest individual she'd ever met in her life, which, considering the ridiculously long life span of most of her mother's relatives, was quite a feat.

They'd managed to find him and a guinea boat just down from the powder hulk. He sat on the pier, his legs dangling over the side while he enjoyed a particularly foul-smelling cigar.

He'd agreed to take them to Calais, asking twice what James had originally offered due to the alleged swiftness of his boat. Clarissa could not help rolling her eyes at his statement. The very idea of speed being used in connection to anything having to do with McGary was more than her dwindling patience could endure.

They waited until it was completely dark then climbed aboard the guinea, traveling the short distance to where McGary kept the cutter anchored. After switching ships, James helped McGary with the lines while Clarissa did as James had instructed and hunkered down belowdeck. She wasn't allowed a lantern, but her eyes had adjusted to the darkness and she made out the contents of her room. A captain's bed, upon which she sat, a small sailor's trunk, and a chair. Clarissa supposed a man as old as McGary hardly needed many worldly possessions at this late point in his life. Still, the room felt cold and lonely.

She tucked her legs under her and leaned against the rough wooden wall. She'd purposefully not asked James whether or not she believed they would catch up to Pettibone. Clarissa didn't want to put him in the position of disappointing her—but more than that, she couldn't bear to hear his answer.

For herself, she feared they were too late. She couldn't know what, precisely, Pettibone planned, but she felt sure that her mother's life hung in the balance. This terror had set in as soon as Pettibone had escaped through the French windows in the library. The fear had grown, expanding rapidly as they'd ridden to Dover. She couldn't think or speak for fear of breaking down along the road from London and never recovering.

"Get ahold of yourself," she said out loud, hugging her arms around herself. She couldn't cry. Not now. She couldn't let the fear win, for then the very little hope that she held in her heart would be destroyed.

They had to be nearly there. They'd encountered no foul weather from what Clarissa could discern and it felt as though she'd been hiding below for hours. She uncrossed her legs and set her feet on the floor. She couldn't wait any longer. She stood and opened the door, hesitating in the doorway while she listened for any troubling noises. Hearing none, she stepped over the threshold and quietly closed the door behind her, feeling along the walls to where she remembered the stairs were.

She crawled up to the main deck and found James and McGary in the bow of the boat, their faces to the wind as the cutter glided across the relatively calm waters.

James turned at the sound of her feet on the deck. "Go back below," he ordered brusquely.

"I want to help. I can no longer sit below in the dark and do nothing," Clarissa maintained, her voice trembling.

"Listen to the man," McGary snarled, cigar smoke enwreathing his head.

"You don't seem to understand," Clarissa pressed, suddenly unable to stop herself as she waved her arms to punctuate the seriousness of the situation. "I literally cannot sit below one moment—"

McGary stood quickly and slapped Clarissa across the cheek. "Get ahold of yourself. I'm not meaning to die tonight, you lily-livered, hoddy-doddy bawd."

Clarissa could not speak. She didn't know if it was the surprisingly powerful force of McGary's slap or the fact that he'd hit her at all.

"I see that he's as useless as you claimed. Now, get 'im below then hie yourself back here—I'll be needing you to outwit them ships," McGary commanded James, then dropped his cigar over the side.

Clarissa looked past the rail and caught sight of a great many hulking ships ahead, all lined up, just waiting for them.

James grabbed Clarissa's arm and steered her toward the stairs. "Please, we're nearly there."

"I'm sorry. I'm trying, I truly am—"

James silenced Clarissa with one rough finger against her mouth. "I know how hard this is for you, and I'm doing everything in my power to ensure that we reach your mother in time. But you must do as I say."

Clarissa nodded, the tears that she'd fought off all day welling in her eyes.

"Go. Remain below until I come for you."

And he turned away to rejoin McGary near the bow as the old man barked out an order.

Clarissa carefully picked her way down the steep stairs and returned to the cabin, where she began to pray.

James paid McGary three times what the old man had asked for running the blockade. The sailor had done a superb job of it, especially for a man his age, and, the excitement of nearly running into the side of a warship had done James some good. He waved to the man one more time, then turned toward Clarissa. "We best make haste for Le Poisson d'Or. There's a chance that someone

might be willing to share news of Pettibone's arrival—
for the right price, of course."

He led her along the rickety pier where McGary had
assured them they'd not be detected. Eyeing the port to
his left, James set off straight ahead, cutting through al-
leyways until they reached the main road. "This way,"
he urged Clarissa, continuing on toward the corner of
rue de la Mer and rue du Havre where the tavern was
situated.

"I'm afraid to ask exactly how you came to know of
such a place," Clarissa said wearily, eyeing the inn with
hesitation.

Corinthians had used Le Poisson d'Or for years as a
resource. The clientele, a mishmash of sailors, merchants, and those well acquainted with the French underworld, had often proved most useful. "It is a long
story. But remember, you agreed to do as I say without
question."

"I'm sorry for my outburst on the boat," she said,
holding tightly to his arm as they crossed the street.

James looked at her, wanting very much to take her in
his arms. "Never be sorry for expressing what you feel.
Agreed?"

"Agreed," she replied, then assumed a look of dull
disinterest. "Shall we?"

James swung wide the door to the tavern and held it
open for her. "We shall."

The scent of fish, salty air, and stale, spilled cider hit
James hard in the face, though he fared better than
Clarissa, who squeezed her eyes shut in reaction. "You'll
get used to it," he assured her, then pushed her farther
into the tavern.

James didn't know how long Le Poisson d'Or had
been in business, but he felt sure it had been centuries.
The crude wooden tables and simple stools looked as
old as McGary, as did the bar along the western wall of

the low-ceilinged room. The deafening off-key song from a group of sailors near the door sent James in search of a quieter spot near the back of the establishment. Clarissa kept her head down while he maneuvered them through the boisterous crowd toward an open table.

They were within three yards of taking their seats when James spied someone in the corner.

"Goddammit," he muttered under his breath. Reginald Meeks, the Viscount of Penderly, was sitting at a table by himself, watching James. James had met the man at societal events before but knew very little of him—beyond the fact that he was the French case officer for the Young Corinthians.

He waited for Penderly to startle at the sight of him, but the man only nodded in recognition and gestured for James to join him.

"Come," James said into Clarissa's ear, then pointed her toward Penderly's location.

Penderly pushed the two chairs opposite him out with his foot. "You've no idea how glad I am to see you, Marlowe."

"I'm at a loss here, Penderly. I was under the impression that no one knew about my assignment," James replied, taking his seat.

Penderly called for the barmaid and ordered two pints of cider. "Carmichael resisted telling me, but with our work concerning Les Moines continuing, it was necessary. Besides, I'll be damned if I don't know exactly what's going on with all of the agents on the Continent. I hope you understand why we kept my involvement from you."

"Of course," James answered. "But I'm assuming our meeting here is more than just a pleasant coincidence?"

The barmaid plunked down the mugs in front of James and Clarissa and asked if Penderly wanted a second. Declining, he paid her then waved her off. "I don't know about that. As I mentioned, I'm deuced glad to see you. After my man at the port told me of Pettibone's return, I didn't know what to think."

"You've seen him?" Clarissa asked, looking anxiously at Penderly. "How long ago? Is he still in Calais?"

Penderly gave James a questioning look, unsure how much Clarissa knew.

"Proceed," James instructed.

"He came into port nearly two hours ago. Secured a carriage and left straightaway."

Clarissa's face fell. "Two hours? How will we ever catch up with him?"

James placed his hand on her thigh beneath the table and gently squeezed.

"Hang on. Just what is Pettibone up to?" Meeks asked.

"I'm not entirely sure. He tried to kill me in London," James paused, taking a swig of cider. "When that failed, he stole a key that belongs to a strongbox in Paris—the very one that holds all of Bennett's money meant to pay for the portrait."

Penderly's brows knitted together as he thought the information through. "He's after the money, then?"

"More than that. He seems to be after Durand. I'm guessing he plans on foiling our mission to try to steal the man's position."

"No matter what Pettibone's plans are, it will become increasingly evident to Durand that my mother is no longer needed," Clarissa added, desperation in her voice.

Penderly nodded. "Of course. I've a man following Pettibone—he'll report in to our office as soon as they arrive in Paris. I'd put my money on the brothel, though—that's where they're holding your mother.

"The Tout et Plus?" James asked.

"The very one," Penderly answered.

James rose quickly from the table, Clarissa doing the same. "I'll need men and horses."

Penderly stood up to join them. "Of course. They'll be briefed as to your true status within the Corinthians and accompany you to Paris," he confirmed. "And Marlowe, welcome back from the dead."

Clarissa was sure that if she ever found herself on the back of a horse again, it would be too soon. Even with the hour's worth of rest that James had insisted they take when they'd stopped for fresh mounts, she wouldn't be surprised if the imprint of the saddle would permanently alter the shape of her backside.

They waited near the edge of Montmartre while one of the five agents who'd accompanied them to Paris went on to confirm that Pettibone had indeed gone directly to the brothel. When he'd rushed back with the news that Pettibone had made straight for the Tout et Plus, a plan had been decided upon to rescue Clarissa's mother, then capture as many of the Les Moines agents as was possible. Reinforcements had been sent for, but there was no guarantee they would arrive in time—and they couldn't wait.

"I cannot let you do this."

Clarissa adjusted the satin gown about her shoulders, pulling in a vain attempt to cover more of her breasts. When the agent had returned with the dress and slippers, many had assumed that one of the male agents would be required to play the part. It had made much more sense when he'd explained his plan, though James had threatened to part the man's head from his body. "You have no choice. Durand knows what you look like. Besides, in all likelihood I'll be able to secure your entry before I encounter the man."

James held tightly to her wrist. "And what if Petti-bone finds you?"

Clarissa had wondered the very same thing. Having failed to secure a reasonable solution, her exhausted brain had conveniently forgotten about it altogether. "James, please. We're running out of time."

He'd listened, though it clearly had taken all of his strength to do so. Only after she'd repeated the plan back to him three times did he release her wrist and allow her to cross the street and approach the back entrance to the brothel.

Clarissa smoothed the skirts of the garish-red gown and took a deep breath before rapping on the door with her fist.

She was readying to knock a second time when the door swung wide and a woman appeared. "*Oui?*" she asked, scratching at the neck of her flimsy chemise.

"I'm Camille. Cozette's friend?" Clarissa answered, feigning irritation. "She told you about me, didn't she? Promised she would."

The woman continued to scratch while she looked Clarissa up and down. "Camille, is it? Well, Camille, Cozette didn't tell me a thing, but you're certainly pretty—and we're very busy. Come in, then." She stepped aside to allow Clarissa entry, slamming the door behind her.

"My name is Joëlle," the woman offered as she quickly walked down a narrow hallway toward the front of the building. "I'll show you to your room."

Clarissa stole a quick glance at the main floor. There was no one about except for one large man at the front door. She avoided meeting his lecherous gaze as she followed Joëlle up the stairs.

"This one will do," the woman said as she pushed open the door of the last room on the right. "Small, but plenty of room for you to maneuver. Freshen up, then come downstairs. The owner will have finished with his meeting by then. He prefers to see each girl before allowing her to meet the clients."

Clarissa nodded appreciatively and waited as Joëlle left the room. Quietly closing the door, she hurried to the window, pushing open the cheap velvet curtains. She looked anxiously across the street, barely able to see the Corinthian agents at the corner. She pried open the filthy window and gestured wildly. She squinted to make out a man's form in the dark as he stealthily ran toward the brothel and stopped just below her window. Putting her arms out as he threw a rope ladder up to her, it narrowly missed her grasp. He tried a second time and her fingers caught on just before it fell.

She tied the top to the bed frame then returned to the window, leaning out and tossing the bottom of the ladder to the waiting agent below.

A rap on the door was followed by Joëlle's voice. "Camille?"

Clarissa waved off the agent, who'd already begun to climb and leaned back inside, hastily pulling the curtains closed. "Yes?" she replied, crossing the room and opening the door just wide enough to see Joëlle standing in the hall.

"I'd forgotten that monsieur is entertaining a special visitor today. He'll have my head if you're found wandering alone. It would be best if you come with me," the woman offered by way of explanation.

Oh, God, could it be Pettibone? "Of course," Clarissa agreed, stepping over the threshold and closing the door quickly behind her.

Joëlle nodded pleasantly and gestured for Clarissa to follow.

Clarissa assumed an expression of polite interest and slowly began to walk toward the stairs, her mind racing.

She could run, but where? If she remained calm and continued on, there was a good chance that James and the others would make their way into the brothel undetected. It was, she realized, her only option.

She descended each step slowly, the sight of the burly man at the entryway tightening her already taut nerves. He looked at them with suspicion.

"She's new—a friend of Cozette's," Joëlle explained, turning to take Clarissa's arm in hers.

"Eh bien," he grunted, his gaze lingering on the creamy expanse of Clarissa's skin as the flimsy strap of her gown slipped from her shoulder.

"Don't let him bother you," Joëlle assured Clarissa, pulling her protectively closer. "He's as big as a bull—and just as stupid. Stay out of his way, and he'll stay out of yours."

Clarissa shook off the terror of encountering the man and allowed Joëlle to steer her down a narrow hallway just off the entryway. She saw the stairs at the end and forced a smile. "I'll do my best."

James was the first to climb the wall, his booted feet landing on the windowsill silently as he pushed himself through. He hastily inspected the room then returned to the window and assisted the other agents as they appeared one by one. The last of them climbed over the sill and into the small room. He pulled the ladder up then fastened the window and shut the curtains.

"Clarissa is gone," James told the gathered men, checking the knife concealed in his boot and the other tucked into the waistband of his breeches. "She would not have gone unless it was absolutely necessary—or if she was forced."

"Pettibone?" one of the men asked, his tone grave.

James's heart constricted at the sound of the man's name. Of course, it made the most sense, but if she'd been identified by the Frenchman? He couldn't finish the thought, the possible repercussions beyond consideration.

"We'll subdue the man at the front before he alerts the others to our presence," James replied. "If we're lucky, they haven't had enough time to call in reinforcements."

If we're lucky.

He'd found Clarissa again, despite all the odds. If that wasn't plain, dumb luck, James didn't know what was. Could God be so kind as to extend His grace, just a bit further?

There was only one way to find out. "Wait out of sight until I give you the signal. Understood?"

The men nodded and James silently opened the hall door. He peered into the passageway. Finding no one, he walked through and headed for the stairs, adopting the half stagger of a drunken client who'd just awoken.

"*Bon dieu,*" he began in a thick Languedoc accent, holding his head in his hands as he tripped his way to the main floor. "Do a man a favor, would you, and find me something to drink."

The Les Moines agent at the door started at the sight of him, his considerable bulk moving with surprising speed. "Who are you?"

James came within three steps of the man and stopped, dropping his arms at his sides. "I'm the poor sod who went to bed last night with an incredibly flexible brunette and only just now woke up—missing my money and my gold watch, that's who I am." His disgruntled voice growled the words with an echo of outrage.

The guard took a step closer. His eyes narrowed as he looked James up and down. "Our girls would not—"

James didn't give him the opportunity to finish his sentence. He slipped the knife from his waistband

and drove the blade into the man's gut, catching the Les Moines agent's weight as he pitched forward and groaned heavily. James lowered him to the floor and signaled for the waiting Corinthians.

"You," James began, pointing at Martin, "hide him. The rest of you, follow me."

He moved quickly toward the hallway that led to the basement stairs. Movement from the back of the house caught his eye and he looked down the length of the brothel's back hall to where Clarissa had entered less than an hour before. Several Les Moines agents crashed through the outer door, increasing their pace at the sight of James.

"Hopkins!" James shouted at the Corinthian agent nearest him.

The man looked to where the enemy agents were fast approaching. "I have this, sir. Go—find Lady Clarissa."

James nodded then raced down the hall, reaching the stairs and taking them two at a time as he ran toward the lower floor. He stopped at the bottom, orienting himself. Durand's office seemed the most logical place to start, so he hugged the wall and moved silently toward the room, aware that the noise from the battle above would have alerted anyone below.

A woman suddenly appeared, her eyes wild with fright. James reached out, pushing her against the wall and covering her mouth with his hand. "The new girl. Where is she? Tell me and I'll not hurt you." He gently released her and moved his hand to encircle her neck.

"In Durand's care, though I would not go any farther, if I were you," she whispered, trembling as she did so.

"Is there a way out on this floor?" James asked in a hushed tone, ignoring the woman's warning.

The woman nodded. "Through the kitchens."

"Good. Use it—now. Do not come back."

She nodded once more as James loosened his hold, then bolted for the kitchens.

James continued down the hall, stopping just outside the closed door of Durand's office. He listened for a moment, the absence of a female voice filling him with dread.

He'd waited long enough. James turned the brass door handle and shoved open the door, not knowing what or whom he would find.

"Do come in, Marlowe."

Pettibone stood just in front of the desk, with Durand seated behind it and another man, whom James recognized instantly, seated in the corner. But Clarissa was nowhere in sight. He tamped down the terror that threatened to take hold and focused on the man.

"Gentlemen," James said by way of introduction, sizing up the opposition in mere seconds. Three on one. He'd faced more threatening odds before.

"You see, Father, Talleyrand, it is just as I said. You hired a turncoat," Pettibone pronounced, his voice thick with satisfaction.

"I thought that was you, monsieur," James addressed Charles Maurice de Talleyrand-Périgord, a French diplomat and valued, though wily, Napoleon ally, as he sat quietly in the corner. "May I assume that I've found the leader of Les Moines?"

The older man nodded his head, his thin lips forming into a bitter smile. "Considering the fact that you'll be dead within minutes, monsieur, I suppose it would do no harm to admit my involvement."

"How kind," James replied, turning his attention to Durand. "And you? 'Father'? Now, that is a shock."

Durand grimaced. "To you and me both, I'm afraid."

"Father, your disgust is hardly warranted, especially considering all that I've done—why, I delivered this traitor to your door—"

"Exactly," Talleyrand interrupted, tapping his fingers on the arms of his chair. "A more monumentally stupid thing to do, I cannot imagine."

Pettibone began to sweat, thin lines of moisture snaking their way down his temples. "But now you know who this man is—what he's capable of."

"The same could be said of you, son," Durand replied, pushing back his chair. "Another of your failed attempts to overthrow me, *non?*"

"I've no idea what you're talking ab—"

Durand stood and took aim at his son, the pocket pistol that he'd been hiding beneath the desk firing off one deafening shot directly into Pettibone's heart. "Now, what are we to do with you?" he asked coldly, lifting a second weapon and taking aim at James.

James stared at the dying man, who'd fallen backward and landed in a boneless heap near Talleyrand's feet. "Where's Lady Clarissa?"

"Locked up tight with her mother. I'd thought to deal with her later," Durand answered, gesturing with the gun. "But right now my associate and I need to be leaving—without you."

"Tell me, monsieur, does your government pay well?" Talleyrand asked of James. "I would think a man of my unique qualifications could do well."

James barely had time to absorb the news that Clarissa was still alive before the man's odd question demanded an answer. "Depends upon the services offered, I suppose."

"You bastard," Durand spit out, pointing the pistol at the older man.

Talleyrand sighed and offered Durand a look of boredom. "That's hardly news, my friend. Come now, did you really think my allegiance is only to the emperor, in these perilous times?"

"But he is the rightful ruler," Durand countered, his pistol holding a steady unwavering line.

"Regimes may fall and fail, but I do not," Talleyrand answered simply. "The Russians are quite fond of me, you see. And I suspect the English would be as well."

The noise from the fight abovestairs grew louder, the thud of bodies hitting the floor intermingled with muffled shouts and curses.

Durand's stony façade cracked and he scrubbed a hand over his face. "Come. I'll not kill you quickly—that would be too merciful." He walked around the desk, motioning both men toward the door. He waited while Talleyrand opened it. He then shoved the nose of the pistol into James's back and urged him on. "To the kitchens," he instructed.

Talleyrand obeyed, walking quickly down the hall. James followed, slowing as they entered the kitchens. Cooks and servants stopped what they were doing to look at the men, though none seemed all that surprised.

They were nearing the back door when James saw his opportunity. A bucket of potato peelings had spilled onto the floor in front of them. Talleyrand delicately avoided the refuse, while James pretended not to see it, stepping directly in the mess. He feigned a slip and pitched backward into Durand, knocking the man and his pistol to the floor.

Durand scrambled for the gun and reached it just as James grabbed it, the two wrestling for control. Durand punched James in the nose with his free hand and attempted to roll away. But James kept hold of the pistol and slammed his forehead against Durand's. They wrestled, moving closer to the stove, the gun between them.

And then it went off.

James looked down at Durand, the man's face contorting with pain. He mouthed something that James could not make out, then his head sagged to the side and he stilled.

The sound of something connecting with metal caught James by surprise and he jumped up, the gun still in his hand.

Talleyrand lay immobile on the floor, the woman from earlier standing over him with a cast-iron pan in her hands. "He was trying to get away. An incompetent lover, that one," Joëlle explained simply. "Took more of our money than he should have too."

Agent Martin appeared in the kitchens, followed by two other Corinthians.

"Under control upstairs?" James asked, poking Talleyrand with his foot.

The man groaned.

Thank God, James thought to himself, knowing Carmichael would have been very disappointed by the untimely death of the Les Moines's leader. He was looking forward to interrogating him.

"Yes, sir," Martin answered efficiently.

James nodded then ran full tilt from the room, his strides eating up the distance down the hallway.

"Clarissa!" he shouted, trying each door as he came upon it.

"James!" The scream erupted from the last room on the right.

He didn't bother with the doorknob. Instead, James kicked the door in and ran for Clarissa and her mother, taking Clarissa in his arms and holding her tight. Her precious body was warm, alive, pressed against his. "Are you two all right?"

Clarissa pulled back and looked into his face. "We are now, my love," she answered, her palms coming to rest on his chest reverently. "But please," she added, relief in her voice, "promise me we'll never be parted again, especially by lock and key. Too hard on the door and frame, wouldn't you agree?"

He smiled, a deep, relieved, loving, laughing grin. "I love you."

"You are our savior," Isabelle interrupted. "Truly, James."

Clarissa smiled brightly at her mother. "He is, isn't he," she said possessively, beginning to cry as emotions overwhelmed her.

"Always have been," James added.

"And always will be," Clarissa confirmed, then tilted her head up to James's and captured him with a kiss that told him she meant it.

"She's more beautiful than I remembered," Carmichael commented as he watched Clarissa sketch her mother. The light through the windows of the front drawing room at 27 Hertford Street in Mayfair, according to Clarissa's comment only moments before, was perfect. And so she'd taken up her charcoal and drawing paper and set to work, everyone in the room agreeing that an artist's intuition is never to be ignored.

"Yes, she is," James agreed. "Funny, that. I thought the very same thing when I first saw her again in St. Michelle's studio."

Carmichael nodded. "Lady Westbridge as well."

"Yes, I agree there too, though my first glimpse of her in France quite frankly stunned me. Those weeks spent with Les Moines left her pale and thin. Since returning to England she's greatly improved."

James and Clarissa had decided against telling her mother about the Young Corinthians. She'd been in far too much danger already, and it wasn't as if it would change what had happened with her husband.

But the day of James and Clarissa's wedding, Isabelle had summoned James to an antechamber in the church and asked for his forgiveness. Her husband's infidelity had torn her in two, she'd explained, and she couldn't let the same thing happen to her daughter. Isabelle had ignored James's plea that fateful day so long ago and failed to tell Clarissa that he'd come to their home. It had weighed heavily on her conscience ever since, and now that they'd found their way back to each other, Isabelle couldn't let another day go by without telling James of her part. Seeing them together, so happy—so complete—had forced her to accept that closing one's heart to the possibility of sorrow also closed it to the likelihood of love.

The man James had been mere weeks before would have tasted bile in his throat at such a revelation. He would have held tight to his bitterness and told the woman, in so many words, that she deserved to be tortured by her regrets.

But he was no longer that man. When Carmichael had recruited James for the Les Moines assignment, James had suspected it would be the most important case of his career. But he couldn't have known that it was to be the seminal moment of his life. He'd found himself—after holding on far too long to the man he thought he was. He'd let go and taken a chance. And he'd won.

"You've not asked after Talleyrand."

James felt his jaw threatening to tense and mentally forced himself to relax. "The man deserved to die. Still, I completed my assignment, Carmichael. You have to know that I can no longer serve in the same role—"

"Talleyrand is very valuable, Marlowe."

James leaned forward in his chair and propped his elbows on his knees. "Do you think he'll hold up his end of the bargain and help dismantle Les Moines?"

"If we pay him enough, yes, I do. Besides, he's the only one who can," Carmichael answered. "You did it, James. You not only completed the assignment, you completed it with more than expected success."

James looked at Carmichael, and his heart, previously brimming with happiness, tipped over and welled with satisfaction. "Thank you."

"You're welcome," Carmichael replied sincerely. "Now,

James, I would be remiss if I did not mention a noteworthy observation I've made during my visit today: Marriage seems to agree with you," Carmichael added, an infinitesimal smile appearing on his lips.

James chuckled, not about to disagree with him. He was, after all, James's superior. And he was right. "You can't imagine the fights, Carmichael," he whispered conspiratorially. "Ah, but the reconciling—well, that makes it all worthwhile."

"Is that all?"

James fidgeted with one of the ridiculously puffy pillows Clarissa seemed so fond of arranging everywhere in the house. "No," he admitted sheepishly. "I love her. Always have. Always will. But then, you knew that already, didn't you, Carmichael?"

"Well, as you know, Marlowe, I'm not one to gloat," Carmichael began in an even tone, turning his attention back to the ladies. "But, yes, I did."

James couldn't help himself. He let out a roar of laughter, garnering the attention of not only Carmichael, but the two women as well.

"You, Marlowe, have never looked happier, truly."

James clapped Carmichael on the knee, hardly able to suppress the emotions that seemed intent on overtaking him. "I've never been better than right now, my good man."

"It's beautiful, is it not?" Clarissa lay against James's chest, the flickering candlelight catching rainbows in the crystals sewn into the bodice of her wedding gown.

James chuckled, his chest hair tickling her cheek. "How long do you plan to leave the gown there—on the chair, displayed like a vase of flowers."

"Perhaps a year—or two, depending upon a number of factors, which I'll not bore you with," she teased, trailing her fingers down his taut stomach to the edge of the silken bed linens, then slowly walking them back to where she began.

"And you're absolutely certain you do not want a honeymoon?"

James had asked after a honeymoon since the day he'd proposed. He seemed to feel that he'd failed her in some way by not packing her up and dragging her across several nations, over large bodies of water, and through battlefields.

"James, I do believe that three Channel crossings within weeks of each other is all the travel I can possibly endure at the moment. Perhaps, when we're eighty and our children have their children—"

"Just how many children?" James interrupted, his interest pleasing Clarissa.

"Four, I believe. Or eight. I cannot decide. Which do you prefer?"

James's muscles rippled in response to Clarissa's curious fingers. "They're both nice, round numbers. Perhaps we should simply go forward with one and then decide?"

"Four it is," Clarissa declared. "Now, where was I? Oh, yes, when we are eighty and our four children have children of their own, perhaps then we'll take a tour of the world."

James sighed. "I can hardly wait until I'm eighty to give you your consolation prize."

"Whatever do you mean?" Clarissa asked, her curiosity piqued.

"Consolation—you have to know that my not being able to give you a honeymoon has been—"

"Hush." Clarissa sat up and placed two fingers on his lips. "Not the definition of the word, James. The reason why you cannot wait to give me the prize."

"Oh," he answered. "That's simple enough. He'll be dead by then."

A faint scratching sounded at the door between Clarissa and James's bedchamber, followed quickly by an irritated "Yeow!"

"Did you?" Clarissa exclaimed, her eyes widening with comprehension. "You did not! Did you?"

James smiled wide and pushed Clarissa gently from his side. "Well, if you're so curious, perhaps you should go and see."

Clarissa, her glowing skin and beautiful limbs bared for James's appreciation, leapt from the bed with robust enthusiasm and ran across the room to the door, pulling it wide with all of her might.

"Meow," Pharaoh said by way of a greeting, rubbing himself about her ankles with obvious feline pleasure.

Clarissa gathered him into her arms and carried him back to the bed. "I must admit, I missed him dreadfully," she said to her husband, her eyes misty with tears.

"Then you're happy with your consolation prize?" James asked, clearly quite proud of himself.

Clarissa kissed Pharaoh on the soft, black fur between his ears then set him on top of one of her favorite pillows.

She threw back the coverlet and climbed into the bed, wrapping herself about James's warm, male form. "Quite so. Shall I tell you how much it pleases me, or would you rather I show you, Mr. Marlowe?"

"For the love of God, please show me, Mrs. Marlowe. Show me now."

"Pharaoh, close your eyes," she commanded the cat, then turned back to James, drawing the coverlet over their intertwined bodies, and spending the remainder of the evening showing her husband just how happy he made her.

ACKNOWLEDGMENTS

Junessa Viloria for her continued support and expert eye. Jennifer Schober for her awesome agent skills and general coolness. Franzeca Drouin for ensuring that I don't make a fool of myself. Lois Dyer for everything. And the Girls for keeping it real.

Read on for a sensational extract of

The Saint Who Stole My Heart

Stefanie Sloane's fourth Regency Rogues novel

Available now from Headline Eternal

"Pardon me, my lady, but I think I'm going to be sick."

Lady Elena Barnes, the daughter of Robert Barnes, the Marquess of Salisbury, had reason to take her maid Rowena seriously. The poor girl had already cast up her accounts three times that day, the carriage ride from Dunwell doing little to ease the agony of Rowena's sour stomach.

"Right," Elena said reassuringly, thumping the roof of the conveyance and yelling for the driver to stop.

The carriage jerked to a stop on the perfectly raked gravel drive of Hardwick House. Elena turned the golden door handle and pushed hard.

Rowena dove from her well-appointed seat, landing safely on her feet, and proceeded to vomit into a manicured patch of roses.

Elena rushed out after her, settling her hand at the base of the poor maid's back. "Oh, Rowena, are you all right?"

"Might I be of assistance?"

Something slithered in Elena's stomach at the sound of the rich, deep male voice. That, or she'd managed to secure Rowena's ailment for herself. "Yes, if you wouldn't mind," she began, rubbing Rowena's back lightly as she turned to look at the servant.

Only it was not the liveried form of a Hardwick House footman that met her gaze. It was Lord Hardwick himself. "My Lord, I beg your pardon."

Now she remembered who Dashiell Matthews, the Viscount of Hardwick, was.

Adonis, she thought to herself.

Looking at the man was not unlike what Elena assumed mere mortals would experience when encountering the gods. His hair was quite similar to spun gold. And she'd never been one prone to flights of fancy, but his piercing blue eyes and sculpted cheekbones found Elena peering about for signs that they'd taken a wrong turn and somehow ended up in heaven.

Or Valhalla, if those cheekbones were to be believed.

What is wrong with me?

"For what, Lady Elena?"

Elena suddenly realized the man was slowly waving his hand in her face. "I'm sorry?"

Lord Hardwick offered her a lop-sided grin. "You asked that I pardon you. I was simply curious as to the offense."

Oh, God, his mouth. His full, full mouth.

She shook her head and strained to take in anything but the sight of Lord Hardwick. "For my maid's . . . For your rose bush, which will most likely require a serious pruning . . ." Elena paused, realizing belatedly that, in addition to making no sense at all, she'd also stopped the carriage nearly a furlong from the home's front door.

She stared at the line of servants in the distance, all waiting awkwardly to dance attendance on her.

"For the vomit, Lord Hardwick," she finally ground out, deciding the most direct course was more than likely the best at this point.

Lord Hardwick looked at her, his brow clouding with confusion. "But you've not vomited, have you Lady Elena?"

Ah, yes, it was all coming back to her now. Of course, she'd never been privy to the conversations of the more desirable debutantes of her day, but Elena had heard snippets of delicious gossip here and there.

And the whispers about Lord Hardwick claimed that the man was as dim-witted as he was beautiful.

Perhaps even more so, actually.

"No, no I have not, my lord," Elena replied, releasing Rowena into the care of a footman who'd made his way across the expanse.

Elena almost, *almost* wished Lord Hardwick had not opened his mouth.

"Shall we ride the remaining furlong, Lady Elena?" the viscount asked, pointing to the carriage's open door. "Seems a waste, after all."

Now she most certainly wished that the man was mute.

Elena watched as the footman escorted Rowena toward the waiting servants, then turned her attention back to Lord Hardwick. "In the carriage, then?"

"Of course, Lady Elena," he replied incredulously.

"I'd hardly ask you to sit astride one of your matching blacks."

She peered deep into his blue eyes, searching for intelligence.

And deeper.

And found nothing.

Oh, God.

Elena sighed. "Actually, if you would not mind ever so much, I do believe I'd prefer to walk."

Lord Hardwick shrugged his shoulders and gestured toward the house. "Suit yourself, Lady Elena."

The two walked in silence to the waiting servants. Lord Hardwick introduced the principal staff in a leisurely manner, finishing with the butler, Bell.

The man bowed politely. "Lady Elena, if you would allow me," Bell began in a low, firm tone, "may I make the proper introductions?"

The short, round man looked as uncomfortable as Elena felt.

Lord Hardwick laughed. "Hardly necessary, Bell. We met over there, just a moment ago. Couldn't you see from here?"

Elena looked at Bell with relief. "Yes, Mr. Bell, that would be lovely."

"Lady Elena Barnes, may I introduce Dashiell Matthews, the Viscount of Hardwick."

Elena dipped into a tasteful curtsy then offered her hand to the viscount.

His lop-sided grin appeared again, and Elena suddenly realized she felt sorry for the man. It could not be an easy lot in life, his idiocy.

The viscount managed a dignified bow and took her hand in his, placing a chaste kiss across her knuckles. "A pleasure to make your acquaintance, Lady Elena," he pronounced, rising once again and finishing the introduction with a wink.

Elena smiled warmly at the man, much the same way she did every time she encountered Peter Hoskins, a pig farmer who lived not far from Salisbury Manor, her home in Surrey. Some years before, Peter had made the unfortunate mistake of coming between a sizable sow and her offspring. The mother stomped the pig farmer into the mud until he could hardly be found.

He'd never been the same in the head after that, nor would he ever be.

"And yours, Lord Hardwick," she replied conspiratorially, noting yet again the man's devastatingly handsome looks.

Such a pity, she found herself thinking, though she could not imagine why.

Dashiell Matthews, the Viscount of Hardwick, drummed his fingers on the arm of the upholstered chair as he looked about the library. He'd promised to give Lady Elena the grand tour of the massive room. Actually, Bell had offered him up then conveniently disappeared upstairs with the woman in tow.

He couldn't help but admire the man. *A right, good agent Bell would have made,* Dash thought to himself as he looked about. Literally hundreds of books lined the shelves, the topics they covered as wide as his father's interests—which were vast, indeed.

Mathematics, religion, astronomy, history—the list went on and on. Dash had always admired his father's thirst for knowledge, but his love affair with the mountain of volumes before him? That was something he'd never understood.

Oh, Dash devoured books as voraciously as his father—if not more, when it came to particular areas of interest. But once he'd read a book, he had no need of it any longer, his mind capturing the information so precisely that Dash could conjure up exactly what was printed on any given page at any given time.

"How on earth will you be able to part with them?"

Dash looked to the entryway where Lady Elena stood.

"Easily," Dash answered, standing and walking to her side.

She nodded in understanding, a small, pitying "Oh" escaping from her lips as she took his offered arm.

Dash fought the urge to add "because I've read each and every one—and committed them to memory, no less," but he didn't, of course. It was never easy to watch the fruit of his labors blossom so easily, the realization that it was simple enough for people to accept his dim intellect hardly reassuring to his ego.

He led Lady Elena across the room to where the books on mythology were housed. "The Greek gods and such live here," he explained, pointing to the volumes. "Romulus and Remus and all of that. Father said you were a student of such things?"

Lady Elena patted him gently on the arm before pulling away. "Romulus and Remus are Roman, my lord," she gently corrected. "But yes, it's true. I am a most enthusiastic student."

Dash watched as the woman reverently ran her fingers over the volumes, landing on a deep blue bound book and carefully pulling it from its place.

Of course, he knew that Romulus and Remus were Roman. But she'd taken the bait, always satisfying when it came to the bluestockings.

And what a bluestocking she was. Her bun was so severe Dash wondered if she was able to actually close her eyes, the tension caused by such a supply of pins surely causing the skin about the sockets pain.

Though the color of the hair imprisoned within the torturous circle was not precisely mud brown, as he'd originally estimated so many years before. Actually, it was closer to a rich sable, he realized, with hints of gold intertwined throughout.

Her face was more fetching than he'd given her credit for as well. He continued to peruse her person as she returned the book to the shelf and walked slowly down the long, carpeted aisle.

Her hair color was reflected in her eyes; her nose was charmingly pert, as was her mouth. Dash paused at her mouth, noting the full, pink lips as she silently read off the titles of books to herself.

She bent to examine the lower row, giving Dash a rather nice view. He could have sworn the woman had been entirely too plump to be fashionable when she came out, but here she was, her deliciously curved backside perfectly complementing two rounded, firm breasts. An hourglass. A wonderfully proportioned hourglass.

Dash was suddenly annoyed. His memory was a

thing of beauty—or so he thought. Of course, Lady Elena's drab dress, a dull taupe color cut entirely wrong for her figure, was what he'd expected of her.

But the curves? Not at all. Nor the mouth or the silky hair . . .

"Oh!" Lady Elena exclaimed in a hushed tone, her excited intake of breath pulling Dash from his thoughts.

She rushed toward the end of the aisle, nearly skidding to a halt in front of a glass case situated against the wall.

Dash couldn't help himself. Her enthusiasm was infectious, and he followed.

"Francois D'Aulaire's *Greek Mythology*," Lady Elena whispered, as though speaking a sacred prayer.

Dash moved closer to the case, studying the book. His father must have acquired the volume shortly before his death, its presence wholly surprising. "Have you read it, Lady Elena?" he asked, the delicate scent of a single note flower reaching his nose as he did so.

"Hardly," she replied, leaning closer to the case. "This volume—the only one still in existence, mind you—was lost for years. Your father was incredibly fortunate to find it, my lord."

Rose? No, the scent was more complex than that. Lavender? He discreetly breathed in the scent of her, suddenly desperate to identify it.

Gardenia! "Ha," he said enthusiastically, causing Lady Elena to jump.

"I beg your pardon, my lord?" she asked, looking at him as though he were mad.

Dash checked himself belatedly, straightening his crisp cravat. "Funny that, wouldn't you agree? My father found a book that so many could not," he replied, looking at the volume with childlike glee.

"Yes, well," Lady Elena began, her voice laced with strained patience. "The late Lord Hardwick was not the man who actually found the volume. But we can all be thankful that he had the foresight to provide such an admirable and efficient home for it. Look here," she paused, gesturing to the case. "See how it is perfectly situated away from the sunlight."

Dash hardly heard a word the woman said, his focus entirely turned to the quality of her skin, a pleasing flush running from her forehead to the dreadful neckline of her dress.

"Fascinating stuff," he interrupted, needing to be anywhere but next to Lady Elena. "But I'm afraid I must be off. I'll leave you to your books, my lady."

She smiled at him as though he was the village idiot. "Of course, my lord. This must all be terribly boring to you," she replied, curtsying.

Dash bowed then turned to go.

"Thank you, my lord," she added. "You've no idea what these books mean to me—and my father, of course."

Dash paused, but did not turn around, fearful that she'd draw him back. "Oh, don't thank me, Lady Elena. It's all my father's doing."

It was the truth, after all. Though Dash was having a hard time being thankful to his father for anything at the moment.

"I look forward to seeing you at dinner, my lord."

The woman could not bear to relinquish the last word. "Yes, Lady Elena," he replied.

"Excellent."

Christ Almighty.

The Devil in Disguise

**A Regency Rogues novel of deadly spy
games and dangerous seduction.**

Lord William Randall, the Duke of Clairemont: A devilish
rake with little regard for society — and an elite spy.

Lady Lucinda Grey: Beautiful, fiercely intelligent
and the target of a vicious kidnapping plot.

Two lives collide in the deadliest fashion with everything
at stake. Will hearts be lost in a world of passion?

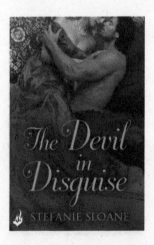

'Smart, sensuous, and sparkling with wit'
Julia Quinn

The Angel in my Arms

**A Regency Rogues novel of lethal spy
games and exhilarating passion.**

Marcus MacInnes, the Earl of Weston: A sinfully handsome
agent tasked with a mission involving a smuggling ring.

Miss Sarah Tisdale: An unconventional beauty
whose family are under suspicion.

Amidst an unlikely case, desires burn and love simmers.
With everything on the line, will passion prevail?

'Utterly delectable and seductive'
Teresa Medeiros

The Saint Who Stole My Heart

**A Regency Rogues novel of danger,
intrigue and steamy seduction.**

Dashiell Matthews, Viscount Carrington: An impossibly
handsome spy on the hunt for a notorious London murderer.

Miss Elena Barnes: A voluptuous beauty
as intelligent as she is fearless.

As fate causes the crossing of paths, will
everything be risked as the two join forces?

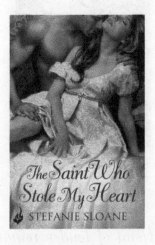

'*Everything readers of Regency romance crave*'
Amanda Quick

The Scoundrel Takes a Bride

A Regency Rogues novel of dangerous spy games and seductive passion.

The Right Honourable Nicholas Bourne: A notorious scoundrel whose help is sought on a dangerous mission.

Lady Sophia Southwell: The secret love of his life promised to his brother, who needs his help exacting revenge.

Together on the darkest of cases, will love overpower vengeance?

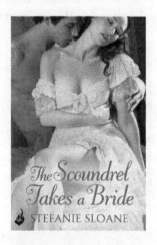

'Perfect blend of tender romance and heart stopping adventure'
Fresh Fiction

The Wicked Widow Meets Her Match

**A Regency Rogues novel of lethal spy
games and intoxicating passion.**

Langdon Bourne: Dedicated spymaster on
a mission to eliminate his nemesis.

Grace Crowther: A woman about who rumours
abound and upon whom he must rely.

As needs and wants become intertwined,
will rules be broken and risks be taken?

'An engaging, refreshingly original storyteller'
Stephanie Laurens

headline
ETERNAL

FIND YOUR HEART'S DESIRE...